CARRYING

CARRYING

Samantha Joseph

4th ESTATE • *London*

4th Estate
An imprint of HarperCollins*Publishers*
1 London Bridge Street
London SE1 9GF

www.4thestate.co.uk

HarperCollins*Publishers*
Macken House
39/40 Mayor Street Upper
Dublin 1
D01 C9W8
Ireland

First published in Great Britain in 2026 by 4th Estate

First published in the United States by G. P. Putnam's Sons,
an imprint of Penguin Random House LLC in 2026

1

A catalogue record for this book is available from the British Library

ISBN 978-0-00-878974-9 (hardback)
ISBN 978-0-00-878975-6 (trade paperback)

Book design by Laura K. Corless

This novel is entirely a work of fiction. The names, characters and incidents portrayed in it are the work of the author's imagination. Any resemblance to actual persons, living or dead, events or localities is entirely coincidental.

Set in Simoncini Garamond Std by Six Red Marbles UK, Thetford, Norfolk

Printed and bound in the UK [using 100% renewable electricity at CPI Group (UK) Ltd]

For Chatham,
my sister,
my daughter,
and, most of all,
my mother

CARRYING

Chapter 1

"Can I get two pounds of bone-in, skin-on chicken breast?"

The butcher wipes his hands on a bloodstained apron, a smile peeking out underneath his mustache. "Coming right up, beautiful."

Martha's a vision in a light blue wrap dress and just the right amount of makeup for a happily married thirty-nine-year-old in Brentwood on this August Sunday. She carries herself like a '50s housewife, except for the Apple Watch and the tasteful hint of Botox.

He returns with the chicken in butcher paper and hands it to her.

"Could I also get a quarter pound of beef liver?"

"You got it."

"And do you have pig's blood?"

"We might have some frozen in the back. What are you making? Blood sausage?"

A smile creeps across her face, revealing her perfectly white Tic Tac teeth. "An old family recipe."

Chapter 2

Still in the wrap dress, Martha sits on her toilet with the lid down, ever so patiently shaping the beef liver with a pair of scissors. She makes small cuts, removing only the tiniest slices with each snip. She doesn't have time to go back to the butcher if she cuts too much.

Martha loves this toilet. When she redesigned the bathroom, she sat on a thousand thrones before she selected this one, sleek and Japanese. She didn't go insane with remodeling when she moved in; she just implemented a few key changes to make it her own. To make it feel like no other woman had lived there. She knew Leon wasn't looking for a new life entirely, only a new wife to make his life whole again. A less savvy second wife would have gone bombastic and torn up the whole house, but Martha picks her battles wisely. It's Enid's house too; no kid wants to live through a major renovation.

But the primary bathroom had to go. This had been her first true wifely duty. Even if it was only different by one single bathroom, the home would never be the same after: It would be hers. It wasn't too difficult, using the guest bathroom during the renovation, being extra careful that Enid couldn't hear them canoodling in the shower.

Martha admires her work. The beef liver is perfect, a small amorphous shape about the size of her big toe. Okay, wait, actually, one more trim. Ah. Now it's perfect. She finds the red-purple totem quite adorable, like the newborn squirrel abandoned by its mother that she found in her backyard when she was six, doomed to perish despite Martha's best juvenile efforts to save it. Her creation squishes gently in her hand. She almost wants to keep it, but it has an important job to do.

She stands, lifts the toilet lid, and drops the liver into the bowl. It hits the water with a gentle plop. She looks down at her little pet, the maroon in sharp contrast to the spotless white porcelain.

With the back of her hand, Martha smudges her mascara a bit. She doesn't want to look too theatrical, only like she'd been crying a little. She looks in the mirror and rubs her eye makeup a touch more. Perfect, lived-in.

She opens the small plastic container of coagulated pig blood, loosened back to a liquid state with a dash of vinegar and a few minutes in the microwave. A delicate splash of blood mixes into the toilet water. She doesn't want to turn the bowl completely red; otherwise you wouldn't even be able to see her creation. Of course she could have just used red food coloring and corn syrup, but that would've been too Halloween. The scent of blood hits so right—tangy, acrid, sharp in the nose. Syrupy sweetness would've given the whole thing away.

She dips her fingers into the blood, reaches under her dress, and pulls off her panties. An old pair, just as she planned. The crimson quickly spreads across the crotch, covering up the floral pattern. She drops the underwear onto the floor. No, no. She fusses, picking them back up. Too haphazardly thrown. She needs to set the scene more precisely.

She sits back on the toilet, feeling strange perched on top of her pet, like the tender thing at the bottom of the bowl might come back to life and slither inside her body, where it supposedly came from. She pulls her panties over her feet and gives a slight kick. There we go. They crumple on the floor by her feet in grisly tragedy—impeccable.

Now this is the part that's going to hurt.

She has to stain the dress. She loves this wrap dress dearly. It makes her breasts look bountiful and perky, her waist tight, her hips perfect for bearing Leon's child. And that's why she must say goodbye to it. To really sell this, she must lose something that she loves. A true sacrifice in this ritual for it to work. It's only fair.

With her unblemished hand, she pulls her dress up. She dabs some blood onto her crotch, cold against the warmth of her loins. She lets some of it drip on her thigh, then wipes it away with a small piece of toilet paper. It has to look wiped, but not entirely clean. She drops the toilet paper into the bowl.

Martha feels no disgust at the pig blood touching her privates, but she winces when the dress falls onto the wetness. This garment was thrifted vintage Cavalli; she'll never find it again. The deep red pools on the periwinkle fabric. Closing the container of blood, she puts it into the small trash can by the sink.

She checks Leon's location on her phone; his handsome picture on Find My races dangerously toward her own blue dot, mere minutes away. She exhales sharply and ties the garbage bag closed, carefully carrying it out.

And through the bedroom, not letting it leak.

Down the hallway, past the guest room and Enid's room.

Past the kitchen. She already composed the mise-en-scène elegantly—smoke trickling out of the oven vent from burning Sunday dinner, rapidly blackening chicken breast and root vegetables.

And, finally, into the dark garage.

Martha yelps, her ankle twisting. She falls forward, right onto her hands, dropping the garbage bag beside her. "Goddammit, Leon."

She quickly pulls herself up and looks down to see the cause of her stumble: her husband's toolbox on the floor. She huffs and picks it up, returning it to the worktable where it belongs, which she has told him to do countless times. She squints, annoyed that she can't even reprimand him for his carelessness this time.

The garage door roars to life.

Shit.

From the slit of the door opening, the light from the outside world bursts through the darkness.

She shoves the garbage bag into the big black can, reshuffles the large kitchen trash so that it covers her evidence, then races out right before she can be seen from the car.

Back in the kitchen, she ignores the increasing plume of smoke from the oven.

She's nearly made it back to the bedroom when she hears Enid enter the house and say, "It smells like something's burning."

Martha reaches the bedroom. She's so close.

The smoke detector blares.

Leon calls out, "Martha! Something is smoking!"

In the bathroom now, she doesn't respond. She closes the door, but not entirely; she wants him to see her through the crack. Setting the scene, she throws herself on the ground against the sink. She spreads her legs and pulls up the dress so that he'll see a hint of the bloody portrait painted on her crotch.

"Martha?" Leon, fearful, calls out over the beeps of the smoke detector.

She works herself up to fake cry, quivering her eyes and lips. No actual tears fall—she's no trained actress, after all—so she covers her eyes with her hand. Her voice crackles, barely eking out the faintest moan: "In here . . ."

"The chicken must be completely bu—" Leon looks through the crack of the open door, gasping at what he finds. He opens it and enters, terrified. "Martha?!" He softens when he pieces together the clues. He whimpers, "Baby."

Hook, line, and sucker. Eagerly waiting for him to hold her, she whispers, "Leon."

He glances at the toilet, shutting his eyes tight when he sees it. He slams the lid closed with a hard clack. The horrible thing out of sight, he reopens his eyes and flushes the bloody mess. He lowers himself to the floor and puts his arm around her. The smoke detector still blaring loudly from the other room, he coos, "My baby, my baby." She isn't sure if he's talking about her or the thing going down the sewer pipe.

Enid screams, "Someone shut off the alarm!"

Martha buries her face in his shoulder. Eyes glossy, he starts to tear up. "Let's get you to the doctor, to Roger."

"I haven't bled in half an hour," she replies weakly. "It's over. I don't need a doctor."

"I AM NOT TALL ENOUGH TO FAN THE SMOKE DETECTOR!" Enid yells. "YOU NEED TO DO IT!" Fully crying now, Leon ignores his child. Enid marches to the doorway, fingers in her ears, yelling: "YOU NEED TO TURN OFF THE ALARM."

The girl's eyes stretch wide as she takes in the scene. At eleven, she might vaguely understand what's happening.

Leon startles. He rushes over to his daughter, hastily wiping his tears away. "Martha is—she's sick. Give her some space." He pushes Enid back slightly and gently closes the door behind him.

With the door closed, Martha stands.

She hears Enid ask, "What's wrong? Is she okay?"

Martha doesn't like hearing fear in her stepdaughter's voice, but she's grateful her husband is already out of the room, before he could really closely examine the blood on her thigh.

She undoes the knot of her bloodstained wrap dress. It falls to the floor.

"She'll be okay," Leon murmurs to Enid, the smoke detector punctuating his words. "Now get a stool so you can fan the alarm."

Martha calls out, "Go with her."

"Okay, I'll be right back."

Naked, she pulls back the shower curtain with a whoosh. She steps into the cool porcelain and turns on the water, extra hot. She stands under the stream, wetting her hair, face, perky breasts, slender waist, firm ass. The blood washes from her thighs, swirling into the drain.

The smoke detector finally stops.

Martha grins—success.

Chapter 3

Martha sits up in bed, warm under her down comforter. Even in a burning hot Los Angeles summer, she likes getting under the blankets with the air conditioner blasting. She and Leon typically sleep Scandinavian-style with separate comforters, a method she found on TikTok—she appreciates her beauty rest.

A show about interior designers in Beverly Hills, a longtime favorite of hers, plays on the television. When she first watched these home renovation shows in her twenties, living in a cramped studio downtown, squishing a never-ending army of cockroaches, it was all aspirational. She dreamed of a life where people were getting into serious arguments over which shade of burgundy the drapes should be. Now her home is more expensive than the ones on the shows. Sure, it's smaller, less gaudy, but only because the people on the show claim they're in LA when they're really in the Valley or Orange County or even dangerously close to San Diego, a fate she would not accept, no matter how many extra rooms she could have there. She loves her chic Brentwood one-story home: modern, elegant, classy, with lots of glass and sunshine. Leon's first wife picked right.

Martha's so entranced by the gay interior designer that she almost forgets she's supposed to be feigning sadness when Leon walks in. She smiles at him for a moment before she adjusts like she's putting on a brave face through the pain.

"Tofu and vegetables with brown sauce from Fortune House." Leon approaches the bed with a steaming plate. He smiles with his lips closed—the lines edging his green eyes make her feel weak. He's a clean-cut, attractive man, his wrinkles making him look even more handsome, distinguished, while hers are to be buffed away.

Martha would normally never eat in bed. She often yells at Leon for indulging in this gluttonous act; breaking her own rule will really drive home how hard this is for her. He hands her the plate of Chinese takeout and sits next to her. He puts a hand on her shoulder and massages. Always affectionate, he's particularly tender with his touch tonight.

Leon never cooks. He admitted that when he was a single father, he always ordered in. The only home-cooked meals then were made by his mother. Nothing was ever going to come out as well as his deceased wife had made it, so Uber Eats and Postmates and DoorDash were his coparents until Martha entered his life.

Martha is a fantastic chef. It's what she lives for. There is truly nothing that gives her more joy than nourishing her family and the praise that comes with it, the *mmm*s and empty plates for her to put in the dishwasher. And since she hasn't earned a dollar in years, she needs to emphasize culinarily just how lost her family would be without her.

To sell the performance, she had to do something she's never done before—burn perfectly good chicken breast to a crisp. Leon disposed of the ashen debris and ordered dinner without even asking her what she wanted. He just knows what she needs.

"Did I completely traumatize her?" She picks up her fork and starts eating, always careful not to speak with food in her mouth.

"No, no," Leon stammers. "Sure, a little startled, but she's okay."

Martha doesn't believe that. Of course she feels bad that she potentially traumatized the girl, but she accepts it as necessary collateral damage.

He adds, "I told her you were dealing with a 'girl problem.'"

She stifles a giggle. Obviously that was a horrible thing to say, but she's amused by his incompetence. How had he ever managed without her? "Now she's going to think that's her future: a bloody mess on the bathroom floor."

"Martha—"

"I'll talk to her tomorrow." Martha will make it a learning experience. "It's best if it comes from me."

"What you need to do is recover."

"I'll talk to Roger tomorrow morning. And I can throw in a little talk with Enid after school."

"What are you going to say?"

"She's eleven. That's not too young to talk about these things."

He massages deeper into Martha's shoulder. In his head, his daughter will always be the five-year-old crying in his arms when her mother died. He doesn't challenge Martha's judgment. "Why don't I take the day off and come with you?"

"You don't need to do that."

"Okay, well, I'll go ahead and cancel dinner with my mom."

"No, I think I can make it." Any other day, Martha would jump at the opportunity to nobly cancel on her mother-in-law, but now it would be pushing her luck.

"Are you sure? I'll make up an excuse, obviously, we don't have to tell her about . . ."

"I'll be okay. It'll be good to be with family."

He nods, his loving eyes like milky jade with flecks of gold at the center. He's taking such good care of her, a hunter in the woods taking pity on an injured, orphaned fawn. She wants to be absolutely ravaged by him, his huntsman prick in her ungulate slit. But it's too soon, despite her intestine-deep growl, yearning for him to fill her up. She does feel a hint of guilt, her husband being so compassionate toward her for something that didn't really happen.

But actually, she decides, Leon is comforting her for something real: She can't get pregnant. That part is true. She does deserve his kindness. She's genuinely mourning her lack of fertility, even if he doesn't know that. Sure, he doesn't remotely understand what she's actually going through, but she'll bask in his care nonetheless.

She gives him a gentle peck, her mouth glossy with brown sauce. She wipes it off his lips with her finger, licking it. He smiles back, so cute, happy that he seems to be healing her. He whispers, "You should ask Roger how long before we can try again."

Chapter 4

Martha lounges on the examination table in Dr. Roger Reeder's office at the Beverly Hills Center for Reproductive Care. Instead of a medical gown, she still wears her regular clothes, which today are a little more casual—jeans, a tight black Reformation tank top, and a small diamond necklace Leon bought her for their third anniversary.

Roger enters without even saying hello. She can tell he's already stressed by her presence.

Martha can hardly contain her excitement when she sees him. "Girl, I fucking sold it!" she cackles. Her voice is freer around him, not so tightly rehearsed.

He closes the door. "I need a drink."

"I can smell the Oscar. The 'For Your Consideration' billboards are getting plastered above Santa Monica Boulevard as we speak, darling."

He sits in front of her. "I don't know how you do it."

"Oh, it was easy! A shred of beef liver, a splash of pig's blood, and a heaping helping of my Best Actress pussy."

Roger doesn't even try to hide the disapproval in his voice: "How did Leon take it?"

"He completely believed it. Like not a single doubt in his mind."

"No. Like was he sad?"

Martha frowns—it's not like she has no heart. "He was crying. You know how bad he wants a baby." She stands, looking around the room, entranced by the colorful poster on the wall about the menstrual cycle.

Roger sighs. He does not approve of her schemes. She does not particularly care that he doesn't approve, but she just needed to tell someone, and he's the only one she can trust, the only one who knows the truth.

She picks up a plastic uterus replica off of the counter, gesticulating with it as she speaks. "What I need from you is a little spiel I can tell Leon."

"Be careful with that. It comes apart."

"Something explaining that the miscarriage wasn't bad and that I'm completely fine, but we should wait before trying again."

He snatches the plastic uterus out of her hands. "I told you to tell him the truth already." He places the replica back on the counter.

She rolls her eyes. "I'm trying to give him the perfect family, just like he had growing up. From the start, we talked about how badly we wanted to have kids of our own. And it's true. I do want them. Badly."

Roger leans against the counter with his arms crossed, completely unmoved. "Faking a bloody miscarriage to your husband—who you claim to love—you don't see how that's a new low?" They've had versions of this conversation before, but this new ploy has pushed him over the edge.

She takes his hands, looking deep into his eyes. "He was going to catch on if I never got pregnant. And if I said I was infertile this whole time, he would get rid of me."

"He would not get rid of you. He loves you. You really don't think—"

She drops his hands, putting on a cloying voice: "Hi, Leon, so your wife, whose pussy you've been cumming in for all these years? You could've been shooting your sperm right into the garbage disposal. She never told you the truth because she wanted to pull a fast one on you: She's actually an infertile transsexual!"

Roger sucks his teeth. He's heard this spiel before. "Your honor, she's carrying."

From their ballroom foremothers: To carry is to do something with so much drama, so much flair, so exceptionally well as to utterly annihilate the competition, even to the point of going overboard, of doing too much, of being *extra* extra. She is carrying to the highest degree.

Martha is a trans woman. She is stealth. Next-level stealth.

Nobody knows. Not Leon, not Enid, not her mother-in-law or any of Leon's family, not any of the mothers at school. Only Roger, Martha's one friend that she kept from her life before. He knows her tea, but he's loyal and sworn to secrecy. She took him in after his parents kicked him out and helped him through college and med school. She's his mother; he, her firstborn. He won't betray her.

She was blessed with a naturally high voice and petite frame. Only five foot six, she hit some sort of transsexual lottery. Martha is fish, high-class expensive fish—bluefin tuna tartare at Nobu Malibu. Sure, she's had a few things carved and plumped, but nothing with an obvious scar except her breasts, and thankfully, living in Tinseltown, breast implants are not clocky. Her work is natural, subtle, just as she asked for. She got her pussy long ago, nearly fourteen years, and she has only the faintest scars that are covered by pubic hair on either side of her picture-perfect labia. She says that her parents are dead, which they might as well be, and that she lost touch with everyone from earlier in her life, which is true. Faking her period isn't all that hard either. Realness, honey.

She shrugs. "Fine, if you want, if you really think I have to, then I'll come clean. I'll tell him everything. And when he kicks my sorry ass to the curb, I'll be very grateful to sleep on your couch until I can get back on my feet. He'll get an annulment—marriage under false pretenses. I haven't worked in, what? Three years? But I'm sure I'll find something eventually. And kicking me out is the best-case scenario. You see what happens to the girls. He could be so furious, so truly fucking disgusted by my trickery, that he grabs me by the neck and wrings the life out of my feeble little . . ." She gets herself all choked up.

Roger relents. "Tell Leon it was a complete miscarriage. The bleeding has completely stopped, and all of the pregnancy tissue has been expelled. And that you need to wait to try again until you get your next period, so a month. Or whenever you decide that is."

She knew that she would bring him around; she just had to get through this little routine first to absolve his conscience. While it does make things more difficult, she finds it adorable that he uses his big scientist brain to think about hoity-toity things like ethics and the Hippocratic oath. She's still his only real mother—the woman who gave birth to him thinks he's a pedophile who'll burn in hell. And while Martha doesn't have as much time for him now that she's married, she still screens potential boyfriends and tries to make sure he's not drinking too much, not mixing substances he shouldn't.

"That's perfect," she chirps. "I'm planning for a bit of an early-onset menopause. Thirty-nine isn't too crazy, right?"

"About five percent of women have it before forty-five, so it's not out of the question." Roger reaches into the pocket of his lab coat and pulls out a bottle of pills: "Here."

She starts peeling off the Estratab label. He refuses to relabel it for her as that would be illegal. He hasn't done anything entirely unethical yet, always voicing his concern. He can't stop her from relabeling it herself when she gets in the car. Leon doesn't see estrogen in his medicine cabinet but levocetirizine, her supposed allergy prescription. She puts the pill bottle in her purse. "The good stuff."

Roger walks to the door and opens it for her to leave.

"This is the home stretch," she whispers. "No more lies. Or no more new lies, just the old ones settling in. Nice and cozy." She grabs his arm and gives his biceps a squeeze, pretending to be impressed. "How do you have the time to look this handsome?"

He can never stay mad at Mother.

Chapter 5

Martha waits patiently in the car line in front of Enid's middle school. After her meeting with Roger, she texted Leon that she felt good and she could take the girl to her grandmother's tonight. Martha wants to talk to her about last night.

She smiles and waves at the babysitters and other mothers picking up their kids. Enid just started middle school, but it's mostly the same families with some new ones added in. They're at a different building on the same campus as the elementary school. Martha is involved, but not to an inappropriate degree. She'll make brownies for the bake sales and volunteer on field trips, but she doesn't make it her whole life like some of the mothers do.

"See you at Power Sculpt later?" Christine chirps, yelling through her open car window at Martha. She's Martha's best mom friend, which means she's really her best girl friend, since she's abandoned all the old ones. Christine is one of the cooler mothers here, working something behind the scenes in Hollywood. She's not the prettiest, but she's fitness-obsessed. She has to be. Her husband ran off with his assistant, one of those bone-chilling events that sent shivers down the spine of every married woman at the elementary school—a power couple torn apart by the twenty-something assistant's business-less-than-casual outfits and blowjob lips freshly pumped with Restylane.

While Christine will be the first to admit that she lost the divorce weight with Ozempic, Christine and Martha often do Pilates together so that she doesn't gain it all back. When Martha sees Christine power through minute-long planks, core trembling, she can tell the woman is really working through something emotionally.

"Not tonight!" Martha calls back with an exaggerated frown. "Taking the kiddo to the mother-in-law."

"I hope she's got wine!" Christine waves as she drives off. "And don't forget Quinton's birthday party on Saturday!"

Martha thought she would feel judged as a stepmother, but she's been completely accepted. Even if Martha is far hotter than the other mothers, they save their judgment for the young new wives, not age-appropriate ones who replace a tragically deceased mother. Christine and some of the other mothers who were around for elementary school really stepped up when Leon's wife died, perhaps trying to sneakily vie for the open spot, but you can only drop off so many sorry-your-wife-died casseroles before it starts feeling less generous and more pushy. The women's kindness petered off as they returned to the minute drama of their own lives, giving Martha the perfect opening, an empty slot to squeeze into.

She notices Emma heading out of the building with her sixth-grade boy. Emma is single, but that doesn't mean you have to completely let yourself go. Martha watches with barely concealed contempt as the woman's frizzy unkempt hair blows in her face, sticking to the sweat on her forehead. Her clothes pucker at the seams after some recent weight gain. Her skin looks sallow with prominent dark circles, like she'd offer you a poison apple.

When Martha looks at other women, she decides what work they should have done, sculpting them like clay. Emma needs a retinoid-heavy skincare routine, a Brazilian blowout, a Fraxel laser treatment, a deep plane facelift, and full-body contouring liposuction. It's become a soothing game, working through a puzzle to make the world more beautiful. Still, Martha's secretly jealous of those dowdy dames. She'd give anything to be completely content wrinkled like a walrus, bramble-bush tangled mane, flab flying wildly in the wind.

But Martha must serve fiercely to survive. She still stops traffic, watching men's heads follow her 180 degrees as she struts past. She considers her body to be her life's greatest work, the thing she's poured the most time, money, and a whole lot of pain into—carving a gorgeous woman from the marble of a boy. While she hasn't been under the knife in a decade, now the upkeep is all on her—diet, exercise, pluck, dye, wax, laser, inject.

Martha pulls up, seeing Enid walking toward the curb. Her stepdaughter enters the backseat, throwing her backpack across it. "You know my friends all sit in the front."

"What do you say we get a sweet treat?"

"What kind of sweet treat?"

"Ice cream?"

"What about fro-yo?"

Enid is a little bigger than the other girls. Obviously Martha herself was only going to have a kids' scoop of vegan ice cream, but she wishes her stepdaughter didn't care about things like saturated fat and calories at such a young age. While Martha takes immense pride in her figure, she feels like it's a choice she got to make: to erect an undeniable monument to her womanhood that nobody can take away. But seeing this sweet little girl who once proudly slapped on her belly while rolling around in the mud suddenly become a calorie-counting preteen in a baggy T-shirt, Martha's heart aches for her stepdaughter.

* * *

Enid jabs her spoon into the swirl of her bright blue raspberry fat-free, sugar-free frozen yogurt. She and Martha sit on a bench in a little park.

"Don't tell your Grandma that I ruined your appetite, okay?" Enid nods. Martha's been going over how to start this conversation all day, but now she's blanking, so she blurts out, "Do you know how babies are made?"

The kid answers matter-of-factly: "Sperm from the testicles. Eggs from the ovaries. How old do you think I am?"

Martha's impressed. "We didn't talk about things so openly back when I went to school."

"They want us to be ready for puberty. Katie got her period already. She said it sucks and showed us her bloody pad in the bathroom."

"Oh, wow. You girls are so, uh, open with each other."

"You weren't like that with your friends?"

"I didn't really have close friends like that." While Roger took care of her after surgeries, that was out of necessity. Martha hates to be so vulnerable, only likes to be naked when there's something to gain from it, like a husband, or, at the bare minimum, an orgasm.

Enid eats another spoonful of cyan yogurt.

"Yesterday I had a miscarriage," Martha says softly, scanning the girl's face for a reaction. "Do you know what that means?" Enid shakes her head. "An embryo, an egg that is fertilized by a sperm, was growing inside of me. But something wasn't right, so my body got rid of it."

"What wasn't right?"

"I'm not sure about that. But the doctor, Uncle Roger, told me that I'm completely okay now. Miscarriages can be scary, but it is completely normal. I wish you hadn't seen what you saw, but I want you to understand what happened and to not be afraid."

"What wasn't right though? Did you do something wrong?"

"No, I didn't do anything wrong," Martha replies, offended that Enid immediately jumped to blaming her for her entirely fictional miscarriage. "Many women have them. Your teachers, friends' mothers, your aunts, some of them might have had them." That seems to affect the girl, perhaps now imagining the scene that she walked in on last night happening with other women in her life, with herself in the future.

"I want to always be honest with you." Martha has gotten so good at this charade that she feels absolutely no guilt saying something like that. "I know that this is a mature topic, but I think you can handle it. We should both be honest with each other, always. I love you very much." She puts her hand on Enid's thigh, satisfied with having a real parental moment, woman-to-woman. She notices the fro-yo dripping. "Get it before it melts!"

Chapter 6

"The little guy has the fattest cheeks I've ever pinched," Amy squeals, her jowls jiggling like tapioca in an earthquake. The aforementioned mother-in-law. "And you know I've pinched a lot of fat cheeks in my day."

When Martha looks at Amy's seventy-four-year-old face, a mess of coarse curly gray hair and a lifetime of improper sunscreen use, she can't help but think of a retiree's sagging ballsack.

Martha knows you look at a man's father to determine how well he'll age; Leon's deceased dad always looks handsome in the photos hanging on the wall. But what exactly are you supposed to determine from a man's mother? Martha realizes the answer is probably to run out of the house as fast as she can, but it's too late for that now.

Martha, Enid, Leon, and Amy have taco night in Amy's dining room. The table is long; they fill less than half of it. The woman loves to host. Martha always feels bewildered being in the place where Leon grew up. He lost his virginity in his bedroom here while his parents were on a trip to Palm Springs. She feels grateful that they did not meet in high school—she was a teenage twink, giving blowjobs to a closeted football player in parking lots the town over, only to watch him marry the girl he knocked up at prom.

Leon's childhood home, Calabasas, is so close, while Martha's is far away in the middle of the country. It's been so long since she's been home, decades by now, that she has trouble fully remembering it—how the rooms all fit together, how the curtains sway, the photos on the wall. She wishes didn't remember anything at all.

"And that's Nicole's ninth grandchild. Nine! Can you believe?" Amy scoffs before taking another glug of a dry white wine. "She could start a baseball team."

"Or a K-pop group," Enid adds.

Leon groans, "We get it, Mom. You're green with envy."

Martha stares at her plate. The in-law made salsa verde chicken. Amy has a special talent for completely drying out any meat.

"Sure, I am! I had four kids. Four! And I've only got three grandchildren," Amy whines. She reaches out to touch her Enid on the top of the head. "Three gorgeous, beautiful grandchildren who I love to the moon and back, but I'm still waiting on my baseball team."

Martha takes a bite of the chicken.

Ew.

She stifles a gag as the poultry hits her tongue. She chews it slowly, wondering how Amy could have possibly messed this up so badly. Her saliva turns to completely rotten sour slop. She's never tasted something so foul. She's worked very hard to never insult her mother-in-law's cooking, but she can't bring herself to swallow it, worried it will make her sick. She tries to discreetly spit it back out into a napkin, her spittle clinging to the chewed-up piece of chicken, but Amy immediately notices.

"Something wrong?" Amy raises an eyebrow, defensive.

Leon, who has spent years dutifully swallowing his mother's terrible meals without complaint, shoots his wife a look: *Don't even think about it.*

"Uh," Martha stammers, not wanting to offend, but not willing to take another bite. "I think my chicken went bad."

Amy guffaws, insulted. "You think I served you rotten meat?"

"The seasoning is lovely, and it's cooked perfectly," Martha lies. "But I think my piece went bad. It's no biggie, really."

"It's shredded chicken," Amy replies, barely holding back her irritation at the accusation. "We're all eating the same chicken."

"It looks fine to me," Leon adds, trying to defuse. He stabs a piece off Martha's plate with his fork.

"Don't. It's bad," Martha insists, not wanting him to taste something so wretched.

He ignores her warning and chews it, curious. She grimaces, preparing for his horrified reaction. But he shakes his head, confused. "Tastes normal to me."

Martha simply can't believe that. She stabs another piece and puts it in her mouth.

Just as vile as the last one—strange, rancid. The spices only make it worse. She spits it out directly onto her plate, a chewed-up mound of saliva-coated shredded chicken sitting next to the rice and beans.

"Martha," he stammers, shocked at his wife's unusually unrefined display.

"Jeez." Enid grimaces, turning away.

"I don't see how only your pieces could be rotten"—Amy puts her hands up—"but I'm happy to make you something else."

"That's certainly odd." He puts his hand to Martha's forehead. "Are you feeling okay?"

"I'm perfectly fine."

He looks concerned, eyebrows raised to signal to her that he's worried about what happened last night. Martha obviously knows it isn't that.

"I'll make you something else then," Amy offers.

"No, no, I'm fine." Martha takes a big scoop of rice and beans with some spicy salsa and guacamole to get the horrid taste out of her mouth.

Enid pushes her plate forward. "I need to start my homework."

"Give Grandma a hug."

Enid stands up and hugs her grandmother. Amy gives her a big kiss on the cheek, wiping off her coral lipstick when she pulls away. "You're still my baby even if your cheeks are less pinchable." Enid walks off. Amy makes sure the girl is out of earshot before turning to Martha. "You know I got really strong food aversions when I was pregnant."

Leon says, "Let's not talk about that." They said they weren't going to tell Amy that Martha was allegedly pregnant, but she suspects that he told her anyway.

Amy sighs, "I'm sorry, dear."

"It's okay. We're okay," Leon responds so his wife doesn't have to.

Amy reaches out and grabs Martha's hand. Martha hates feeling Amy's old papery skin on hers. She wonders how Amy would've reacted to her precious oldest son marrying a transsexual. She may be a liberalish Angeleno, but tranny-in-law is probably a skosh too far.

"It must be so hard not having the family you both always dreamed of," Amy says with a sympathetic face. Martha nods, pulling her hand away slightly, but the crone holds on. "I know my Leon always pictured having a big family, just like he had growing up. And after everything he's been through."

Martha stares at him, telepathically begging him to end this conversation. He catches on. "Yes, Mom. Did you make dessert?"

Amy powers through. "But you have to keep your chin up. It will happen for you when it needs to. It's not your fault biology isn't on your side right now."

"Thanks for the pep talk. Dessert?"

"But you have those eggs frozen, right?" Amy continues. In a prior moment of panic, Martha told Leon that she had frozen eggs when she was thirty-two. She does not have a plan for if and when this becomes relevant. "I know you've been dragging your feet on IVF, and you did get pregnant the old-fashioned way, but you're past the age where—"

"Dessert." Leon raises his voice. Martha feels thankful to him for ending the discussion.

Amy lets go of her hand with a defensive shrug. "I made a chocolate torte."

* * *

"Did you know that Los Angeles's palm trees were planted for the 1932 Olympics and they're all reaching the end of their life? They don't live past a hundred," Leon says, cozy under his comforter, nose deep in a book on the hidden lives of trees.

"What happens when they die? The palm trees start falling on us?" She's heard this trite Angeleno fact before but lets him have his moment, as she always does.

"You better watch where you're going."

Leon is nothing like the men Martha used to date as an openly trans woman. He is boring, gloriously boring, giddy to tell her facts. He has a job she doesn't quite understand that makes more money than she could ever have imagined; he plays tennis and golf; he likes nonfiction books about subjects so dry they would make her brain dehydrate. Everyone says he's such a nice guy. He makes love well, very well, eager as a Boy Scout for cunnilingus.

She never dated a nice guy before. She's sampled every dirtbag, loser, and jerk-off in the city like a deadbeat pupu platter. She can't imagine any of those scumbags reading a book, not even sure if many of them were literate. Even the ones with high-paying jobs, the ones with wives and kids, they'd never share a fun fact with her. She was used to getting booty calls at odd hours—lunch breaks, when their girlfriends were at drinks, when the kids were at karate. No matter how disrespectful the ask, Martha always went. She'd known that a lot of the dolls were getting paid for what she did, but she didn't ask for money. She was no hooker; she had a college degree and an office job and felt she was above that, even if that made her an idiot for doing it for free. She did it for love, or scraps of sexual attention that, if she squinted and tilted her head, she could make herself believe might be a type of love. It was only with Leon that she had more than scraps—a full meal—breakfast, lunch, dinner, and dessert.

And those losers were the better of the men. There were men who were worse, much worse.

Leon grabs her hand and kisses it. "I'm sorry for what my mom said. Not about the food. The other stuff."

"It's okay."

"But I've swallowed her overcooked dried-out meat for my entire life without a word! That's what you do at her house," he gripes playfully.

"I'm telling you it went bad! She hates me now, doesn't she?"

He kisses her hand again, looking up at her with those kind green eyes. "No, how could anyone hate this face?" He reaches out and gently takes her chin, turning her to face him.

In moments like these, she does think of telling him. He looks so sweet. How much easier would everything be if she blurted it out? If she told him the truth, this unbreakable knot of tension twisting her intestines would finally unravel.

But no, her mouth dries and puckers when she even thinks about saying the words to him.

Still holding her face, he continues, "And thank you for talking to Enid."

"Of course."

"You're always so intentional with her. You don't know how much I appreciate that, the effort, all your effort."

She turns her face down to kiss his palm. "I learned from the best."

While she's more than happy to have taken on many parental duties, Martha loves watching Leon be a father. Caring, calm, firm, present, he loves his daughter so immensely, with every fiber of his soul. Martha knew he would be a good husband if he could love her even a fraction of that. Sure, he isn't always the best with specifics, at remembering the after-school schedule and doctors' appointments, and can be a bit fumbling with the girl stuff—that's where Martha comes in. He would never in a million years raise his voice at his daughter, lay a hand on her, do anything that could make her feel anything less than wholly safe and deeply loved.

Martha's father had been either frigid, silently drinking a Busch in front of a baseball game, or cruel, beer-filled veins popping out of his forehead, screaming at her for the sway in her hips and at her mother for creating such a defective child. She would've given anything to have a father like Leon, who would play princesses with the utmost commitment when Enid was younger. It was intensely attractive, watching him giggling, flaunting a terrible posh British accent, sipping imaginary tea, pinky out.

He lets go of her face and asks, "How did it go with Roger?"

She swallows. "He told me that the bleeding has completely stopped, and all of the pregnancy tissue's been expelled. My vitals look good."

"That's good. You think your body was still having pregnancy symptoms with the chicken tonight?"

"It's possible, I suppose."

He waits a moment before saying, "I know it's soon, but when can we try again?"

She conceals her annoyance—he's already pushing again after one night? She thought the miscarriage would've bought her a lot more time. He must be getting nervous, desperate. "At least a month. Or until I get my next period, whenever that will be." There's the spin. She can decide when her next period will be, delay it for months.

"I think it's time we seriously look into IVF."

Her heart drops to her surgically constructed vagina. "Because your mommy told you it was time?"

He pouts at her harsh tone. "I said I'm sorry she even said anything. She shouldn't have."

"No, she should not have," Martha repeats, trying to throw this conversation off course.

"But we should've been prepared for this much earlier. I know we had this idea in our heads that we would do it the natural way, but there's no shame in artificial insemination."

"This is all so soon, so sudden." She needs to buy herself more time. She has no idea how she could fake it without massive help from Roger, who has thus far refused to get his hands truly dirty.

"This stuff does have a timeline, whether we like it or not. And it only gets more difficult. You're almost forty."

Motherfucker. The mention of her age comes as a kick to the stomach. "I am in my thirties. I literally just turned thirty-nine."

"Your birthday was three months ago. Baby, I don't care about your age, but the doctors do."

"They are men of science, so they will want to be accurate with the numbers: I am not forty." Even though she has no capacity for reproduction, she's still made furious by the inequality—Leon's forty-six-year-old body gets to keep producing children, no clock ticking away inside his ever-drooping testicles, while her organs supposedly wither up if they don't act fast.

"I know we can try IVF after menopause, but—"

"Oh, now I'm already menopausal?" Shit. Martha's plan for early menopause won't even be the end of all of this. Damn you, modern science.

"Hey, it was too soon to bring up. I'm sorry." He kisses her on the cheek. "And you are the youngest, most beautiful, youngest woman I know." He kisses her again.

She sighs, "I'm getting dinner with Roger tomorrow, I can discuss it then."

"Always working him off the clock," he teases. Martha knows her husband thinks it's strange for her best friend to also be her doctor. Of course Leon's completely right to think it's inappropriate, but she insists Roger's the only one she trusts. "We have a month. Let's just get it in our heads."

Chapter 7

Martha walks into the kitchen in the morning, the air fragrant with toasty coffee; Leon is an expert with the Moccamaster she got him for his forty-third birthday. He freshly grinds the beans and times it perfectly for her arrival. While she knows he would prefer a darker roast, it's always to her liking—light arabica, never bitter. He already left for work. She kissed him goodbye in bed, hiding her anxiety about the threat of IVF. Clouds of steam catch the late-morning light as she pours a hot cup into her favorite mug, painted palm trees on it.

She takes a sip.

Jesus Christ. It's fucking disgusting.

She spits it onto the counter, gagging, wondering for half a second if Leon is playing some practical joke on her, but he's not the type. Could he have somehow messed up the coffee? He's made it since they met and has never failed. While the chicken tasted rotten, the coffee tastes chemical, unnatural, inedible.

She goes to the sink, runs the faucet, and bends over, sticking her tongue under it, letting the thick LA tap water spill over her taste buds.

"What are you doing?" Enid asks, entering the kitchen expecting her breakfast.

"Dad messed up the coffee." Martha returns her tongue back inside her mouth, though the unpleasant, almost synthetic flavor lingers. "Let me get your cereal."

* * *

On the drive to school, Martha tries to figure out what the horrible taste was. It certainly wasn't like anything she's ever consumed before, but there's something familiar about it. Something she knows very well but can't place.

After she drops Enid off, she spends the rest of the day nervously thinking about how she can pull this IVF thing off, although nobody in her little routine at Whole Foods or the gym or school can see that she's cracking. While the miscarriage was a solo performance, she will need a full cast for IVF.

Even though she's getting dinner with Roger, she's still on her heaviest housewife shit. She prepares her family roasted salmon, carrots, potatoes, an arugula salad, and a lemon-tarragon yogurt sauce. And cleans the kitchen after—she does not come to play. She actually enjoys cleaning, finds it relaxing, although the maids who come every Wednesday do all the hard stuff.

She makes life so easy for Leon, so beautiful, so delicious. That's the deal. She cooks, cleans, does school pickups, keeps her body tight, and has sex whenever he wants. She loves every second of it. Other women who bristle in the housewife role, finding it lonely or unstimulating, are spoiled brats. No stupid boring job and your sole purpose is making everything lovely? That's the peak of human existence, Shangri-La Dee Da every day.

While other little boys dreamed about becoming baseball players, astronauts, or rock stars, little Martha dreamed of one thing: becoming a woman. It was a desire she felt such deep shame about that she thought it was completely impossible, like hunting a unicorn, even more outlandish than the Little League kid making pro one day.

She went to a state school for communications, nothing fabulous, just to get out of her hometown. She moved to LA after she graduated with no dreams of superstardom, only a warm place completely foreign to her Midwestern upbringing.

It was her first night in the city, leaving Union Station, when she saw them for the first time in the flesh: the dolls, trans women. Looking at their bright lips, big hair, and firm breasts, Martha realized her deepest juvenile wish was no impossible fantasy. It would be painful, expensive, and lonely, but unicorns were real, even if they needed a team of doctors to get the horn to stay on.

She was the only one from her hometown who actually went on to live their childhood dream. Once she became a woman, it dawned on her that she needed a new dream. That's when she started dreaming about love, about men. But a healthy relationship with a man who loved her, who truly saw her as a woman, turned out to be the real unicorn, more fantastical than changing sexes.

* * *

"It's not like I actually want to sit in a church in Fresno in hundred-and-four-degree heat, but the fact that I'm disinvited to my own niece's baptism is downright spiteful," Roger groans, draining his third dirty martini at the upscale modern American restaurant by his condo. He reaches out to the waiter. "Can I get another one?" He's lucky he can walk home.

Martha slowly sips her second margarita. "Your family doesn't deserve you. I don't know why you still want to see them."

"Get her another too," he orders the waiter.

"I need to drive home, hon."

"Get her a refill." He loses some of his usual composure when he's like this. "My sister isn't a nutjob like our parents, even if she still sees them all the time. And I want to be a part of her family, it's only my mom that's refusing to let me attend. So, I called her."

"You're supposed to be no contact! What good possibly comes from talking to that bitch?"

"She was screeching, saying that I'm a groomer, so I hung up the phone before she could get to any other choice words."

"I can't even imagine what my mother would call me. Not that I even know her number anymore." The last thing Martha's mother ever said to her was that she would end up a corpse on the sidewalk and nobody would even come looking for her. She finishes her drink. "Why would you talk to her?"

He looks around for the waiter, already impatient for the refill he ordered moments ago. "Even after she kicked me out, even after she refused to see me, even after every name she's called me, I still miss my mommy." Frowning, his eyes glisten.

Martha bristles. Her son has contacted his birth mother. "How could you possibly miss someone that's so cruel to you?"

The waiter returns with their drinks. As Martha thanks him, they make eye contact for just a second too long, his eyes lingering on her face. She fears she's been clocked, but no, he's just checking out the beautiful woman before him, even if she's over a decade his senior.

Roger grabs his cocktail before the waiter even puts it fully down on the table. He always drinks even more when family stuff bubbles up. He hasn't answered her question, focusing on the martini instead, the toothpick with the olives poking him in the upper lip.

In the silence, she launches into the dilemma: "Leon wants to start IVF."

He blows out his lips, making an explosive sound effect. "Welp, it was fun while it lasted. I hope."

"Roger."

"Honey, just tell him. You're being actually ridiculous."

"I took you into my home when your mommy kicked you out. You had no money, and I asked for nothing. I loved you, I love you. And now I have to ask you to return the favor."

"Cool it, Mother-tucking Teresa. 'Return the favor'? Meaning what, exactly? Enlighten me."

"I need you to help me fake IVF."

"Houston, we have a problem," he cackles. "Diva, let's bring it back down to planet Earth."

"I already said I froze my eggs, so we just need Leon's sperm in a cup, which he'll be more than happy to provide. Then you pretend to squirt the embryos up my noo-noo. It's not that much really. The embryos will fail, don't worry. I won't fake another pregnancy. And hey, as a treat, you can guzzle Leon's leftover jizz!"

Roger finishes his drink and slams it on the table a little too roughly. Others look over. "I would lose my fucking license."

"How could you lose your license? You're not even doing anything. You are literally not doing a medical procedure."

"You want me to risk my whole life, my whole career, maybe even jail time—"

"You would not go to jail."

"Fraud, Martha! Malpractice. It's very serious, unlike this moronic plan you've concocted on estrogen fumes." He's always been a catty drunk.

"Fine, I'm a bad person, I'm crazy, I'm stupid. Let's quit the song and dance and you can agree to help me already, okay? Dinner's on me."

He drags his hands down his face. "Tell him. Just tell him. That man is so in love with you. He would understand."

"This is what a relationship is. You minimize the less desirable parts of yourself in exchange for love. That's what everybody does."

He softens. "I don't think he would hurt you. Or kill you. It will be okay, whatever his reaction is, you will be okay."

"Just stop. I will never do that."

He hardens again, his eyes rolling back, unable to bite his tongue anymore. "Honey, if he really was so special, if he actually was this dream man you act like he is, he would accept you. And if he doesn't, you're not giving up all that much. It's not like that man really understands you. He loves a cardboard cutout of you."

"I was so lonely before him. Truly, deeply alone. I'm not going back to that."

Roger throws his hands up, absolving himself of her. "I'm not helping you."

His voice is stern, and she realizes he really might not help her this time. Her precious son is ready to wash his hands of her and throw her back into the wilderness for the wolves to devour, tearing the meat off her bones with their canines.

Tears welling in her eyes, she tells him something she's never said: "He would never see me as a woman again. Even if he somehow didn't kill me, didn't hurt me, didn't kick me out of his life, even if he got over the deception and against all odds wanted to stay together, he would never see me as a woman again. I'd forever be some demotion, some sick deviation from the real deal. He's the man who matters most to me in the world. Not telling him is the only way Leon loves me for who I am, with nothing else between us."

The waiter returns with their food, putting their plates on the table. "The pasta for the gentleman and the steak for the lovely lady."

"Thank you," Roger says softly, her speech still in the air.

It's the irony of passing, of wanting to be truly seen as a woman. Martha feels zero guilt for waiters, coworkers, friends, strangers, anyone else, assuming she's a cis woman—that's the entire point. She does not want to live life on the margins, forever marked by some cruel joke at birth. By passing, she undoes her own monstrosity. Nobody looks at her differently, as less than, as a perverted freak, as something to spread scary stories about.

No matter how much she tries to shove it down, she does feel a sting of guilt with Leon, always thinking about how much easier life would be if he knew. But he is the very last person in the world she wants to tell.

She looks down at her food, unable to look at Roger after being so vulnerable. She first takes a bite of roasted asparagus—delicious. Then she grabs her steak knife and cuts a slice of buttery filet mignon. She puts it in her mouth.

Yuck.

The steak tastes completely rotten too. She spits it out immediately.

"You good?"

"I think something is wrong with me," she sighs, disappointed that it wasn't Amy's cooking after all. "Food has been tasting really off for me."

"Off how?"

"Chicken tasted rancid last night. And this morning my coffee tasted like, like chemicals or something. And now this steak, it's nasty."

He reaches over and stabs a slice of steak with his fork. He puts it in his mouth—no reaction. "It's good." He mulls it over. "Dysgeusia. That's what it's called. Can be caused by new medication, dental problems, head injuries, even a cold or sinus infection."

"I don't think I have any of those."

"If it's a weird taste every now and then, that's not too concerning. But maybe you should see another doctor. One that isn't me."

She slumps into her chair, dismayed to lose the delectable taste of meat, now seemingly forced into coffee-less vegetarianism. And suddenly all alone.

He grabs her plate and switches it with his own, a mushroom pasta. She twirls some spaghetti on her fork and eats it. "Yum." He now eats her steak. But he won't help her. Maybe he needs more convincing, but she fears she'll have to figure this out on her own. She sighs. "You're a good kid."

Chapter 8

Martha does her best to ignore her hangover as she drives Enid to school, her Dior sunglasses not doing enough to block out the gleaming early-morning sun. When Martha got home from dinner, a drink or two past tipsy, Leon commented that she probably shouldn't have driven home like that. She shrugged it off.

She lied and told him that Roger said that they can use her frozen eggs, which makes IVF easier, but they still need to wait before she should get pregnant again. Leon accepted that. She successfully bought herself a little time, but she will have to figure out something once the month is up.

In the backseat, Enid looks out the window, mouthing the words to the last chorus of a Taylor Swift song. When the song ends, she turns forward and asks, "Were you pregnant on purpose?"

She has caught Martha off guard. She glances at the girl in the rearview mirror, staring right back at her. Leon should really have led this discussion with his child a lot earlier, but Martha doesn't want to lie to her. "Yes. Your father and I want to have a kid together. He's always wanted that big family that he grew up with, your uncles and your aunt." Enid exhales softly. Martha can't read her properly through the rearview mirror. "We think you'd make the best big sister in the world. Wouldn't it be fun to have a little brother or sister?"

The moments it takes Enid to answer stretch on for Martha until the girl finally replies, "That could be kind of cute."

Martha looks back to the road. Why were she and Leon so afraid of telling Enid right away? He was worried that his daughter—still five years old in his head—would think that she was going to be replaced, but she's old enough to know that it would make their family feel fuller rather than push her aside.

The road in front of Martha suddenly starts to blur.

She rubs her eyes, confused, scared to have her eyes falter with an eleven-year-old in the backseat. Is the hangover that bad? "It would be really cute."

She blinks firmly. Her vision returns to normal. That was weird.

"Aren't you too old? My mom was twenty-eight when she had me."

Old?! That little twerp. Martha tightens her thirty-nine-year-old hands on the steering wheel. "I'm not even forty," she responds a little too harshly. "You have friends with moms who were older than me."

"Did you flush the baby down the toilet?"

A headache sears the front of Martha's forehead. She puts a hand to it, pressing, trying to push this sudden pain out of her head. Her vision goes blurry again, the cars in front of her out of focus.

"It was not a baby," Martha stammers, blinking her eyes hard, trying to get her vision back while she zooms across the freeway. "It's, it's a clump. It was a clump of cells."

The lines of the road duplicate, the bumpers in front of her glittering and shifting. Even her hands on the steering wheel seem to have cloned. She keeps blinking as hard as she can, willing her vision to return to normal.

But when she opens her eyes, it's worse than before. Oh God, oh God. She can't die here; Leon can't have another wife die in a car crash.

"But it was going to be a baby."

She wavers at the wheel, barely able to make out where the road stretches forward and where the concrete divider wall stands. "Well, yes, but, but it's, but—"

She swerves, losing control, unable to really see where she's going.

Enid startles, putting her hand on the roof of the car as she screams. "Martha!"

But Martha still can't see straight. Scared, she babbles, "Sorry, sorry," not sure if she's apologizing for what already happened or what's to come.

HONK.

She swerves across multiple lanes of traffic, trying to pull over to what she thinks is the side of the road, praying they make it there in one piece.

CRASH.

Metal clangs against metal as a speeding car nicks into the side of theirs, sending them spinning, the whole world swirling in flashes of honking cars, asphalt, blue sky, and palm trees in the distance.

"WHAT THE FUCK?!" Enid shrieks with all the might of her terrified little lungs.

Tossed around like a sock in the dryer, breathless, Martha loses any last shred of control, closing her eyes to try to block out the chaos. The only thing she can think to do: She stomps her foot on the brake. The car collides with the barrier on the side of the freeway, an awful shriek of crunching steel into concrete, violently throwing the girls forward.

Martha's airbag goes off. She prays that her breast implants don't pop as she falls into it. Enid yelps as her seat belt stiffens across her chest, knocking the air out of her.

Martha pants heavily, shocked to still be alive. With her eyes closed, she tamps down the airbag. "Enid, tell me you're okay."

Tears trickle down the girl's face. "I don't know."

"Does anything hurt?"

Stunned, she feels her neck with her hands. "I think, I think I'm fine."

Martha finally flutters her eyes open, the world now back to its singly rendered state. She looks at her hands in front of her—just the normal two. She turns around, feeling terribly guilty at the Enid's tearstained face.

The girl mutters under her breath. "My neck hurts a little."

Martha shakes her head. "I couldn't see right. And then . . . I'm sorry. Call your father. Now."

Enid whips out her phone. Martha looks at her in the rearview mirror, allowing herself to believe in the God of her childhood for just a moment so she can thank Him for not killing the girl in a car accident. She takes a deep breath to calm herself, hand over her quickly beating heart, returning to the godless world of the 405.

"Wait, did you say 'fuck'?"

Chapter 9

I'm so sorry. I've successfully traumatized her twice this week."

"You don't have to keep apologizing." Leon drives Martha home after dropping off Enid very late at school. He takes a deep breath, the seconds counted out under his breath. Martha can tell it's some trick a therapist once taught him. It's not just Enid; Martha's traumatized him too. He knows how quickly your loved ones can disappear. He wouldn't make it if it happened again.

He left work as soon as Enid called. He insisted on taking her and Martha to the hospital to get them checked out, despite his daughter's protests that she was fine, even with a dark bruise from the seat belt across her chest. The doctors, not very busy on a Wednesday morning, released them quickly with no reported injuries. The doctor recommended Martha see a specialist for the migraine. They dropped off Enid after lunch for the second half of the school day. She must be telling all her friends about the crash, who will surely tell their mothers, who will surely assume that Martha's getting her Starbucks with three shots of Baileys and two squirts of barbiturates.

She can feel her husband trying to conceal his total panic as he gives calm, reasonable advice: "Maybe it's best if you take a break from driving for a bit."

"That might be a good idea." In the mirror, she examines the red bruise on the bridge of her nose from the airbag.

"We can afford for you to Uber until we figure out what's going on."

She knows that when Leon closes his eyes, he sees his family's bloody bodies, mangled on the freeway. He admitted that he used to be on antianxiety medication after his wife died. He would wake up in the middle of the night and have to run into Enid's room and wake her up, worried she'd stop breathing in her sleep. He could barely send her off to school. Some days he even kept her home, only to soothe his morbid thoughts. If Amy hadn't given him a good shake and forced him to see a therapist and psychiatrist, Enid would have been trapped in the house, monitored 24/7, protected by Leon from the many dangers of the world that he couldn't stop envisioning.

He didn't tell Martha the story for a long time. She knew better than to ask. It wasn't all that much of a story anyway. The hospital called him and said that his wife had been in a crash and that it was dire. She was dead before he even arrived at the hospital. Nothing unique or spectacular.

Martha never asked about her. She knew he would tell her when he was ready. Nearly a year into dating, right before she moved in, Leon reached into the medicine cabinet in his bathroom for some dental floss and noticed Martha looking at the Xanax. She obviously had seen the pill bottle before, having looked through his medicine cabinet as soon as she had access to his bathroom, but this was the first time that they acknowledged it together. He told her the story, looking at her through the mirror. Once he was finished, she turned around and hugged him, her arms around him, his arms down at his side. He cried, really cried, the way that only a grown man who has not cried in a long time can. In that moment, she knew he would ask her to marry him. He'd told Martha that he'd been off the meds for a while, only had them around just in case. She worries this incident will put him back on the stuff.

He asks, "Do you think it might've been like a panic attack? Because of . . . what happened?"

"I've never had one before. But I guess it could've been."

He responds with a nod. He puts his hand on her shoulder, not so much to comfort her as to steady himself—she's still here, she's still here.

She doesn't know if she should say it yet, but she's still so high on adrenaline that she goes for it: "But now with all of this health stuff, whatever it's from, I don't know how soon I'll be ready to try again. The natural way or IVF." She'll use this to buy more time.

Leon's face falls, but he says nothing, squeezing her shoulder. She worries that this was the wrong move. He's already stressed; why would she use this moment to throw that at him too? Everything rests on precise timing.

She's breaking the contract. He said early on that he wanted more kids, and she eagerly agreed. She should've said immediately that she couldn't have them, but she found it endearing that a man cared so much about having a big family and she didn't want to lose him. Martha, an only child, doesn't know what it's like, but it had to have been better than being alone with her parents. She also knows that without another child, they are still stuck in a pale imitation of his original family—a mom, a dad, and a daughter, with Martha slotted in where his first wife once was. A baby would mark a totally new family arrangement, one unblemished by death.

While Leon sees carnage when he closes his eyes, Martha imagines a different sort of doom: a woman with a flourishing fertile womb. Her greatest enemy is this Imaginary Fertile Woman. She fantasizes about this female in many different forms. Sometimes she is young, gorgeous, undeniable, with pouty pliable lips and milkable breasts in tight-fitting crop tops. Sometimes she is very kind, older but still younger than Martha. In a cardigan and a loose cotton dress, she's not a total showstopper, but she already has a kid of her own; that's how Leon knows she's good at it, procreation. Sometimes she is ugly and desperate. But he is desperate too.

While the exact specificities of this mate are imaginary, she is a very real threat. She sees the way women look at him, tall, handsome, kind, and great with his own kid, even if he comes with baggage. She recognizes the look on their faces very well: *Fill me up with your seed, sire my child, protect our brood in this violent world.* She sometimes wishes she had picked someone else, somebody less desirable, but really, it was Leon who had picked her when first he sat down next to her at the bar.

The only way to defeat this Imaginary Fertile Woman is for Martha to play her part perfectly. By the end of this, he needs to feel that they've been through so much together that he'll accept not having another child. He needs to feel awful for even thinking about leaving her. Maybe they'll consider adoption. It isn't just that she fears he will desire some Imaginary Fertile Woman; it's that he feels he deserves a child, that he is owed one. Leon is progressive enough, but some primitive part of his brain is howling that he must be fruitful and multiply, his birthright as a successful male. She's the secretly infertile wife, cruelly preventing him from fulfilling his destiny. Like Amy said, he's been through so much. A baby, a beautiful new life, will cast away the last cobwebs of grief, and maybe he can return to the man he used to be. He can be normal again.

She does want a child just as badly as he does, maybe even more. She would love to be a mother, to raise a baby with him. When she sterilized herself long ago, chopping off her original reproductive organs to fashion them into the nonreproductive organs of the fairer sex, she didn't care in the slightest about her genetic lineage. But now that she's found a man she truly loves, she wishes she could turn their love into something real, something you could touch, hold, cuddle, kiss, bathe, and feed. But she's used to accepting limits, well aware that life does not offer her what others get so easily; he has never had to accept such harsh realities. Even when his wife died, surely an unfairness, he found a new one.

Fearing she might've made some grave error in that last statement, Martha retracts. "I'll see a specialist this week. Try to get my health in order so that we can get back on track."

"I'll pick up Enid this afternoon." He pulls up to their house to drop her off before returning to work. He parks the car and turns to kiss the top of her head. He does still care about her; she hasn't lost this just yet. "I want you healthy."

* * *

The tissue paper on the examination table crinkles under Martha's butt. Dr. Gina Listero looks over her chart. Martha gave a million blood samples; took an allergy test, a vision test, a CT scan; and provided both her urine and stool, embarrassed as she carefully maneuvered her shit into a white plastic container for the lab to dissect.

"We don't see anything obviously wrong with you," Dr. Listero starts. "We do see that you have slightly elevated C-reactive protein, which indicates some inflammation but doesn't point to anything specific. Your liver, heart, kidneys, thyroid, and immune system all seem normal. Vitamin levels look good. Negative for mono, COVID, hepatitis, and all STIs. We didn't see anything on the CT scan. It could be some sort of passing virus that we didn't test for." Dr. Listero finishes reading the chart and looks up at Martha. This doctor was recommended by one of the moms at the school, supposedly the best around, which she better be, considering she accepts no insurance and charges $2,000 for a consultation. "I know you want an answer, and I don't really have one. But what I can do is refer you to other specialists and prescribe something for the migraines—sumatriptan. Take one as soon as symptoms start."

Martha deflates. "All right. Thank you."

The doctor looks back at the chart. "And how long have you been on hormone replacement therapy?"

Martha's face flushes. The only doctor she's seen in years is Roger. Since she previously had no health issues, he could easily do her annual checkups. She hasn't had to discuss her transsexuality with anyone besides Roger in a long time, since before she met Leon. She hates it, picking at her manicured fingernail, knowing that this doctor no longer sees her as a true woman but as a semi-successful science experiment. "About two decades."

"That is quite a long time."

"Is it?"

"We don't have extensive research on health outcomes for male-to-female transgender women who've been on cross-sex hormone replacement therapy for over a decade."

Martha scoffs, "I know plenty of women, much older than me, who've been on hormones for decades with no issue." She doesn't mention that she doesn't keep up with any of those women.

"That's well and good, but it's still not well researched at this level."

"What would the solution be? I can't go off estrogen. I have a vagina."

"I wasn't suggesting anything like that. But it's something to consider."

Martha chews the inside of her lip. The doctor seems to be implying that hormones are the cause of her ailments. Should she simply consider all of this pain a consequence of her own actions, her selfish shortsighted decision to transition?

"I'll take the pills for the migraines. Thank you." Martha hopes her curt "thank you" will end this clearly useless appointment, but now the doctor seems to be in a panic trying to recover from what she's hoping will not be filed as a formal complaint.

"With symptoms like this, we should consider that you might be experiencing something psychosomatic," the doctor offers, moving away from the touchy subject of oversensitive transsexuals.

"Psychosomatic? Like I'm imagining all this?"

"Not that you're imagining it, no. I know these symptoms feel very real."

"Feel real? They are real."

"Yes, they are real." The doctor smirks, uncomfortable, only bringing herself closer to a complaint being filed. "Are you under a lot of stress?"

"No, I'm very relaxed," she lies.

"Stress is normal. You're a parent, a wife." Martha notes the use of "parent." It's a pointed demotion from "mother," degendered. Maybe it's a medical term, as Martha has not given birth, but it still stings. "Life can be very stressful, it's not shameful to admit that. We women put a lot of pressure on ourselves."

"Yes, that's very true, but I'm not particularly stressed," she replies tersely, knowing that the doctor wants her to feel grateful to have been included in the category of women.

"Well, I'm very envious of that."

Martha notes all the fine lines on the doctor's forehead—she really is stressed, despite all the money she hauls in from this racket. "I'll take the migraine pills." Two thousand dollars down the drain for a prescription she could've gotten at urgent care—thank God it's Leon's money.

Chapter 10

"Let's get a good night's sleep before Quinton's birthday party," Martha suggests, a polite way of telling Leon that she does not want to have sex on this late August Friday night. She's too anxious, not just from the health stuff but from openly talking about her transition, like somehow the words are still hanging in the air and will fly into her husband's ear.

He closes his book on trees, gives her a peck on the lips, and rolls over to his blankets. "A kid's party without sleep is considered torture by the Geneva Convention."

She laughs politely, then turns off the light and pulls on her eye mask, trying to sleep off her anxiety.

But as Leon snores, she lies awake, begging for slumber to come.

She spends the whole night tossing and turning. She feels tired, but she can't turn her brain off. She takes some of Leon's liquid melatonin, dropping it right onto her tongue. She was the one who easily drifted off to sleep, while he struggled. That's why they started the Scandinavian sleep method in the first place. But he figured out the right combination of melatonin, magnesium glycinate, and a low dose of trazodone that seems to knock him out.

* * *

At 4:30, she gives up on trying. She puts her AirPods in, goes under the covers, and scrolls through TikTok. She does feel her brain rotting, but she keeps her content mostly educational—makeup, cooking, dieting, workouts, and plastic surgery recovery timelines.

She gets a lot of pregnant mothers. She likes the ones who give it to you straight. It's only the really Christian ones who act like every step is a gift, not something that makes you fat, gassy, and irritable. She likes the horror stories. Women who have painful pregnancies only to give birth to stillborns, turning their bodies inside out for nothing, something dying inside of you. And even if you give birth to a perfectly healthy baby, there are still so many twisted ways that it mangles your body, turns you into something unrecognizable.

There was one popular TikToker who used to post constantly. She even made a video when her water broke, getting driven to the hospital. Then there was silence. People kept commenting on her old videos asking for updates. Months later, her husband finally posted. He looked ragged, unkempt, not camera-trained like his wife. With tears in his eyes, he read a prewritten speech: His wife died during childbirth, but they managed to save his son, who he now raises alone.

Martha presses her face against this window into a stranger's life, her breath fogging up the glass, always imagining herself on the other side. She loves to hear the bad stuff. Maybe she's not missing out after all; maybe it's better on her side of the window.

TikTok is a time thief. By the time she comes out of her scrolling trance at 6:26, she thankfully feels the silky pull of slumber as the sun starts to come up. She tugs her sleep mask back on and finally manages to will herself to unconsciousness.

"Good morning." Leon kisses her, and it feels like she only just closed her eyes. She groans. "You didn't sleep?"

"Uh-uh."

"You can get another hour in before we have to get ready, sorry."

But Martha's brain has already turned back on. It's too late. She takes off her face mask and checks the time: 8:47. The Geneva Convention will be broken today.

* * *

"What a precious little angel," Emma coos, holding Kayla's darling baby. Martha notices that Emma does look a little nicer on the weekend. She's at least managed to get a brush through her hair. Martha wonders if the mothers are looking at her funny because they heard about the crash or because she looks terrible for the first time in front of them, eye bags dark from her sleepless night.

"Grover may look like an angel, but you should see his *diapies*," Kayla titters, a big gummy grin, yellow foundation that doesn't match her chest.

Martha fakes amusement, concealing her disgust at this twenty-seven-year-old using the word "diapie."

"Do you want to hold him, Martha?" Emma asks, holding out the baby.

"Oh, I don't know," she says, stalling. She would love to hold a baby, but this one is the enemy.

"Please! I could use a break. Grover is so needy." Kayla flashes that gummy grin again.

Grover obviously did nothing wrong, but is a mortal enemy nonetheless as the offspring of Kayla, the assistant who Christine's ex-husband, Kent, ran off with. Well, not only ran off with, but also married and impregnated. Not even thirty yet, Kayla doesn't seem to care how people look at her and her baby's father, who is well into the second half of his fifties.

"Oh, all right." Martha smiles as Emma hands over the baby to her. Grover stares at her with big blue eyes—her heart melts. She would steal this baby, run away if she could.

Christine complained all week about having to invite Kent, Kayla, and Grover, but she knew that Quinton wanted them there. Kayla strikes terror in all the mothers, still with their husbands. She's wearing a Victoria's Secret push-up bikini to the pool party six months after giving birth and looks fantastic. It's not just Christine who would kill her. Martha would look hot in a bikini too, but she has enough respect to wear a pink Free People maxi sundress instead.

"He's always staring at the beautiful ladies." Kayla is sweet in her own way, even if she's the exact embodiment of the Imaginary Fertile Woman.

"Hey, little guy," Martha coos. Grover giggles, the most beautiful little trill. It feels so right, it hurts. She curses the cruel God that decreed that some floozy can so easily produce something so pure, so magical, so full of boundless love, while her own body produces nothing but mucus and feces. She can feel Christine's eyes on her, fraternizing with a terrorist.

Kayla bites her lip like she's about to say something really bad: "The pregnancy was so easy, I barely showed. The nurse said Grover literally slid out of me. He makes me want baby number two."

Martha can't imagine Kent having a third child. He will already be over seventy when Grover goes to college. She turns to look at Leon, throwing a football to the middle school boys in the pool. He has that perfect drool-worthy dad bod—firm muscles under a little pudge from eating so much of Martha's cooking. She turns to see Kent, lounging in a pool chair, beer belly proudly protruding as he smokes a cigar.

Emma warns, "That first one is sent to trick you. Having multiple kids under three is a torture I don't wish on anyone."

"When Quinton goes to his mother's, it gets so lonely though." Kayla shrugs. "But you love only having one, Martha? Or did the hubby just say no more?"

Martha shakes her head, bewildered by this hussy's ignorance. She would have thought that Kayla knew the whole story, but she must be so ostracized by the other moms that she's out of the loop.

"I'm also a stepmother." Martha's face flushes with shame. Especially because, with Grover, Kayla undid her own stepmother status—she's just a mother now, no prefix.

"Wait, what?" The girl tries to recover. "Enid even looks like you kinda. I legit had no idea."

"Oh, really?"

An off smell thankfully ends the conversation. Martha holds out the baby, making a funny face as he fills his diaper. "Grover!" Kayla shakes her head, taking him back. "I told you his *diapies* are nuclear." She rushes him inside. Kent has not held his child once today.

Martha wanders over to Christine, standing guard around the pool, making sure none of the kids become liabilities. She fought fiercely for the house in the divorce, refusing to let the bastard kick her out of her own home, unwilling to give up the succulents around the swimming hole.

Martha whispers, "Who wears a bikini to a kid's party? Is she looking for someone else's husband too?"

"I can't believe I let her come." Christine puts her arm around Martha and leans on her shoulder. "Thanks for coming, really."

"Her foundation is so orange, like a clown fish."

Christine laughs. Martha often wonders how she would react if she told her the truth. Christine loves *Queer Eye*, but it's different when a real-life transsexual has infiltrated your ranks. She would probably do the classic older-woman thing, getting mad that you're prettier than her.

Christine snickers, "I sure wish Pete could've come today."

"Pete? Which one is Pete?"

"Oh, he's only my new boyfriend!"

"Boyfriend? Like capital-*B* boyfriend?"

"We've only been on a handful of dates, but we've been texting and FaceTiming for months. He's always out of town for work."

"I knew you had a little extra pep in your step at Pilates," Martha teases. "So tell me everything. How'd you meet?"

"Tinder." She shrugs. "I admit it: I'm an app user! I'm a middle-aged woman on dating apps. And it worked! Got me a good one."

"Show me, show me."

"He doesn't photograph well," she prefaces before she pulls out her phone and finds an acceptable image of her suitor. "Pete." A picture she took of him at dinner, the candlelit portrait is incredibly unflattering to his serious face, much older than Christine. He's bald, but not brave enough to shave off the sides.

"He looks like he really likes you," Martha offers. "What does he do?"

"Medical sales. He travels for it. No kids. Never married. No baggage! No ex-wives or other people's kids I have to raise. I really hit the jackpot."

Pete could not be further from Martha's definition of a jackpot. "Has he met Quinton yet?"

"No, not yet. It's still early. Kent, that bastard, was lucky: Quinton already knew the tramp as Daddy's assistant." Christine grimaces.

"But we all need to get together sometime. You'll really like him. He's loads of fun."

Martha can't imagine how the dowdy man could be loads of fun. "Let's do it!"

She looks around to find Enid sitting outside of the pool, chatting with a few of her girl friends. Enid didn't even bring a bathing suit. She hasn't had her period yet, but she wears a training bra. She's already so aware that her body looks different from her friends'. Martha wishes she could give the girl more confidence, but she would feel like a total hypocrite, only comfortable with herself after intensive plastic surgery and a Spartan workout routine. It's hard being a pudgy middle school girl anywhere, but LA must be a particular hell. Martha feels a sick pride that she'd absolutely stunt on every woman from her hometown, not that she'd ever return.

Leon pulls himself out of the pool, a twinkle in his eye. He grabs a towel and approaches them. "How are you, ladies?"

"Fabulous," Christine replies.

Leon grabs Martha's hand. He's cold and wet, but Martha doesn't mind. He glistens in the sun like marble. "You're doing good?"

"I'm good."

"Do you have wax in your ear?!" Christine barks, chasing a kid at the other side of the pool. "I said no running!" The kid turns bright red and runs away from Christine. "No running!" She races after him. Leon and Martha both smirk at the scene.

Leon puts the towel around his neck and pulls Martha away from the pool, walking toward the house, away from the noise of the party. He whispers, "You're feeling good?"

"I'm fine. I'm tired, but I'm good."

He tenderly brushes her hair behind her ear. They both notice Kayla walking out of the house holding Grover, freshly diapered. "I loved seeing you hold him."

"I didn't realize you were watching." How did she ever get so lucky? That this gorgeous man's biggest wish is to see her holding his baby. Something delicious bubbles inside her. "You know, I don't think anyone will notice if we disappear for ten minutes"

"Where would we disappear to?" He's usually the one to initiate, so he goes absolutely rabid when she does. He reaches his hand down, quickly adjusting his growing hard-on in the netting of his bathing suit.

She bites her lip. "I have to go to the bathroom." She turns around and walks away, letting him watch her for a moment. Without looking at him, she adds, "That was an invitation."

He skips closer to her, walking inside. She grabs the waistband of his swim trunks and pulls him into the bathroom. He closes the door behind him. "We can't have Enid's friends all whispering about us."

"We're fine," she says, kissing him to shut him up. She puts her purse on the back of the toilet.

He kisses her, pressing her into the wall. She opens her eyes for a second to soak in the scene in the mirror, the way his shirtless body wraps around her. She can already feel how hard he is through his swim trunks, the outline of his erection soaking into her dress.

"Take this off," she orders, not wanting to exit the bathroom with her clothes damp.

He unbuttons her dress, kissing her clavicle. She takes off her bra and lets it fall to the floor. She strips off her dress and throws it onto the back of the toilet on top of her purse.

She grabs his cock, still rock-hard in his forties, something that fills her with pride. She knows that many of her friends' husbands can only get the old kielbasa three-quarters torqued on a good day, softened by failing vascular systems and waning attraction. As Leon moans, she covers his mouth with her hand. "Quiet. And quick."

He pulls his shorts down around his ankles—no time to even

fully take them off. He lifts her leg around him, pulls her panties to the side, and enters her. She needs this bad, so bad. He covers her mouth with his hand. "You said quiet."

He fucks her hard against the wall. She digs her nails into his back and watches him in the mirror, his ass flexing as he thrusts. She can feel an orgasm building up quickly. She can feel his too, his breath quickening, his face getting red.

It must be the lack of sleep because she feels loose, wild, unfiltered: "Put a baby in me."

He thrusts deeply three more times and then grunts. His cock throbs inside her, filling her with his semen. She gasps, about to cum, staring at herself in the mirror.

The migraine strikes her head, a brick to the skull. She sees herself and Leon intertwined in multiples, the world spinning around her. A beast with a million backs, too many to count.

"Oh God," she groans. He pulls out of her slowly, but when he lets her go, she crumples to the floor, her eyes closed tightly, hand on her forehead.

"Baby, what's happening?"

A knife in her cranium. "Migraine."

"What, what can I do?"

She wants him to crush her brain, to kick the pain out of her head. "Pill, the pill."

He nearly trips over his trunks, still around his ankles, as he scrambles to pull her purse off the back of the toilet seat. He moves so quickly that he knocks her dress right into the water in the toilet bowl. "Oh, shoot. Shoot."

"Are my pills not in there?" she asks, eyes still closed, not yet aware that her $312 dress has fallen into the toilet.

"I got it. Here."

She blinks her eyes open to see three hands holding out the pale pink tablet. Delirious, she reaches out and grabs it, dry swallowing. She closes her eyes again and puts her head to the cold hard tile floor, trying to will the pain away.

Leon, flaccid again, finally pulls up his trunks. He rubs her back. “Breathe through it, just breathe.”

After a minute or so, the worst of it is gone. She still has a horrible headache, but when she blinks open her eyes, she sees his concerned face looking down at her, only one of him once again. “Thank you, I’m okay now.”

He looks terrified, like he really thought she might die right there on Christine’s bathroom floor. “Let’s get you some water. Can you stand?”

She nods. He grabs her arms, helping her stand. In only her panties, she sees herself in the mirror, mascara smudged. She looks down to find her once pink sundress now soaked to red, swimming in the toilet bowl.

Chapter 11

As quickly as Martha fell into this dream of a life, so quickly does it slip away. She had to leave the party early in Christine's old T-shirt and sweatpants. Everyone stared at her, the other mothers now sure of their Baileys-and-barbiturates theory, but Martha was in too much pain to care.

She doesn't want her life to change, but it isn't up to her. She forces herself to continue. She goes with Enid in Ubers to school. A total waste of money, but Leon will take no risks with her driving. Obviously he wouldn't. Especially not with his daughter in the car. But at some point, her costs to his wallet will outweigh her benefit.

She takes the pills the doctor prescribed, but the migraines and blurry vision always break through, returning at random. She tries to figure out a pattern.

She goes to Power Sculpt with Christine. The migraine strikes her in warrior two, her knee at a ninety-degree angle and her arms spread apart. A bullet in her forehead, she sees women clad in Lululemon and Skims in doubles and triples, their colorful yoga mats now a kaleidoscope on the floor. She nearly falls over, folding herself into child's pose until it's over.

"Tough class?" Christine asks as they walk out. Maybe the migraines only happen when her heart rate is up. Fine, she'll stop working out as hard. Low-impact exercise only.

But no, migraines come whenever they please: while she cooks, while she kisses Leon, while she helps Enid with her homework, while she mops the floors.

"It's okay, I just need to lie down" becomes her catchphrase.

Sumatriptan doesn't work. That stupid doctor—*expert in the field, my ass.* She knows nothing. And this can't be psychosomatic, it can't. Martha's crazy, but not that crazy, right?

Christine says her cousin's husband swears by antihistamines for sinus-pressure headaches. Martha pops a Claritin and prays for salvation that never comes, a migraine still striking her in the grocery store. Maybe the lights are too bright in the aisles. She'll have to order grocery delivery.

It strikes again while she cooks dinner. She burns the grilled cheese. She was already doing an easy dinner, a sandwich far beneath her usual repertoire, but now she doesn't know if she can keep cooking. They start ordering in.

She watches her family chow down on ribs ordered from Postmates. It seems bizarre to make barbecue travel in plastic in the back of a stranger's car, but she can't make those sorts of judgments anymore. She takes one bite, just in case, and—no, no, no—disgusting as ever, the rot breaking through the slather of barbecue sauce.

She lies awake at night, staring at either the ceiling or the sleeping lump of her husband, wondering if she'll ever have her life back, wondering when he will finally leave her. This isn't what he signed up for. He needs a wife, and Enid needs a mother, not an invalid.

She tries to get appointments with specialists, but they're all booked months in advance, if not years. She makes the appointments anyway, but she doesn't know if she'll make it that far.

She naps during the day and stays awake at night. She tells herself it's merely one bad day; she's allowed to have one bad day. And then it's been a whole week of bad days and, oh no, she's turned herself completely nocturnal.

She gains weight. Without meat, she shovels carbs into her gullet but never feels truly full. She can't bear to know how much she's gained, but she can tell that Leon has noticed.

She tries to hide it to anyone outside of the house, underplay it as best as she can, but the cracks start to show. Amy's visits have always been covert inspections of Martha's skills as a homemaker. She used to pass them with flying colors, but she can't bring herself to dust off every window shutter slat like she used to.

Amy grimaces as she rifles through the fridge. Martha finds her health inspector in the kitchen, jaw agape, face furrowed in disgust, holding a package of pork chops, mottled with gray and green, little white tufts of mold. Her face feels flush, red with shame—she never would've let something go bad before. Martha apologizes and snatches the meat from her mother-in-law, who's now lecturing her on the dangers of rancid meat in the fridge.

About to throw out the spoiled swine, her hand hesitates above the trash can for a moment, unable to let it go. She can't quite tell what's compelling her, but she feels a sudden affinity for the rotten slabs. Perhaps it's sympathy. She too was once good, beautiful, delicious. Now, like the pork chop in her hand, she is corrupted, contaminated, worthless. Her mouth wet, she wills herself to drop it into the trash, sure that's what her family will soon do to her, toss her away and take her out to the curb on Monday for the garbage men to dump in a landfill.

She sees the lesser doctors who are available on short notice, racking up medical bills that insurance only sometimes pays for, but no answers materialize. She will do anything, take any prescription or suggestion. Everybody around her has a recommendation, and the internet adds a thousand more: milk of magnesia, acupuncture, muscle relaxers, an herbal suppository that "looks a lot bigger than it feels," anticonvulsants, aura massage, immunoglobulin, sound baths, infrared saunas, pre- and probiotics, therapeutic screaming, meditation, ice baths. She even makes Leon install something in the office so she can hang upside down.

But nothing cures her.

TikTok has become both a lifeline and a cruel joke. She can't bring herself to focus on anything more substantial, not enough brain power for even the dumbest reality TV show. She only has the concentration for bite-size pieces of the world. While the workout and cooking and makeup videos used to be helpful, now they are merely sources of content to be vicariously consumed at the scratch of her fingernail, her only connection to the fantasy of the life she used to live. The influencers mock her, their lithe limbs, young healthy bodies, fresh blood pumping under taut skin on the other side of the screen.

The app figures out Martha's new form. It shows less of the healthy bodies and more of the sick ones—women with chronic pain, Parkinson's, long COVID, mast cell activation, POTS, Ehlers-Danlos, Crohn's, terminal cancer, and more. They post front-facing camera videos of themselves hysterically crying, shaking on their musty carpeted floors, in empty beds, in stained hospital rooms, in tiled bathrooms, feeling so utterly alone, hating every doctor and friend who tries to help them, nobody able to ease their burden. Martha finds them all hideous, utterly embarrassing, so desperate for attention and sympathy that it makes her stomach turn, shamelessly turning their pain into a cyber spectacle. But she knows that whether she broadcasts it or not, she is now one of them.

September slips away, and the only silver lining is that discussion of pregnancy and IVF has ceased. She feels useless, impotent, unable to do anything she used to love, unable to do anything she needs to do. Martha has always been a doer; whether it was working to get enough money for surgery or working to keep her husband happy, she has always been active, never content to sit on her ass. Sickness forces her to be alone with herself, with her ailing mind, body, and soul, all withering away at exponential rates. Her life becomes unimaginably mind-numbing and completely unstimulating. For the first time since before she met Leon, she actually feels lonely. She now spends her days, once a thrum of activity, alone, half asleep; her evenings struggling to move the articulated limbs of her marionette; her nights alone, lying in the dark next to her unconscious husband.

She feels as though she is scratching off the days on her prison cell wall, but rather than waiting to be free again, Leon will release her to whatever gutter she came from. She can't go back to her old life, the studio apartment teeming with roaches, the unending loneliness. She can't even handle an office job like this. But she would understand if he can't do it anymore. He's been patient with her, eating takeout, bumping up the maids' hours, funding her efforts, not belittling her pain. But he is only human.

They signed a prenup. Leon said it was what his lawyers told him to do to protect Enid. Martha had no problem signing it, sure they'd be together forever. But now that stupid prenup means that she won't even get to live off his teat if he gets rid of her. She was so naive to stop working, but it seemed like such a fabulous idea when she was laid off and Leon suggested she could run the home.

But more than the house or the job or the money, she loves him; she truly loves being his wife, being a stepmother to Enid. She can't take the way he looks at her, with sympathy, scorn, pity, contempt—she can't always tell which. When she first transitioned, she knew it would be a lonely road, but she told herself that she could live without love. But now that she's had it, now that she's drunk the syrupy nectar for so many years, growing fat and greedy from the rich taste, she would perish without it, dying in the cold of a sick broken heart.

The Imaginary Fertile Woman grows less imaginary with every passing moment.

On the first Tuesday in October, a headache shatters through her skull in the middle of the day, the worst she's felt thus far. She collapses onto the floor, unable to even crawl to the couch. Maybe this is her punishment for having it too good for too long. Maybe her mother was right: A person like her could never live a good life.

Lying on the cold hardwood floor, among the layer of grime she would have never previously allowed, for the first time in a very long time, thoughts of suicide creep into her head. Suicide had been her constant companion before she transitioned. She didn't see a world where she would get older, didn't see a world where she'd survive. Suicide was the only way she imagined her life ending. But once she crossed to the other side, those thoughts faded; she said goodbye to her old friend. She took her body by the horns and forced it into something she could live with. Even when life was hard and painful, she was a woman.

But now she finds her old friend knocking on her door once again. She doesn't see a future for herself. She can't live like this. She's not really living at all. Maybe nothing else could get her body to obey, but she still knows one thing, one undeniable thing, that would.

She tries to push the thought out of her head. She can't do that to

Leon. But when she sees the way he looks at her, she wonders if it it's better to have your wife kill herself than to watch her wither into nothing. Maybe it would be the kind thing to do for him, the noble thing.

She would do anything to get better. Anything.

Chapter 12

Martha snoozes in bed, sleep mask on, afternoon sun beating on the curtains. She originally picked the curtains, willowy and light, because they were pretty. She hates them now. She needs something sturdy to turn day into night, but in early October, she's thankful the days are getting shorter.

"It's nearly five," Leon says as he flicks on the light. He clearly doesn't care that Martha was getting some rest. "You obviously didn't see my texts. Or calls."

She wakes up, confused, getting her bearings. Sleeping at random times makes waking up even more bewildering. "No, I didn't. Sorry."

"Keira's mom had a work thing come up, so she couldn't take Enid home today. I called you to see if you could Uber to her, but you didn't answer, so Enid had to wait hours at the school until I could get her."

"I'm sorry, I didn't see."

"You still need to communicate with me. I didn't know if you were—"

"I'm sorry." She lifts off her eye mask, terrified of him. She has not heard him sound like this, so upset with her, in the entirety of their relationship. He doesn't fully understand how much power he has over her.

"Did you even wake up today?" Before, he would've asked this sympathetically, but now it's an accusation.

"Yeah, yeah." She nods, trying to wake herself up. "I didn't mean to take a nap, it just happened."

"You need a sleep specialist. You're nearly nocturnal now."

"I don't think I have it in me to see another doctor, specialist, proctologist, whatever. But I should. I will."

He sits next to her on the bed, softening. He puts a hand on the lump of her knee under the blankets. "What are we going to do with you?"

"This won't last forever."

He sighs, not responding. Why should he? She doesn't believe what she said, so why should he? "Is your period still regular?"

Her face goes white. "My period?"

"Has Roger checked you for endometriosis? Or PCOS? Those can cause very confusing symptoms."

She hasn't seen Roger at all since this started. "No, I don't have that."

"The only way to really confirm endometriosis is with surgery. It's underdiagnosed."

"My symptoms don't really line up with it."

"It's a constellation of symptoms. I googled it. A lot of women have migraines with it."

How could she possibly fake invasive surgery to investigate a uterus she doesn't have? "I would know if I had endometriosis."

"You should at least get a second opinion. Roger is your friend, but he might not be the best choice for all this. And getting the surgery could help with conception." That's what this is all about. He's wondering why she can't conceive a healthy spawn. "I've booked you an appointment with another gynecologist in Fairfax. She's very highly rated."

"You booked me an appointment?!" She gasps, furious. He's never been so involved.

"You're stressed and tired, so I made it for you. With all the doctors you've seen, you still haven't seen another gynecologist. I can drive you. I'll go in with you too, I can help explain the situation."

"You don't need to book my appointments for me." She sweats.

"Maybe it's not endometriosis, but I'm sorry, with the miscarriage, it seems like a likely source of your ailments."

Not knowing what else to do, she goes for a frantic Hail Mary: "I haven't even had my period since the miscarriage."

"You haven't?" He looks very concerned. No period means she's officially infertile. "I'm glad I got you the new doctor, Roger's clearly not on top of this."

"It might be the start of menopause."

His face falls, pulling his hand back to his lap. "Aren't you young for that?"

"Five percent of women have it before forty-five. Maybe all the health stuff triggered it early." He won't look at her. No, no, this wasn't smart. What was she thinking? Throwing this at him when he was already upset? Wrong move. "Or maybe it is just a few weird weeks in my body. It might not be menopause. Maybe it will come back when I figure this out."

He simply sighs in response. Why should they both sit around speculating? Neither knows what will happen, but they do both know that forty is hurtling toward Martha at breakneck speed. Anything over thirty-five is technically considered a geriatric pregnancy, so over forty must be an ancient pregnancy. Or maybe it's a corpse pregnancy. That's what comes after old age: death.

* * *

That night, Leon sleeps soundly while Martha stares at him in the dark, wishing that she were tired. The gynecologist appointment will be the end of all of this. They will divorce; she will have no money, no job prospects, no love. She'll be too sick to get a job or a man. Nobody will ever love her again. She will spend the rest of her life sick, poor, and alone.

She will not fall asleep anytime soon, no matter how badly she wishes for it. She goes to the living room couch to munch on potato chips while scrolling through TikToks.

"Laura Mercier powder is overra—"

She scrolls past.

"You won't believe what's in this chocolate ca—"

Scroll.

"I've had it too. Strange symptoms. Migraines. Taste cha—"

Scroll.

"I'm going to tell my parents that I—"

She scrolls back up.

A scruffy man with an inviting face speaks directly to the camera: "I've had it too. Strange symptoms. Migraines. Taste changes." He's well lit, his location like an office or something. The video has no hashtags and only twelve likes, but here it is, like it was meant to find her, the algorithm using all of the data they've mined to bring her to this very video. "Vision problems, and that's just the tip of the iceberg. Nothing helped. We know that doctors don't know shit. Your friends don't know shit." She appreciates his honesty. "I believe you may be suffering from ROND. Rapid-onset nutrient deficiency." ROND. That piques her attention. Something with a real name, something so real that it has an acronym. "For those of us in the Los Angeles area with severe symptoms who feel like we're out of options, we meet at 3:30 a.m. Yes, we know that you've become a night owl. Fill out the form in my bio for the address."

She's never done something as completely unhinged, ludicrous, and downright brainless as clicking the link in anyone's bio, but she did say she would do anything.

Chapter 13

Martha pulls into the parking lot of a rundown office building in one of those bizarrely empty parts of town—possibly Boyle Heights, but she isn't sure. She doesn't know this neighborhood as well as she used to. The first time she's driven in nearly two months, she feels grateful to go in the middle of the night because traffic is nonexistent, only a brisk twenty-five minutes to traverse the whole city. She doesn't want Leon to see a charge for the Uber, and if a migraine does strike, there's barely anyone on the road, so she could easily pull over.

She felt so confident and filled with adrenaline when she started this adventure, but now she feels extremely silly. She should be scared, a woman alone in the middle of the night at a location that she got from a TikToker, but she just feels stupid. She used to meet up with strangers on the internet all the time, but never for something like this—she feels dumber for thinking that these people will heal her than for hoping that some dirtbag from Tinder who cums in milliseconds will want to be her boyfriend. But she feels that same hope again, that same twinkle that this mystical person will completely transform her life, save her.

She gets out of the car and looks up at the warehouse. The building is empty, dark. She finds a door and tries to open it. Locked. What is she doing? This is ridiculous. Maybe this isn't even the right warehouse.

Next to the door, she notices a doorbell. She presses it.

Nothing happens for a moment, and then the door buzzes, unlocked. She opens the door, unprepared for whatever may happen on the other side.

To her surprise, she walks into what looks like the waiting room of any other doctor's office she's been to, the lighting soft, inviting.

"Welcome to the club." The man behind the receptionist desk smiles, nobody else in the waiting room, but she thinks she can hear people deeper in the facility.

"I saw your video." Martha approaches the desk, recognizing him as the TikToker. It's that surreal dating-app moment, when someone who moments ago was behind a screen has suddenly materialized in front of you, this time someone cute, mid-twenties, short, light stubble, baby face.

His voice is warm, alluring: "I'm glad I'm getting the word out! I'm Bruce."

"Martha." In front of an attractive man, she suddenly feels underdressed—hair in a clip, sweatpants, a sweatshirt, no makeup.

"I'm so happy you're here, Martha," he says with deep, inviting eye contact. "Well, I'm sad you're suffering, but I'm glad that you'll be getting the help you need."

"I would try anything at this point."

Bruce pulls his Hanes black tank top to the side, revealing a long deep pink scar under his hairy pec. "It's great to have another trans person with us."

Her heart fills with roiling black terror. Her whole life depends on being unclockable. And this man, this random man she only just met, has the nuclear codes to her entire existence, one button away from denotating the whole thing to oblivion. She should deny it, slap him across the face, walk out and never look back, pay any price for his silence, or kill him with her bare hands.

Seeing her face, he tries to backpedal. "Oh, sorry, I didn't mean to assume anything."

Stunned in place, she has to know. "How did you know?"

"I'm really sorry, I shouldn't have said anything."

"But how did you know? I haven't been clocked in . . . I can't even remember the last time."

"Sorry, I shouldn't have said anything. But we're all chill here."

She needs to know exactly what it was—the tilt of her brow bone, the timbre of her voice, the slope of her shoulders—so she can demolish, polish, destroy it.

He smirks. "I mean, they don't make cis women that beautiful."

She giggles, not from being so swept off her feet but from pure incredulity. Her whole life is flashing before her eyes, and this man has the audacity to flirt with her? It's so outrageous that it somehow works to calm her.

He powers forward. "So, tell me about your symptoms and why you think you may have ROND."

"Everything you said in your TikTok. Taste changes were first. Meat tastes completely rancid, coffee tastes chemical, like, uh . . ."

"Gasoline?"

"Yes! Exactly." A lightbulb goes off as she finally puts a name to the bizarre flavor. This guy knows what he's talking about. "Blurred double vision. Migraines, really painful. My sleep schedule is erratic, basically nocturnal. And I have tried everything, but still no." Martha tears up, finally recounting this to someone who actually understands. "I want my life back. I would do anything to feel better."

He comes out from behind the desk. "Can I hug you?"

"Uh," she stammers, holding back tears. "Yes?"

He pulls her into a deep embrace. She feels held, truly held, for the first time in a long time.

"We're going to get you better." His breath balmy in her ear, he squeezes tight.

She pulls away, embarrassed to have been so vulnerable in front of this total stranger. For once, she's grateful that she didn't put on mascara. "Sorry, sorry."

"Don't be." Bruce puts a hand on the side of her arm. "Follow me to Room A."

He opens the door leading out of the waiting room to the rest of the facility. She doesn't quite comprehend the layout of this place: They're in a warehouse, but it has regular ceilings?

She can see that there are more rooms farther down the hallway, but he stops at the first one. She can hear a few voices inside. He opens the door.

Room A looks like how she imagines an AA meeting is set up: ten chairs in a circle with a table with refreshments on the side against the blank white wall. Five people sit and chat, but they all stop and turn when Martha and Bruce enter.

"This is Martha," Bruce announces. "She'll be joining us for treatment tonight."

They all greet her warmly.

She notes the word "treatment." He still hasn't said what that is. She was expecting people far crazier, but they all seem sane, normal.

Maybe not the typical people she has in her life, but nobody she would look twice at on the street.

Except Angie. She'd look twice at her.

"Angie," Bruce says. "I hope there's enough for Martha as well."

"Oh, great, you've brought another tranny," Angie laughs. She has one of those old transsexuals' faces, of street queens and ballroom dolls who transitioned in hotel rooms, bedrooms, and back alleys rather than doctors' offices like Martha had. Angie clearly has had some professional work done in more recent years, which gives her an older yet undefinable look. Wearing some cheap sparkly thing from Santee Alley, she could be anywhere from forty-eight to seventy-nine. "Is that the only people you bring here? Gorgeous women you want to—"

"Hey, she found me," he protests. Ah, so he flirts with everyone. He motions to one of the open chairs. Martha sits. "This is Level 1 of our treatment regimen. Many of us have a full recovery with this alone." He takes the seat next to her.

Angie grins, her filled lips stretching. "Mother brought more than enough bounty for us all to feast."

Feast. Is that literally or figuratively?

Warm in this little room, Martha takes off her sweatshirt, observing the others. There's a young man in his twenties, a straight tech guy, scrawny, nerdy. There's a hippie-looking young woman, piercing-loaded ears and an arm covered in tattoos that look like doodles. And then a gay couple in their sixties, holding hands, two bears. Martha feels immense jealousy—they get to be fat and bald and hairy and completely in love. She's struck by their normalcy. She almost feels disappointed, like they all should be wearing *Eyes Wide Shut* masks.

Angie fiddles with a duffel bag under her chair. She pulls out a large tin, covered in aluminum foil. "Rescued tonight's cuisine from the back of a Vons."

She peels back the foil, revealing a pile of whole chickens that look completely raw. Maybe they've been very lightly poached? Angie rips off a leg with a wet tear. Martha confirms that it is in fact as pink and raw as a freshly waxed asshole. She watches in confusion as Angie passes the tray. The tech guy rips off a breast, the hippie girl tears off another leg, while the bears pull out a whole raw chicken to share.

"You can really tell it's organic," one of the bears comments. "Or it was."

The bigger bear leans over two empty chairs to pass the tray to Martha. She takes it, confused.

The smell hits her.

Angie gleefully says, "The label said these babies are three weeks past due."

Martha gags, looking down at the rancid chicken. There was already an odd smell in the air, but now that it's right in front of her, the stench of rotting flesh is unbearable. Yellow-green-gray rot streaks through the opaque pink flesh, littered with soft spots of white, black, and green mold. Her eyes water from the odor of death and decay steaming off the carcasses.

She has to look away. She laughs, hysterical. Of course the people she met off of TikTok in the middle of the night are insane. Just because they look normal doesn't mean their brains aren't as rotten as the fowl they're devouring. "What, what is this?" Martha holds out the tray for somebody else to take.

Bruce stands, taking the tray from her but still holding it in front of her face. "Hey, that is a completely valid reaction, but I urge you to taste one."

"This is insane!"

Everyone else looks at her, unperturbed by her panic as they chomp. Bruce urges, "Just taste one."

"This will make you all sick." She feels insane for having to state something so obvious.

"Martha, you're already sick." He holds out a drumstick. "You said you'd do anything to feel better. Now take a bite."

For a second, he sounds so convincing, so caring, that Martha parts her lips ever so slightly, salivating, looking into his alluring eyes.

But the smell hits her again.

She stands up, flustered, embarrassed that she'd considered it for even a moment. "You people are psycho."

"It's not like we're doing some Satanic ritual," the hippie woman scoffs, punctuating the sentence with a cartoonish chomp of her chicken leg, slurping up the silvery ligaments.

Bruce puts the tray down and takes a step toward Martha. She jumps back slightly, the realization hitting her that nobody knows where she is. These people could kill her right now. Leon would have another dead wife, and he wouldn't even know what happened to this one.

Bruce puts his hands up. "We've found solutions that work for us and we believe would work for you too. We're all consenting adults. If you don't want to participate, see yourself out."

* * *

She exits the warehouse to the cold dark night, out of breath. She shakes her head. This was a mistake, a huge mistake. She needs to go home right now and forget about all of this and never tell a single soul. But how could she ever forget what she saw in there?

Bewildered and exhilarated, her heart pounds.

It strikes her swiftly, the streetlight in front of her multiplying and blurring. She wishes this were happening anywhere but here. The pain in the front of her skull becomes overwhelming. This is the worst by far. Her legs go weak; she thinks she might faint. She starts to fall over, and, oh God, she's going to hit her head on the concrete and bleed out and die right on the pavement.

Strong arms wrap around her, holding her up. "I've got you. I got you." She looks up at Bruce's face, appearing to her in doubles and triples. "I got you."

She closes her eyes and leans against his firm body, waiting for the pain to subside. He pats her hair. She feels better quickly this time; perhaps a knowing touch makes the pain ease faster. She flutters her eyes back open, the world normal again. She looks up at Bruce, his singular handsome face.

"Thank you." She stands up on her own, embarrassed.

"I used to get really bad migraines too."

"But not anymore?"

Bruce holds out Martha's sweatshirt. "You forgot this."

Chapter 14

Martha and Bruce reenter Room A. Everyone has mostly finished their chicken, gnawing on the bones now.

"They always come back." The tech bro smirks. The others laugh. It seems they always do.

The shorter bear grins. "Oh, you know we ran away when we first saw all this."

The other adds, "We were ready to call the cops on this whole thing, but . . ."

"They always come back," the bears say in unison.

Angie cackles, her mouth full of chicken bones cracking on her molars. She motions to the tray. "It won't bite."

Martha reaches into the tin to take one, trying to overcome her disgust, but once she feels the slimy rotten flesh, she pulls her hand away. "Oh God, I can't."

"Sit," Bruce instructs her. "Close your eyes. Don't breathe in through your nose. I'll feed you."

Martha takes a deep breath to calm herself, just like Leon does. She sits, eyes shut tightly. Hasn't she put a lot worse things in her mouth? In her Tinder days, for sure.

Bruce takes a drumstick with one hand and her chin with the other, softly lifting it up. "Open."

She opens her mouth, sticking out her tongue. She can't believe she's doing this, but his voice is so sure, forceful yet doting. He positions the drumstick in front of her open mouth. The rancid stench hits her nose even more intensely, eyes watering from the stink so thick it tickles her trimmed nose hairs. Her lip trembles with anticipation.

"Take a bite."

Shaking, Martha takes a very small bite. Her teeth slice through the slick coating of mucus, biting through the stringy muscles of the uncooked flesh, tearing off the smallest nibble of meat. She prepares to spit it out, but when the clammy morsel hits her tongue . . .

Holy shit.

Her disgust shifts to surprise: pleasure, immense pleasure. It's so incredible that she thinks it must be a mistake. Has this all been psychosomatic the whole time? Emphasis on the "psycho."

Martha opens her eyes and grabs the drumstick from Bruce. She takes a massive bite, as big as her mouth can take. It's delicious. More than delicious. It's the best thing she's ever eaten. This can't just be in her head. It really is that good.

He nods, smug. "We believe the taste changes are your body's way of telling you what it needs. This tastes good because you are finally properly feeding your body. We call it rapid-onset nutrient deficiency. There are at least a hundred people across the country who are doing this exact same treatment and surely thousands more who need it who aren't getting it."

"But why, why would my body suddenly need rancid chicken?" she asks.

"We don't live in a harmonious society. We're surrounded by poisons," he explains. "This is our antidote to the poison."

She doesn't quite understand, but she can't deny what just happened. "But like, what exactly is the poison?"

"Modern life is the poison."

"It's the microplastics," the hippie girl says confidently. "They're in our bloodstream, they've crossed the brain-blood barrier. We're semi-Plasticine creatures now."

"Lacey, you don't know that it's from plastic," he replies.

She rolls her eyes like it's so obvious. "All our grandparents were eating produce covered in DDT for nearly three decades before they realized it fucked your shit up and the babies were coming out weird. *Silent Spring* came out in '62, and it still took a decade for them to actually ban it. The same thing's going to happen to plastic."

"It's the 5G signal," the shorter bear says nonchalantly. "The waves changed our DNA,"

"Definitely the 5G," the other bear echoes.

"I think it's not any one thing. It's all of this shit in this so-called modern world," Angie says, gesturing vaguely. "All of it combined."

"Or it's possible this disease has always been affecting people," the tech guy suggests. "We all know that modern medicine has major blind spots."

"Whatever the reason is," Bruce says, regaining control of the room, "we know that there's a chemical change when meat goes bad, processed by bacteria that we normally consider harmful. But now our bodies love those rotting chemicals. You'll immediately function a lot better with proper nutrition. The treatment for ROND is simple: Give your body the right nutrients."

"Why isn't this being studied?" Martha asks. "This is a major medical breakthrough."

"You really think a bunch of white coats are going to take the crazy curdled-chicken eaters seriously?" Angie scoffs. "All that matters is feeling better."

"I've thought about taking this to medical professionals. It would help a lot more people if it was taken seriously," Bruce admits. "But then I get scared. Eating contaminated meat could be considered a threat to my life, suicidal self-harm. If I present this to a doctor and they don't believe me, they would be in their rights to detain me and shove me in some inpatient clinic, preventing me from getting the medicine I really need."

"It's a real threat, getting sent to the insane asylum. It's happened to some of our other members," Angie warns. "When spouses or family members find out."

"How did you even find this solution?" Martha asks.

"I was so sick I couldn't keep my job waiting tables, but I didn't have insurance to see real doctors, not fast enough," Bruce recounts. "And with no money to pay rent, my roommate was furious with me, knowing my promises to pay her back were empty when I had no job in sight. And she yelled at me to clean out my crap in the fridge. I left a chicken breast in there far too long. It was completely rotten. But I was hungry, no money for food. When I went to throw it out, it looked kind of . . . appetizing."

"I felt that too," she remembers. "With spoiled pork chops. I thought it was sympathy, but I guess it was hunger."

He continues, "I started posting online. I couldn't be the only one, I had to find others like me."

"I found him on Reddit," the tech guy adds.

"I don't try to go viral or anything, don't want to put this all at risk. But I know this is my duty, helping other people get better."

"But how do we know it's safe?" She still takes huge bites of the drumstick, getting quickly to the bone.

"Girl." Angie sneers harshly. Martha feels deeply comforted by an older trans woman saying "girl." "You shoot up with cross-sex hormones, and you draw the line at a little old poultry?"

"But that's safe. That's through a doctor. It's been studied."

"Not too long ago, we were pumping back-alley silicone and popping horse-piss 'mones." Angie's right—she has the lips to prove it. They're overfilled yet loose, almost square in the center. They remind Martha of so many of the women she met when she was first transitioning. Before hyaluronic acid facial filler went mainstream, it was trans women pumping each other with silicone caulk or corn oil, whatever they could get their hands on.

"Horse piss?" one of the bears asked.

"Google it!" Angie barks. "And c'mon, even when it's a prescription from the doctor, do we really know what all the 'moning does long term?"

"We know hormone replacement therapy is safe," Bruce says. "It has been heavily researched now."

"Generally safe, but maybe something happens to one in a million girls who've been on decades of juice. We're not at that yet. Sample size!"

"That obviously hasn't stopped you," he replies.

"Bingo."

Martha finishes the drumstick, licking her fingers. "Can I have another?"

Chapter 15

Martha wakes up feeling fan-fucking-tastic.

"Good morning," she bubbles, turning over to Leon, his alarm going off. She pulls off her sleep mask with glee at the possibility of a normal day once again.

"Oh," he replies, startled by her enthusiasm. He shuts off his alarm. "You're up early. When did you end up falling asleep last night?"

Visions of rotten meat and a hunky trans man flash in her head. She drove back after the meeting, the sky still dark, and returned home as quietly as she could. Leon, fast asleep, had no idea. She brushed her teeth thoroughly, scrubbing her mouth out like she said a dirty word.

"Maybe around like four?" she lies. "But I actually feel good. Refreshed even."

She stretches, in disbelief. Could the rancid chicken really have done the trick? Was the answer lying in her trash can this whole time? She gets out from her comforter and slides into Leon's, holding him tight.

He smiles, happy to have his lively woman back. "What's gotten into you?"

About a pound of rotting poultry.

"Nothing. I'm just, I'm feeling good. Really good."

"I'm glad," he replies, going to get up out of bed.

She pulls him back. "Not yet." She kisses him deeply. More than a good-morning kiss. A fuck-me-in-the-light-of-the-sun kiss. She grinds her pelvis against his morning wood. His tongue worms its way into her mouth.

Oh no.

She pushes him off.

"You don't like the tongue?"

She rips off the sheets and runs to the bathroom, hand covering her mouth, now filling up with squirts of acid. She throws herself to her knees in front of the toilet, vomiting intensely, pea-soup bile pouring from her stomach in painful bursts. Obviously the rotten chicken was going to make her sick.

He walks to the bathroom, an erection still tenting his boxers, and leans against the doorway. Martha, eyes wet with tears and yellow-green dribble clinging to the corner of the mouth, turns to face him. He's smiling, looking down on her. Why is this bastard smiling at her sickness? He chirps, "You know what happens when women throw up in movies. Especially in the morning."

"It's definitely not that," she replies a little too quickly.

"Well, why not?"

"Uh . . ." She racks her brain, barely able to think after puking so hard. "Because we haven't had sex in a month."

"We had sex not too long ago. Morning sickness starts at six weeks."

She turns her face back into the bowl and vomits more. She feels bad. He's so crazy about this baby thing that he's made himself think his sick wife is pregnant, filled with new life. But really, she's rotting from the inside out.

He opens the cabinet under the sink, pulls out a box of pregnancy tests, and places them on the edge of the basin. "Pee on a stick for me and I'll feel a lot better, okay? What if your rabbit died?"

"Excuse me?"

"They used to inject women's urine into rabbits to see if a woman was pregnant. It was a common misconception that the rabbit only died if the woman was pregnant. All the rabbits were killed and biopsied to see if they were exposed to human chorionic gonadotropin. The tests actually had a ninety-eight percent accuracy rate. And now modern pregnancy tests look for the same hormone, but without the bunny murder. But the phrase is still 'the rabbit died.'"

"Where did you learn that?"

He bends down to kiss her forehead. "A book." He exits the bathroom to get ready for work, the tests staring her down.

She bought them to stage the first pregnancy, the one she miscarried. She thought about buying a pregnant woman's pee online, but that would've been too obvious of a paper trail. And Leon is no rocket scientist. She merely took a little pink marker and drew the positive line herself. You'd have to be pretty insane to accuse your wife of faking her pregnancy test, so it worked well.

She gags over the toilet, but nothing comes out, her stomach completely emptied. With all of that out of her system, she feels surprisingly good. Perhaps the vomiting was more like a cleansing release than a sign of illness? She still feels awake, filled with more energy than she's had in a long time. She closes the door and brushes her teeth thoroughly.

She looks back to the box of tests. She could just wet it under the faucet and she'd get the same result, but she's trying to avoid unnecessary lies. She might as well pee on it.

She exits the bathroom and hands him the freshly urine-soaked stick. "Hot off the presses. Let it marinate."

He takes it, excited. "You could've left it on the sink, but thank you."

She shrugs, puts on her robe, and walks to the kitchen. She makes herself a cup of tea, absent-mindedly scrolling on her phone and thinking about last night. She's obviously never going again. She does feel amazing, it's undeniable, but it made her ill. It will be one insane night that no other soul will ever hear about. Maybe she'll delete TikTok, just to be safe.

"You're up early," Enid says, surprised. "Are you taking me to school?" Leon has been taking Enid lately since Martha hasn't been awake early enough to do that. They didn't discuss if that would change this morning.

He yells from the other room, "MARTHA, GET IN HERE!"

"One second, babe," Martha says to Enid. She returns to the bedroom. Panic sets in, wondering if there's some way that the pregnancy test betrayed her. It didn't just say negative but *The test taker is a big fat stinking lying male.*

She's surprised to see Leon with a beaming smile. He grabs her by the shoulders and squeals, "Your rabbit is ding-dong-dead!"

Chapter 16

One of the nurses at the Beverly Hills Center for Reproductive Care draws Martha's blood. Martha stares intently at Roger, who is barely concealing how annoyed he is in having to participate in this charade in front of Leon.

"False positives on at-home tests are rare, but they're not impossible," Roger comments. "Could be a defective or expired test. Even certain types of laundry detergent can mess up the results."

Leon nods. Nothing Roger can say will bring him down. After the first positive test, Martha took a second at-home pregnancy test to shut Leon up—faking another pregnancy and miscarriage was not part of her plan. The first was obviously defective. She peed on the second one as Enid finished getting ready for school.

By the time the second test turned positive, they had to take Enid to school. Leon was celebrating already. The only thing she could think to say was that she'll get a professional pregnancy blood test. He said that was a great idea and insisted that he would take the morning off, claiming a family emergency so that they could get the official results together. She said that him coming wasn't necessary, but he was adamant. She had hoped that when she called to make an appointment, there wouldn't be one available, but the nurse said there had been a cancellation if they could come in immediately.

So off they went, dropping Enid off first. Leon was giddy, kissing Martha's hand excessively, her skin glistening with his spit. Enid didn't ask what was going on, but Martha wondered if she could guess.

Roger adds, "If you recently had a miscarriage, that could also lead to a false positive."

The mention of the miscarriage is the first thing that makes Leon's smile drop. Martha conceals a smirk; Roger confirming the miscarriage right to Leon's face now makes him a full-on accomplice.

The nurse finishes drawing the blood.

Martha knows Roger must be annoyed at making the lab give her a pregnancy test, but she's paying for it so he might as well. It would be more unethical and more annoying to doctor up negative test results. "We'll have an answer shortly."

* * *

Martha and Leon get brunch at a fancy diner nearby. She picks at a chicken Caesar salad while he excitedly inhales a tuna melt. She had hoped that her experience last night rebooted her taste buds, but the properly grilled chicken tastes horrendous, so she eats around it.

He holds her hand tenderly. "I know I'm breaking every rule by saying this so soon, but I have a really good feeling about this."

Her heart breaks for him. She doesn't do all of this to be sadistic. She hates how broken he's going to be when they get the inevitable news. Those faulty ones at home gave him false hope. The disappointment that is sure to follow will push him closer to the Imaginary Fertile Woman.

Her phone rings—Roger. His personal cell phone instead of the office. She wonders why he didn't have a nurse do the deed. She feigns a hopeful sigh. "This is it."

Leon squeezes her hand, but she wriggles from his grasp. In public, this charade feels somehow worse than faking the miscarriage. That had planning, artistry, pageantry; this is just cruel. She takes a sip of tea before she answers, nervous.

"Pick up already!"

She answers, still holding the teacup like an English lady. "Hello."

Leon says, "Put it on speaker."

But she is too shocked. Roger tells her the news. She doesn't say another word while he rattles on and on, baffled at the results.

She drops the teacup. It falls to the floor with a shatter of porcelain. Black tea spreads out like an oil spill. The whole restaurant gasps and looks to her. A concerned waiter rushes over.

Leon stands up, celebrating like his team won the big game. He pumps his fists in the air: "I'm going to be a daddy!"

The whole restaurant cheers for him.

* * *

Martha sits on the examination table with her shirt lifted over her belly, waiting for Roger to prep the ultrasound. Since the call, her mind has been buzzing, droning with anxiety, waiting for Roger to examine her abdomen and reveal to Leon that there is nothing there but intestines, nothing that could create life. She's only full of shit marching to her rectum. But underneath all that, she has this deep undulating feeling that there *is* something there, something rooted inside her—that her life is about to change.

Leon holds her hand. Since the call, he's been so excited, blabbering on about what a good feeling he has. She's remained quiet, vacant, answering him with nothing more than a nod. He can't stop holding her hand today. She feels like he's got her on a leash.

"Now this is early for an ultrasound, but given Martha's, uh, history," Roger says, hitting "history" so it reads for both of them, "I really want to see it with my own eyes. It's possible that you're just having a hormonal abnormality. If your body is overproducing HCG, that could result in all of these false positives and would also be a big medical concern."

"Why would that happen?" she asks, fearing that this is some side effect of ROND or whatever they called it. Or maybe of ingesting rotten poultry.

"Kidney failure, some types of cancer. Some people take HCG supplementally for weight loss, although you're not supposed to."

Leon says, "She's been gaining weight, not losing it."

Martha is immediately offended until she sees he's smiling about that—weight gain means baby to him now.

Roger squeezes the jelly onto her stomach. She shivers at the cold squelch. He roughly pushes her back against the table, positioning her body. Leon squeezes Martha's hand, brimming with anticipation. "We're going to see our baby."

Roger presses the ultrasound against her abdomen, hard. She winces. He stares intently at the screen, producing grainy black-and-white images she can't quite comprehend.

The image starts shaking—Roger's hand is trembling.

He takes a deep breath, steadying his grip. His voice flutters as he speaks, "So right here, the spot over here, that is your ovary."

"What, what do you mean an ovary?" she stammers.

"There is an ovary present," Roger replies tersely, pretending he's not losing his mind.

Leon doesn't quite catch on. "Is there something wrong with it?"

"Nope. Nothing wrong. It's there," Roger replies. "The ovary. Looks . . . normal."

Leon forces a laugh, confused by their reaction.

Martha is speechless.

Roger moves the wand lower. "And here is, well, here is what looks like your cervix and uterus."

"My, my uterus. Right, right. There's my uterus. My uterus."

Roger moves the wand slightly. They all watch as a small black oval appears, a little almond-shaped thing nestled at the side of it. He drops the ultrasound wand like he saw a ghost. "Sorry, sorry!"

"Roger!" Martha yelps. "What, what was that? That black thing?"

He picks up the ultrasound wand, scrambling to find it again.

Leon kisses Martha on the cheek. "I know what that is. I remember with Enid."

Roger finds it again—the black oval and little almond inside of it, the blackness like a hole boring inside of her.

Leon grins. "That's our baby."

Unable to quite believe that the blur of static on the screen is a real thing happening between her internal organs, Martha stares into the black hole of a baby growing inside of her.

She faints.

Chapter 17

"Easy there, girl. Just give me some deep breaths." Leon's voice is low, soothing, calling her back to land from the sea of unconsciousness.

It reminds her of waking up from surgery. You go under in the operating room, it feels like you merely blinked; then your eyes flutter open with a searing pain in your loins, and the nurse tells you to be careful with your new vagina.

Leon coos, "We need you nice and calm. Don't want you riling up the baby."

"The baby," she whimpers.

The baby, that's it, that's what's happening. Roger turns the computer monitor to Martha, showing her screenshots of multiple angles of the ultrasound of the fetus. Speechless, her mind blank in a state of shock, she stares into the depth of the dark hole gnawing inside her.

"There appears to be a fetus growing inside of what appears to be your uterus," Roger says in staccato beats, cold sweat glistening on his forehead. "You appear to be carrying a child."

"You don't need to do all that doctor-speak. She's pregnant!" Leon smiles. "How far along is she? Has to be at least six weeks, I think."

"It appears to be at seven weeks."

"Where is that developmentally?" Leon asks.

Roger replies factually, concealing his shock well. "The embryo is 9.93 millimeters, the limb buds are starting to form, the nerve cells are developing into the brain and spinal cord. We may be able to hear the heartbeat as early as next week."

"We can hear the heartbeat next week." Leon rubs her hand with anticipation. "When is the due date?"

"It would be around the first week of June."

Leon swoons. "A summer baby."

Roger forces a grin. "Leon, why don't you go to the front with Nurse Lia to finish up some insurance stuff while I wrap up with Martha?"

"I'll see you in a second, my love." Leon gives her hand one last kiss before getting up and following the nurse out of the room.

Roger stands by the door, listening for Leon's footsteps walking down the hallway. He waits until Leon's returned to the waiting room, then softly closes the door. Roger sits and takes a deep breath, putting his hands together like he's praying. Martha still stares at the black hole on the screen.

He wheels his chair suddenly toward her. "What the actual fuck. No, seriously. What. The. Fuck?!" He grabs her by the shoulders and whisper-screams into her face, "I don't know what the fuck I'm seeing, but it looks an awful lot like you have ovaries and a uterus and a fucking fetus. How the fuck did that get there?!" He wipes his face with his hands in pure exasperation. He looks back up at her. "Say something."

She lays a hand gently on her lower abdomen and looks at him. She whispers softly, "I am so cunt."

"Martha—"

"I am one-in-a-million cunt."

"I don't understand how this is remotely possible."

"I'm sample-size cunt." She has an eerie calm, like this is the first thing that has made sense in a long time.

"Be serious, please. I am freaking out. Freaking out! How, how is this possible?"

"Sample size," she explains like it's obvious. He stands up, trying to wrap his head around it. He rifles through the wall cabinets looking for something. She continues, "It's not like there are one billion transsexual women. Or even a hundred million. Or anywhere close who've been on hormones as long as me. And think of all the genetic factors, environmental factors, weird health shit going on with me. Maybe one in a billion trannies grow a uterus. And I'm one-in-a-billion cunt."

He finds what he's looking for, pulling out a silver flask. He downs it, not even making a face as the liquor slips down his throat. He wipes his mouth with his white lab coat sleeve and returns the flask to its hiding spot.

He seems to consider this. "You have an X chromosome in every cell in your body that has the genetic code for building a uterus and ovaries—everybody does. They just need to be activated." He nods, clearly willing himself to believe it. "So, this is really just a unique intersex condition. Which means having XY chromosomes and a newly constructed uterus with a fetus growing in it. That's not, no, that's not so crazy after all."

"I'm fertilized-cunt cunt."

He sighs. "So how are you going to tell Leon you have to get rid of it? Fake another miscarriage?"

She gasps like she's been slapped across the face. "Get rid of it? Absolutely not."

He looks very serious. "This is a freak accident, and we have no idea if it's safe, if this baby will be viable or healthy or—"

"I am not getting rid of this baby." She's never been surer of anything in her entire life. She will not let this go.

"This baby could kill you. In a regular pregnancy, a baby can easily kill you. And this time, we wouldn't even know what to look for. We have no idea how this could affect you or what kind of fetus would develop from this. This could be a death sentence. You could be growing some monstrous freakazoid infant, with claws and wings and a tail."

"You said it yourself: A pregnancy can kill you. Any pregnancy can. No woman knows what's going to happen when she gets pregnant. I don't see why it's any different for me."

"You can't be serious," he groans, rubbing his brow.

There is simply nothing he could say that would change her mind. She's never been a big believer in fate or destiny, especially distrustful of that supposed God that her parents kept talking about, but now she sees that everything she's been through has been leading her to this. With an almost religious zeal that she would have found deeply embarrassing not even ten minutes ago, she feels enlightened to the truth of her purpose on this planet after wandering in the desert for thirty-nine years.

She holds his hands firmly. "This is all I've ever wanted, to do this thing that other women get to do, and I've had to accept that it would never be me. You know I've had to fake it. And it hurt. It really hurt doing that. But now, by some actual miracle, I get to do this for real. I can't let this go. I am having a baby with the man I love."

He looks into her eyes, twinkling with hope. She has faked a lot of things, but this is very real.

He turns to his clipboard and writes rapidly, ordering tests, making a game plan. "We are going to monitor you extensively. We need to check your vitals constantly, check for hemorrhaging of the uterus, check for any blood abnormalities, check for, well, check every single thing we can think to check. If this is what you really want, I am ready to buckle up and go on this ride with you, but you need to know that if there's anything alarming, we must prepare to terminate the pregnancy to protect your life."

She ignores the warning, giddy. She claps, feeling as though everything in the room, even the plastic replica uterus sitting on the counter, is clapping for her too. "We're really doing this!"

"I'm going to contact experts from every area I can think of. This is a historic medical case. We need all the help we can get."

"No experts." She shakes her head. "Don't you think Leon is going to notice if all these doctors fly in to monitor me all the time?"

Roger stands up, looking furious. "This is the biggest medical case of the millennium. We can't brush it under the rug. I refuse to do that. It would be unethical."

The door opens—Leon.

They stare at him, deer in headlights. Leon smiles, a big oblivious dad smile. "Finished with insurance."

She stands up and pulls Roger in beside her. "He was just telling me how happy he is for us."

"Aw, buddy. Bring it in," Leon says as he gives them both a big hug, each of their heads on either of his shoulders.

Roger glares at Martha—he wasn't finished with her. But even he can't help but seem excited. "This is certainly going to be something!"

Chapter 18

Martha looks out the window from the passenger seat at streets she's passed many times, highway on-ramps she knows like the veins on her thighs she wishes would go away, but it all looks different now. Even the day itself feels illuminated, no longer just a Wednesday in October. Everything's changed: Now she's a mother.

"Erasmus for a boy," Leon says, his hands steady on the wheel. "Janine for a girl."

"Erasmus? Is that even a real name?"

"Erasmus was a philosopher."

"What was his philosophy?"

"I don't remember."

"And Janine? Is that your high school girlfriend?"

"I just like Janine. No girlfriend, I promise."

"Okay." She smiles, only teasing him.

"I know I shouldn't be thinking of names so early, but I know what I'll be calling you," he giggles. "Mommy."

She cackles. Men used to call her Mommy all the time, on dating apps or in bed. She always found it immensely cruel. Not only a dig at her age, despite these men saying it to her even when she was in her twenties, but also a callous joke, calling her something she desperately wanted but thought she'd never be. Until now. Now her husband calls her Mommy, his baby in her belly, and it is the truest word ever said. "Yes, Daddy."

The Imaginary Fertile Woman has been defeated.

Now she gets to imagine something else—herself as a mother, as the mother of a baby that is her own flesh and blood. She thinks about the clothes. She and her baby will be the best dressed pair in Los Angeles—a high bar. She won't go for costumey, cloying toddler outfits—far too suburban—or for perfectly matching herself with the baby—far too tacky, bordering on cultish. They will wear perfectly tailored, incredibly fine fabrics, still with a sense of personal flair. For herself, she will combine a sort of boho-hippie motherhood with flowing florals and a '90s-movie-star red-carpet glamour, just the right amount of bountiful life-giving cleavage. The child will be swaddled in Ralph Lauren and the chicest baby couture, a balance between New England old money and a '70s Laurel Canyon carefree tot. She imagines that strangers will look at her with her child and immediately recognize that they are a pair like no other before, that she is the motherest of all mothers.

But no, it's not just the fashion that gets her; she realizes that her whole orbit is going to shift. Martha has never been the center of anyone's life. No, not even her parents'—they hated her ever since her toddler wrists went limp. She thought about this constantly when she was single, figuring out the gaping maw of weekends and Christmases and life all alone. It plagued her, the frigid loneliness only interrupted by the temporary warmth of others, nobody ever staying. And even after she found Leon, Enid was already the center of his life; Martha only joined their tribe. But as a mother, finally, finally would she have someone who is truly hers, and she theirs.

He interrupts her fantasies: "And I'll have to cancel that other gynecologist appointment. So much for menopause or endometriosis. We were both so wrong. I couldn't be happier to be wrong." He beams. "Hey, maybe some of your weird stuff has actually been pregnancy symptoms. You clearly had morning sickness. Pregnant women do get super strong reactions to different foods."

"Wow, that would make sense for me." She hadn't considered this. If the baby is at seven weeks, then the symptoms started well before she got pregnant, but perhaps it was a reaction to her cells constructing the reproductive organs. Surely such a major change would take a toll on the body.

"Have you been craving anything weird? Pickles and ice cream?"

Her mouth waters now, remembering the delectable taste of the rancid chicken. "No, nothing strange yet. But you know my girlfriends would tell me the weirdest pregnancy side effects. One of Christine's cousins, her pussy turned blue."

"Blue?!" he laughs. "That has to be some sort of urban legend."

"Christine looked at it herself! Honest to God, it turned blue."

"How could it even turn blue?"

"It wasn't blue-blue like the ocean or a robin's egg. She said it was a deep purplish color."

"Let's hope yours stays nice and pink." He puts a hand on her thigh. "You said you felt good this morning, before the vomiting, at least. Did you do something different last night?"

She gulps. "I tried, uh, a meditation technique. I think it really worked."

"Must have been powerful."

There's silence for a moment before Martha breaks it with a joke: "Scheherazade for a girl and Squilod for a boy."

"What is Squilod from?"

"I made it up. You don't like it? It sounds distinguished."

"Squilod," he practices, letting the sound fill his mouth. "Squilod."

Her phone buzzes in her pocket. She pulls it out and checks it discreetly. A text from Roger: *Cedars Sinai 9:30 AM tomorrow. I'll see you there. Can't change the time, so figure it out. If we're doing this, we're really doing this. With the experts.*

* * *

The next morning, Martha sits in a hospital gown, kicking her legs back and forth like she's excited for the first day of school. The room is chilly, her hard nipples chafing against the cheap paper of the medical gown.

Roger introduced the doctors, lining them up like reproductive-anomaly Avengers. Dr. Nanjani, a man in his fifties, studies stem cells. Dr. Folstein is a sixty-year-old woman and an expert in abnormal pregnancies. Dr. Rockford is the premiere fetal-development doctor in the US, a man in his eighties with hair sprouting out of his ears that Martha desperately wishes she could wax. The last is Dr. Kim, a man in his late forties who is apparently an expert in trans endocrinology, but Martha had never heard of him. Martha made Roger and the experts swear that they would not publicly announce anything yet. Roger agreed, since he said Martha's safety was his main priority. And for such a landmark case, the doctors agreed—for the time being.

"I must be jackpot to you guys," she laughs, trying to warm up the icy room.

The doctors do not laugh. They only glance at her while they read the medical packet Roger made. She feels like they're reading her diary.

"It's a medical miracle, but it looks completely legitimate," Dr. Rockford says to the others, pointedly not speaking to Martha, only a few feet away. "A pregnant male."

"Male . . . ?" she mutters under her breath.

Roger corrects, "Transgender woman."

"And advanced maternal age," Dr. Rockford adds.

"Advanced?" she hisses. "Am I ahead or something?"

Roger shoots her a look. "It's a medical term."

Dr. Nanjani looks to her. "Because we did not monitor you before, we may never know exactly what happened, but we believe some of your stem cells got the green light to become the uterus and ovaries, likely from prolonged feminizing hormone usage. That is not supposed to happen outside of the womb, and definitely not supposed to happen in someone with a neovagina."

Martha smiles and raises her eyebrows. "Cool."

"Isn't it possible the patient was intersex and that went unnoticed?" Dr. Kim asks.

She laughs, "I really don't think so, honey."

Roger explains, "If there were significant internal or external genital abnormalities, they would've been noticed by Dr. Medford, the UCLA surgeon who performed her vaginoplasty."

"Let's run chromosomal testing on the patient," Dr. Kim orders.

"We have that test ordered for her today. Among many others. Please let me know any other you'd like me to add," Roger says. Martha hates how he acts around these people, clearly sucking up to them, these supposed geniuses. It's weird to see him like this, the same man she's watched drunkenly fellate countless strangers' cocks in WeHo back alleys.

“How much is this all going to cost me? I can’t have this on my insurance,” she pointedly asks Roger—code for *Leon cannot find out.*

“You are part of a research study now. You don’t need to deal with insurance anymore. Every test and doctor will be completely covered.”

For the cost of nothing, Martha gets poked, prodded, and probed. They take samples of her blood, urine, feces, sweat, mucus, throat, hair, and vaginal discharge. They perform an EKG, MRI, and many other acronyms that Martha can’t even remember. The morning quickly passes, being shuttled to different nursing stations and medical machines. She feels like a two-headed calf, groped and gawked at under the microscope.

After many hours and surely a pound lost in fluid samples, Martha and Roger finally exit the building, walking back toward their cars. Feeling an almost zealous thrill, she says, “I’ve spent so much time trying to prove my womanhood, I kind of like having to prove I’m a bona fide transsexual. A real-life miracle.”

“You’re the real deal now, diva.” He gets serious again. “Now that your ovaries seem to be producing all the hormones you need, let’s get you off the pills.”

“Oh, that is fierce.”

When he picked a specialty in med school, she had her fingers crossed for plastic surgery, envisioning free facelifts. She felt spurned when he told her he went with gynecology, taunting her with the reproductive system she didn’t have. She thought it was his way of rebelling against her, his mother, but he did list only LA hospitals as his residency preferences to not fly too far from her coop. She never thought that she would actually get to use his services.

“You know that if all of this goes well, you will need a whole squad of doctors at the birth,” he continues. “And after the baby is born, we will want to be studying you and the baby for the rest of your lives.”

She stops walking. "Jesus Christ, the rest of the kid's life? That seems a bit much." Constant medical examination is certainly not what she imagined for her precious child.

"Other people would be going on the *Today* show for this, but you do have the right to keep your identity private."

"I'm not telling Hoda and Kathie Lee shit."

"Well, they both retired, but no matter what, the doctors will keep wanting to publicize this case. You have a right to privacy, and we will obviously keep your name out of it, but—"

"Wait, you know that even if I let those doctors talk about it one day, you are never allowed to talk about this, right?"

"Not allowed to? You are my patient."

"No, no, no. If you get famous for finding the freak tranny pregnancy, that's too obvious. Leon will have questions about your sudden celebrity."

"But I did find the freak tranny pregnancy. And I can lie to Leon if you really want. I thought you didn't have any problems lying to him?"

"Don't be catty."

"You're a miracle, Martha, and you know I don't like saying things that make your ego even bigger that it already is. I know it's scary, but don't you think he'll have to support you? You need to tell him."

"All he'll hear is six years of me conveniently forgetting to tell him that he's been fucking a shemale. Use that big doctor brain: Do you think men like being told that? Whether I'm a miracle, medical, religious, or otherwise?" She sips her iced tea, annoyed. Gay men think they "get it" with trans women, to overidentify with what they see as a shared male femininity. While they both may live in a straight man's world, Martha sleeps with it, she makes love in it, she has a home and a child in it. He'll never understand what it means to lose that because he gets to build a life without heterosexual men in the equation.

Roger sighs. He may resent her for not letting him accelerate his career through this, but he won't do that to her if she puts her foot down. Not yet, at least. He adds, "You shouldn't drink too much caffeine while pregnant."

"It's just tea," She takes one last sip before tossing it in the trash. She puts her arm in his, leaning against him. "But I appreciate your concern."

Her Apple Watch buzzes on her wrist. She glances at it—a text from Bruce. Her breath stops as she reads: *How are you feeling?*

She discreetly puts her hand in her pocket, hiding the watch. "I gotta go, baby. Do a little shopping."

Chapter 19

I have a bit of a strange request," Martha says with a big smile, acting like her headache hasn't gotten worse.

"Stranger than pig's blood?"

She is flattered that the butcher remembers her order from months ago, but she also makes a mental note that he is perhaps the only paper trail to the faked miscarriage. She laughs, "Yes, it is actually stranger than pig's blood. Do you have any rotten meat? Like meat that has fully gone bad? I know that sounds insane, but my daughter needs it for a science experiment."

"No rotting meat," he scoffs. "We are a highly sanitary establishment."

"Yes, please don't take this as a dig or anything. But I thought maybe you have something in the trash out back?"

"We don't have rotting meat. Sorry."

* * *

Moving with a manic energy, Martha slams the door to her car. She wears sunglasses, a baseball cap, medical gloves, and a mask to hide herself. She carries a tote bag. She feels as though she is about to commit a robbery, walking with such purpose through the Ralphs parking lot. Although to anyone who notices her, she looks more like a germaphobe than a thief.

She is hungry.

Yesterday she was torn. Could the meat really be working? She had felt better, undeniably better, since her trip to the warehouse. And now she feels the craving in the pit of her stomach that will not be satisfied by anything on the shelves in the grocery store.

And she isn't just thinking about her own health: She's eating for two.

She watches intently as other patrons walk toward the store. She spots the dumpster by the side of the parking lot, near the truck loading zone. Even with her getup, with really only her nose visible, she went to the Ralphs in South Central to get far away from anyone she could possibly know.

The Ralphs is busy with families speaking Spanish and USC frat boys pushing carts filled with cheap beer and hard seltzers, the greasy scent of grocery store fried chicken lubricating the air. Her scalp already damp, she sweats heavily under the baseball cap. She googled to make sure that dumpster diving is not illegal in California; it's only illegal if you're trespassing, but the dumpster is in the parking lot, which is open to the public, right? Still, she doesn't want to take her chances with getting caught. She watches as an employee tosses bags of trash into the dumpster, heaving them over his head. She waits for the employee to return to the store and then she makes a mad dash for it.

She makes it to the dumpster and double-checks that the coast is clear. Nobody has noticed her; no frat boy has even batted an eyelid at her. She reaches up to pull herself into the dumpster, but it's too high. Crap. There must be another way in.

She spots some wooden pallets nearby, leaning against the fence. Hurrying over, she drags the pallet, breathing heavily, and pulls it toward the side of the dumpster. She hasn't had a workout this good in a long time. With every passing second, she gets more worried that someone will spot her.

She stands on the wooden pallet and reaches up, but still can't reach the side of the dumpster. Normally she is incredibly thankful for her short stature—she feels extra womanly when Leon has to reach things for her—but now she is pissed.

What else can she use? Ah, a trash can. She drags it over. She puts the trash can on top of the wooden pallet and then carefully climbs onto it. It wobbles beneath her. She swings one leg over the side of the dumpster, straddling it. Getting her second leg over, she accidentally knocks down the can—she'll deal with that later.

She drops from the side of the dumpster into the piles of black trash bags and stray garbage. The horrendous smell makes her wretch, even with her mask on; she should've put a sprig of lavender in her mask like a plague doctor. But even with the overwhelming stench, her stomach rumbles, starving.

She starts ripping open garbage bags, thankful for the gloves on her hands, though she still feels the grimy texture. The bags are mostly filled with rotten produce—limp lettuce, wrinkly tomatoes, mushy apples. The flies feast, swarming at everything she frees. Her gloves are quickly covered in slime. When she bends over, her sunglasses fall into a pile of brown, nearly liquefied bananas. "Damn it."

She reaches to grab them, but her hands are so slimy that it would be disgusting to put them back on her face. The Dior sunglasses will have to be a casualty.

She keeps digging, praying she finds something soon, worrying there might not be any here. She could leave fresh meat out to rot, but it would take too long to get it as bad as she ate in Room A. No, the meat has to be here. Angie said she rescued hers from the back of a Vons. She'll find something if she keeps looking.

The sun beats hard on the back of her neck. The dumpster emanates heat like a living, breathing thing. Not a sentient creature exactly but a massive organ, as though she's rifling through the innards of some primordial underworld behemoth.

She finally finds it, ripping open a garbage bag to reveal a trove of plastic-packaged steaks. She lifts one up, elated to see completely gray-green meat—jackpot.

"Yes!" she cheers, doing a little happy dance, shimmying her booty back and forth, as she picks up the rest of the meat, shoveling them into her tote bag.

Time to get out of here.

With the bulky tote bag hanging on her shoulder, Martha tries to pull herself up the side of the dumpster, but it's too heavy. She tosses the bag over. It lands with a hard thud on the asphalt. She's nervous, separated from her stash, like it's something precious, but the only thing that would try to steal it is a stray dog—she would kick any dog's ass back to the pound if it tried to eat her dinner.

Without the tote bag weighing her down, she's just barely able to heave herself out of the dumpster. She lands on the hot black asphalt, cushioning the fall with her hands. Carefully removing her soiled gloves, she tosses them into the dumpster. She grabs the bag and pulls it onto her shoulder. She glances at herself, checking that everything is okay—her implants are still intact, and the baby doesn't seem too shaken up, not that she can feel it yet. She checks the meat in the tote bag, making sure it survived the fall. She giggles—of course it's okay; it's rotten meat.

"Martha?"

She turns to see a frizzy-haired woman with a cart full of grocery bags.

"Emma! Wow, it's so good to see you. What are you doing here?" Martha asks, pulling off her mask, making her voice as big and saccharine as possible, kidney-twistingly embarrassed for someone from the school to see her like this, already imagining the rumors Emma's going to spread. Maybe if she acts like this is completely normal, Emma won't register it as anything else.

"I'm a professor at USC." Emma stares in utter confusion.

"Yes, I knew that," Martha laughs. "What do you teach again?"

"Computer science."

"Right! So smart, wow. Women in STEM!" Martha, completely covered in dumpster juice, wonders why this woman hasn't found the time to put in any conditioning oil.

"I'm sorry, but were you, uh, dumpster diving? Are you a dumpster diver now?"

"Dumpster diver? No, no?" Martha guffaws, stalling until she comes up with something. "Definitely not a dumpster diver."

"But you came out of the dumpster, yes?"

"Oh yeah, yeah. But I'm not like, a dumpster diver. I was diving in a dumpster, yes, but because I, I lost my wedding ring."

"You lost your wedding ring in the dumpster?"

"Yes, I did. Well, uh, no. I lost my wedding ring, and I realized I might have accidentally thrown it out with the paper towels when I washed my hands. I never want to use a grocery store bathroom, but when duty calls." Emma obviously doesn't believe her. She must think Martha has had some sort of psychotic break. Perhaps she isn't entirely wrong. "But by the time I noticed my ring was missing, they had already taken out the trash. I asked if somebody, an employee, could help look through the dumpster, but they said no way. So, it was up to me, so much for customer service! But I found it! Isn't that a miracle?"

"Wow," Emma replies coldly, seeming unconvinced by this fabrication.

"Look, I've got to go," Martha chirps, marching past Emma, holding the tote bag close to her so that nobody can peek in.

"Martha, are you okay?"

"I found my ring! I'm great," she cheers, making a beeline to her car.

"I have a change of clothes in my car," Emma offers. Martha feels a little bad for her earlier thoughts. Maybe she should just buy Emma a conditioning oil as a thank-you.

"You're too sweet!" She turns around, now yelling. "And don't tell Leon about this, please! I don't want him to know I almost lost the ring. Let's get coffee soon!"

Martha hustles to her car. She's had quite the workout—she's starving now.

Chapter 20

Martha frantically drives up a parking structure, going to the highest level. She googled "parking" so that she could go into her own hidden den for her feast as quickly as possible.

Once at the top floor, she pulls into a space, not bothering to straighten out. There are only a few other cars around. She parks and puts her phone on Do Not Disturb.

She pulls out the first package of meat. The label says beef loin top sirloin: $11.99 per pound. The use-by date was three days ago. She tears open the plastic with her nails, inhaling deeply through her nose, taking in the scent. It's off, but it's not terrible. She wishes it were worse.

The first bite fills her with such immense pleasure. Her face flushes, life returning to her. It's good, it's so good. The steak has a richer taste than the chicken. It's not as delicious though, not yet—it hasn't got enough rot.

To tear into the raw steak without utensils, she shakes her head back and forth with the meat in between her teeth. It's still tough, not broken down enough by decay. She chews it, the gray-maroon juice dribbling down her chin. Moans squeak out while she gnaws away at the sirloin, grinding it with her back teeth to get every drop of flavor. The first steak quickly disappears into her gullet. It helps, but she still needs more.

She pulls out another, ripping it open without a care in the world. Only when she is about to bite into the second sirloin does she notice there is another car on the same floor, not too far away. A group of teenage boys are staring at her, their car filled with smoke from a blunt in the hand of the driver. Her display has been so bewildering that she stopped the rotation. Polite, she raises her steak to them, like a toast. The boy in the driver seat raises the blunt to her. We all have our vices.

* * *

Martha pulls into her garage and parks. With a spring in her step, she gets out of the car with the tote bag of meat.

On the way home, she changed clothes and got the inside of the car cleaned. The car cleaners were bewildered by her, this beautiful woman with a car that reeked of unadulterated garbage, but she didn't bother giving an explanation. She will have to be smarter about dumpster diving in the future, but she does have a hefty stash of meat that should last her a while. And if she has to, she can go back to the warehouse.

She opens the garage freezer—that's where she stores meat and Leon never looks in there—but then she realizes the obvious: It won't rot.

The office/gym/storage/guest room is cluttered, filled with objects and boxes from each of its iterations. The elliptical collects dust in the corner, not even plugged in. Leon used to use this room to work, so his desk and a computer take up one corner, but there are boxes of random crap on the chair. She's pretty sure the couch is a pull-out, but that too is covered in containers.

She keeps telling herself that she must fix up this room, but something always comes up. She looks to the pile of boxes in the corner, next to the door to the en-suite bathroom. She lifts the boxes to get to the bottom one. In there, she finds a bunch of old blankets. Perfect. She pulls them out and finds a photo album. She doesn't remember putting that there. Leon must've packed this box.

Martha opens the photo album, and there she is, smiling brightly on her wedding day: the first wife. She flips through—the proposal, honeymoon, pictures of her barefoot and pregnant, baby Enid, the three of them in front of the house. A whole life, a whole family, now only living in a photo album.

Martha has seen pictures of her before. When Martha first started coming over, there were pictures of her everywhere. She was pretty, although truthfully—and she's not just being petty—not as attractive as Martha. Even in these pictures of their wedding day, Leon, young and dashing, upstages his bride. That's rare, especially in LA. That's how Martha knew Leon was a good one.

Leon and Martha had a courthouse wedding, with only Enid, Amy, and Roger in attendance. Martha was the one who'd suggested a small ceremony, trying to come off humble, but really not wanting to reveal too explicitly that she'd cut off all of her family and friends besides Roger. Leon, who already had a big wedding, was happy to save the money for the honeymoon in Anguilla. On Enid's suggestion, she and Leon went to the grave a week before the wedding. That was the last time.

Martha knows she is probably not the love of Leon's life, even though he is the love of hers. She doesn't pester him about it. He does love her, and he is not looking for anyone else, and she has decided that is enough. She has the man, the house, the kid, and now even his baby—she doesn't need to be greedy and demand to be his soulmate too.

The more Martha came around, the more the photos of the late wife started disappearing, signaling to her that he was ready for a new woman. He wasn't going to completely throw her away, but the love of his life could live the rest of eternity in a box with the blankets in the guest room. It wouldn't be smart to use this box for her stash since he might look at the pictures from time to time. She puts the photo album back, insulating the memories in layers of fleece.

She opens another box and finds only blankets this time. She places her decomposing ambrosia in its tote bag at the bottom of the box, placing the comforters over it. She closes the box and sniffs. Hmm. Maybe not enough coverage.

She takes a quick trip to the kitchen pantry and returns to the office, armed with Ziploc freezer bags and Febreze.

"FUCKING HELL!" Martha screams, looking right at Enid about to grab the tote bag out of the box. Enid, who Martha did not even think was home.

The girl turns around, confused by her stepmother's bewilderment.

"Sorry, sorry. I didn't know you were home," Martha says, trying to feign calmness. She walks toward Enid, trying to get herself between the child and the tote bag.

"That bag smells weird."

"Don't you have, uh, swimming today?"

"I called to tell you that my stomach hurts. I texted. You didn't answer, so Keira's mom drove me home."

"Oh, shoot, I'm sorry. My phone, yeah, my phone died. I'll have to thank Keira's mom for that. I've been busy freshening things up around here. It's a mess, as you can see, that I'm trying to whip into shape." She holds up the Febreze and Ziploc bags, hoping that will answer the question of the peculiar scent. "But your stomach hurts, you said? Is it something you ate?"

"It's more like a cramp." Enid puts her hand on her lower abdomen. She looks pained, almost wincing. Then she looks shocked. "I think I got my period."

Martha gasps. "Oh, oh. Go to the bathroom right now. I'll meet you in there. I just have to finish this."

"I think I'm bleeding. I'm bleeding like right now. I'm literally bleeding. Come with me." Enid, who normally holds that preteen air of put-on self-assuredness, seems so young right now.

"Bathroom now. Go. Sit on the toilet. I'll be right in."

"But I—"

"Go."

Enid races to the bathroom.

Martha wipes the sweat on her forehead with the back of her hand. She quickly puts the packaged meat into Ziplocs, sealing them tight. She sprays each bag with a spritz of Febreze before they go in, then sprays the whole thing after she piles them all back in the box. She puts the other boxes on top so the one hiding the meat is covered.

Enid yells, "Come already!"

Chapter 21

"Take the adhesive wings of the pad and wrap those around your underwear so they stick. You need to check every few hours to see if you need a new one," Martha explains. Right after her vaginoplasty, she used pads as a bandage, absorbing her bloody discharge. When it got really bad, she used adult diapers too, but the pads made her feel less infantile, maybe not a full-grown woman but at least a teenager.

Martha looks at herself in the mirror to give Enid some privacy. Her skin looks taut, plump. Whether it's the meat or the pregnancy, it's a good look.

Enid grumbles, "I think I did it right."

"Do you want me to check?"

"No, I said I did it right."

"I can check if you want."

"I did it right." The start of those temperamental teenage years.

Enid doesn't know it, but she should consider herself lucky that they even have pads in the house. Martha doesn't need to use any sanitary products. At first, she just told Leon that he didn't need to worry about cumming inside of her. He assumed that meant she was on birth control. He brought it up one time to assure himself that he was not going to have an accidental child, and Martha affirmed she was taking it. He didn't ask further questions.

A little while after they got married, Leon had a smirk on his face, holding her in bed, and said, "What if you stopped taking the pill?"

"What pill?" Martha replied, panicked that Leon had realized that the pill she took every night was relabeled estrogen.

"The *pill*," he emphasized.

Martha almost confessed right then and there, but thankfully, it hit her: birth control. That's the pill for women, cis women.

Never in her life did she ever think a man would want to have a baby with her, and here was a handsome guy who really loved her, asking if she'd carry his child. It meant more to her than the marriage proposal. "Yes, yes, yes." They had some of their best sex that night, deep, passionate, looking into each other's eyes with her hand on his collarbone as he came inside her.

That's what kick-started the whole production, Martha's game plan to ward off the Imaginary Fertile Woman. Since one version of the birth control pill stopped your period entirely, once she claimed she got off that pill, she told Leon that she's always had an extremely light flow. She tracks her fictional period in a tracker app, but she makes it the first week of every month to keep things simple.

She bought a box of pads, the very box that Enid is currently using. She has to be very careful about maintaining a proper vaginal biome; given hers was man-made, she couldn't go shoving tampons in there all willy-nilly. So she did what any woman would do: She'd prick her finger with a needle and squeeze out the blood onto the pads. She'd hock a loogie and smear it in for the discharge, then wrap the pad in toilet paper, entirely covering her masterpiece.

Her life got a whole lot easier when one of the moms at school started raving about the DivaCup. The mom wasn't sold on it at first, she thought it was "some crap for Gen Z hippies with shaved heads and unshaved armpits," but then the mom realized it was actually quite user-friendly and comfortable. The mom was, of course, only vocally advertising to the older mothers that she still got her period, but it was a lifesaver for Martha. She could simply pretend that she emptied out her menses into the toilet.

"It feels kind of weird. Like a diaper." Enid grimaces, uncomfortable as she stands, waddling over to the sink.

Martha takes a step back so that Enid can wash her hands. "These pads might be a size too big for you. They're small, you probably need an extra-small. And they're for a light flow."

"How do I know if my flow is light?"

"It depends how long it takes you to soak through the pad. It's definitely better to be safe than sorry. Don't want you staining my couch." Martha laughs. Enid does not.

"I think they told us to change our pads every four hours or so?"

"You're an expert already."

"Wait, can I get the poison thing? How long do I have to leave it in for the poison thing?"

"Toxic shock syndrome?" Martha asks. Enid nods, terrified. "I don't think you can't get it from a pad. Those are like horror stories of women leaving tampons in for days. Don't worry about that." Enid dries her hands. "How do you feel?"

"Am I supposed to feel some big thing? I feel, I don't know, achy. Am I supposed to feel like a woman now? How do I know if I feel like a woman?"

A question Martha also asked herself during puberty. One she didn't think she was allowed to ask. "Whatever you feel, that's what a woman feels like."

Enid leans against the sink, finally looking up at her stepmother. "Did your mom help you with your first period?"

Martha lies through her teeth: "A camp counselor helped me, actually. I got it in the middle of a kickball tournament, so embarrassing. A boy pointed out the stain in the back of my shorts and the counselor had to help me in the nurse's office. You're lucky you got it at home."

She feels bad—Enid wants to have a tender moment with her, and Martha has to fudge it. It comes so easy to her. She never even went to camp, but Martha isn't going to give her own mother credit, not even in a lie.

She was so jealous when the girls in her class got their periods in middle school. They spoke in whispers to each other. Sometimes they'd talk about them in front of her—she was like one of the girls to them anyway—but she knew they were holding their tongues a little with a boy present. The girls hated their periods, wished they'd never had them. Martha didn't tell a soul that she cried herself to sleep because she'd never get a period of her own to complain about.

Enid comments, "You never talk about your mom."

"We weren't very close." Martha's mother was a homophobic nutjob who didn't give two shits about Martha, who refused to see her daughter for who she was, covering her six-year-old kid's back in welts from her brown leather belt when little Martha said she wished she'd been born a girl. "I don't think she was a very good mother to me."

Enid looks away, staring at her feet. She winces as she adjusts her pad through her pants. She speaks softly, "I don't even really remember my mom. I feel like I only even know what she looks like from pictures. I've lived more of my life without her than with her."

Enid rarely brings up her mother at all. Martha's heart aches for her—her first period, and her mother isn't here to help. Martha lives out of spite toward her own mother, that crone, in defiance of the life that her mother thinks that Martha must be living. But for Enid, her mother is only a wound, scabbing over but never healing completely.

Martha doesn't know what to say, so she says what in her wildest fantasies she wished her own mother would say: "I know she'd be very proud of the woman you're becoming."

She has a sudden realization, so powerful it brings tears to her eyes. If she has ovaries, after the baby is born, she will have a period—her first period at forty.

"You're crying," Enid says.

Martha's emotions swirl, bubbling up from the pit of her abdomen and out through her eyes. She must be hormonal because the tears really start flowing. She feels it all, deeply—Enid, her mother, Enid's mother, all of their periods.

"I'm so happy, so grateful, that I get the privilege of watching you grow up," Martha gushes from the very bottom of her heaving heart.

Enid pushes off the sink and into her stepmother, wrapping her arms around her, her face pressed snugly against Martha's stomach, just below her breasts. Martha hugs her back tightly. Still squished against Martha, Enid squeaks out, "Should we eat ice cream and watch rom-coms like they do in the movies?"

Chapter 22

Enid and Martha, sunken into the couch, eat Häagen-Dazs directly from the tub—chocolate for Enid, strawberry for Martha—and the incredibly gorgeous man on the television keeps taking his shirt off for them both.

"I think this really is helping," Enid says. Martha lifts up her ice cream. Enid taps hers against it—*Cheers.* "Can I start posting on TikTok? Now that I'm a woman?"

"Not until you're at least thirteen. You're still my baby."

Enid slurps the ice cream off her spoon. "Wait, so why does the guest room smell so weird?"

"I stupidly left some food in there from who knows when. So that room might smell a little funky for a while. That's why I was cleaning."

"Would that be the baby's room? If you had one?"

"It would be."

* * *

Later, Martha performs her nighttime skincare routine at her vanity, rubbing lotion across her chest. This time, she rubs the lotion onto her stomach, feeling the baby. She wants to minimize stretch marks, so she must be oiled up at all times.

"So Enid had some very big news today," Leon says with a dad-in-over-his-head grin as he enters.

"She's growing up so fast," Martha sighs. She thinks about telling Leon what Enid said about her mother, but she decides that should be a private moment between them. It makes her feel more like a true parent, not just Leon's sidekick.

"My little girl is really growing up. She still can't wear makeup until junior year, but—"

"Oh, come on! Let the girl have a little freshman glam, it won't hurt."

"No boys until she's in college."

"We're not going to be locking her away like some Brentwood Rapunzel. It'll only make her crazier. You raised a good kid, let's trust her." She realizes something very strange—they will be parents to both a teen and a young child at the same time. Potty training in one room and sex talk in the other. And then, in twelve years, they'll be going through all the puberty stuff again, hopefully with more wisdom the second time. And then, before she knows it, the kid will be going off to college. Her heart falls, imagining how empty the house will feel. It's still a tiny thing in her womb and she's already mourning her empty nest in twenty years.

He goes over to her, takes her freshly moisturized hands, and pull her up to face him. "You're such a good mother."

While she's been mothering Enid in many ways, she has always taken a backseat to Leon's fatherhood. With this new child, she will be the sole mother, fully in control, a fully equal parent to Leon, if not actually the primary parent, like most mothers. The whole household will shift as Martha fully takes the reins, no longer needing to defer to a man. She holds back a smirk, giddy for the power, to be the superhero and not the sidekick. "And you're the best daddy."

He kisses her softly. "You're going to be so sexy pregnant. Showing, I mean."

She fantasizes about herself with the big swollen belly, bountiful breasts, rosy skin. "Is that one of your kinks? The bigger the belly, the harder you get?"

He laughs, shaking his head. "No, no. It's not like that."

"Then what's so sexy about it?"

He puts a hand gently on her lower stomach, the same spot he presses down on when they make love. He mutters, voice gravelly, "Knowing that wherever you go, you're growing this little part of me, of us."

She leans her head against his chest, his chin on her scalp. "And everyone is going to have to be so nice to me. Especially you."

"I'm always nice to you."

"But now you need to give me daily foot massages, kissing each and every toe."

"As you wish, my princess." He smirks and goes down to his knees, bending over to cradle her size-seven foot and kiss her pink-painted toes. She giggles at the tickle of his lips. She imagines being pampered by not just him but the whole world: everybody telling her she's glowing, cutting lines at coffee shops and bathrooms, free food, and strangers giving up their seat on the bus for her. Not that she would ever take the bus.

Still on his knees, he looks up at her. "Enid also mentioned something about a smell in the guest room?"

"Oh, it was one of those stupid health things I was doing. Didn't want either of you getting to it." She sits back down in front of her vanity, moving her foot away from him, continuing her nighttime routine.

He kneels, eye level with her. "What was it?"

"Probiotic cheese. I dealt with it."

"I should start clearing out that room."

"Don't!" she blurts out.

"Why not? You know that's going to be Squilod's room."

She reels it back: "I know. But let's not right now. I'll deal with that room."

"Why not start building our perfect little nursery together? Nest a little?"

"If you do that, Enid will immediately know that I'm pregnant. We should wait until at least the end of the first trimester to tell people."

"You're right, you're right." She gets up, but he stops her. "You know you probably shouldn't eat any weird cheese like that anymore." He leans forward and kisses her belly. "And say goodbye to sushi."

"How will I live?"

He kisses her stomach with each new proscribed food: "No oysters. No coffee. No white wine."

"I thought a glass of wine was fine!"

"The American Academy of Pediatrics says that no alcohol should be consumed."

"Damn those pediatrics!"

"No sushi. No raw eggs. Not even a runny yolk." He stands back up, now face-to-face with her. "No steak tartare."

* * *

In the dead of night, Martha creeps into the office, careful not to let the door squeak. Guided only by moonlight, she goes right to the stack of boxes in the corner. She delicately disassembles them. She pulls out the blankets from the box, then one of the Ziploc bags.

Dinner was good—Leon and Enid ate tilapia while she had a salad—but it wasn't enough.

She sits on the floor for her nocturnal feast. She pulls out one of the packages of steaks, ripping off the plastic. The moist rust-colored surface of the steak glitters in the dark, beautiful almost. She bites into it, slowly at first, savoring every second. The slime on the sirloin is thicker than on the chicken with a more complex gamey taste, like fresh semen from a man who smokes cigarettes, bitter egg-white tang coating her throat. Once she gets the flavor in her mouth, she devours it. It already tastes better than before, more rotten, more decayed, like Wagyu, so tender. She grunts, low and quiet, guttural, filling her carnal desire for flesh. She feels like a wolf, tearing into her prey under the stars, her lips covered in myoglobin. If it wouldn't wake anybody, she would howl.

Chapter 23

At 2:41 a.m., Martha pulls up her car, laughing when she sees Roger passed out on somebody's lawn on the north side of West Hollywood. She was never as bad as him, but a lifetime ago, she'd passed out on WeHo lawns too; Friday nights look different for a married woman.

With Leon and Enid sound asleep, Martha planned to feast, but tonight she was interrupted by a call from Roger. He hadn't done it in a while, but she still knew what was coming before she answered and heard his slurred speech. Like any mother, she ignored her needs to help her baby boy.

She hopes Leon doesn't notice her absence, because when Martha's had to do this before, he's commented that it's weird that a grown man needs someone to take care of him when he gets too drunk and he can't believe that she would actually still trust his medical opinion. Leon would be even madder now that Roger's stewarding their child, but she doesn't have to tell him.

She parks and gets out of the car. "Honey, I think you're trespassing."

"Honey, I think you're already getting fat," Roger slurs. She chuckles, helping him up, not taking his barbs seriously. He's an inebriated cat, always looking for something to swat at, to sink his teeth into. He plants a big wet vodka-soaked kiss on her cheek. She wipes it off and leads him to the car.

"Please, please don't vomit in my SUV," she pleads, getting him into the passenger seat.

He burps in her face: "I'm a professional, bitch."

She feels bad for him, a limp-wristed drunkard stumbling alone on a Friday night, none of his gaggle of gay party friends caring enough to get him home properly. They both know this is why his relationships never last, but with each new beau, he can only hold off the beast for a few months before he finally drinks himself to cruelty again. He is only thirty-four, but just as Martha's pregnancy is geriatric, so too is Roger for a single gay man.

She used to spend so much time with homosexuals. She used to be one, a very long time ago. Even after she transitioned, she still spent so much time at gay clubs, dancing in peace without worrying about a man flirting with her and murdering her once he found something unexpected between her legs. But once she met Leon, she cut her gay men down to only Roger. She didn't really live in their world anymore anyway. They were all a liability, their big mouths and love of drama a threat to her very existence. She did think about cutting off Roger too, but she loves him too much. And alone with him, she gets to keep a little spark of her old self alive.

He holds down his vomit, head out the window like a spaniel, as she drives him home. She leads him into the elevator and right to the door of his condo, and that's when he lets it loose, puking a thousand vodka-with-a-splash-of-crans over his rainbow-striped entry mat.

“You were so close,” she whines quietly, not wanting to wake up his neighbors. She takes his keys from his pocket and opens the door, making sure they both step over the barf-covered mat. “Let’s get you to the bathroom.”

“Don’t tell me what to do. You’re not my mother.” He haphazardly throws off his shoes, strips off his pants and shirt, and walks into the bathroom in only his socks and underwear like it was his idea all along.

She pulls the vomit mat into the apartment, careful not to get it on herself or the floor. She hears the sound of him gagging, thankfully now into the toilet. She calls out, “Good boy, in the potty.”

She steps into his kitchen, takes a fresh trash bag, and shoves the mat inside. His kitschy rainbow welcome mat was not worth saving. To the chorus of retches from the bathroom, she grabs bright yellow multipurpose cleaner and paper towels, and quietly cleans his spit-up off the hallway floor. She gets a glass of water and a piece of white bread from his pantry and enters the bathroom, a tart stench thick in the air. He kneels before the toilet, his skin red and splotchy. She sits next to him, crossing her legs. She gently rubs his back, clammy.

While she’s done this for him many times before, she won’t be able to once the baby is born. She wouldn’t feel comfortable leaving her child in the middle of the night until the kid is at least thirteen. She savors this moment, knowing it may be the last time she can do this for him.

He groans and turns his head to the side to face her, resting his cheek on the toilet seat, pink puke dribbling down the side of his mouth.

“Don’t put your head on that,” she says, grimacing.

“You used to say you were going to have my baby.” He’s sobered up a bit, words clearer, eyes less vacant.

“And our little George Michael was going to inherit his parents’ insatiable hunger for cock.” She swoons.

"Look at you now. Liar."

"I miss mornings with you. You were supposed to sleep on the couch, but somehow I'd always wake up to you cuddling me in bed, all one hundred twenty-five pounds of sharp edges. It feels like forever ago."

"That was back when you had a dick!"

She feigns offense and smacks his shoulder.

He mutters, "And back before you left me."

"Babe, you were the one who moved out once you got doctor money. Didn't even ask me to live in your fancy condo."

He mumbles, "You left me." He presses his forehead against the toilet, facing the floor, eyes closed. "I think I was too afraid to ask why, but I knew you were doing bad, really bad, right before you met Leon. You tried to hide it, but I know you were lonely, even lonelier, like you had given up on the world. I should've asked why, but I didn't, too self-involved probably."

"I didn't know you noticed that."

He lifts himself off the toilet seat and sits upright, wiping his mouth with the back of his hand. "So I always understood why you don't tell him. He loves you so much, so ooey-gooey for you it makes me queasy." Roger's grown so much since they first met. He was merely a fetus then, a little twink who she let sleep on her couch after his parents abandoned him, making sure he ate more than a Ritz cracker and Malibu for dinner. Now he's a grown man with a mortgage. "I don't think you're a bad person, not at all. I worry about you because I fucking love you. I'm the one who loves all of you."

He doesn't understand that love has changed for her. Love as a gay man means finding your twin flame, that vivacious spirit who you can spend hours dissecting pop divas or A24 movies or the psychopathology of your friend group with. Someone to drink and dance and fuck and flirt with who matches your zing and zest, who gets it, who gets you. But when you're a woman dating straight men, those priorities shift. Heterosexuality has a different premise, an ancient one—men are from Mars and women are from Venus, beings from two different planets who can never truly comprehend the other, but who must create a partnership, build a home, continue the species. She doesn't need someone to understand her soul, but a man who will hunt beasts in the wilderness for her to cook in their hand-sawed Lincoln Log house.

"That's why I need you by my side for this," she whispers. "Because I love you too."

They've never spoken like this before, not so directly. Their relationship is played out in quips, shade, and cocktails, not heartfelt speeches. He curls into himself and flops onto her. This muscular nearly naked man leans into her chest, into her lap. He nuzzles his head into her shoulder. She puts her arms around him, squeezing him tight. Her stomach grumbles, hungry without her usual nightly meal, but she ignores it. She gently rocks him back and forth, knowing that, by the morning, he'll only have the faintest drunken memory of it all.

Chapter 24

Pumpkin gnocchi with brown butter oyster mushrooms and braised leeks topped with toasted hazelnuts and an herbaceous scallion sauce. Homemade sourdough bread. A light salad with seasonal farmers' market veggies and a yuzu kosho vinaigrette. Martha's back, baby.

For the next week, she is restored, revived like Jesus from the tomb with a better blowout. The migraines and vision problems are gone now that she's properly feeding herself.

To the rest of the family, she acts like she's eating vegetarian and not drinking coffee, while at night, she chomps into sirloin, getting riper and riper by the day. She's still somewhat nocturnal, staying up all night until she crawls into bed at four or five in the morning and sleeps for a couple of hours, waking up feeling completely refreshed.

The moms at school have been happy to see her again, Leon quickly relieved of his duties after Martha makes him confident that the migraines are fully gone. She acts like she just had a nasty cold that wouldn't go away. She hasn't even fully told Christine what was really going on; Christine's just overjoyed to have her buddy back for Power Sculpt.

All the results from the pregnancy scans and tests come back normal, positive. Roger calls her to explain the results and apologize for Friday, but Martha says no apologies needed. He adds that they're not quite able to test for claws or a tail yet for her little demon baby, a joke she does not find funny.

Tomorrow she and Leon will listen to the heartbeat together. He doesn't have to know that the heartbeat is later going to be being broadcast to a handful of other doctors.

She never responds to Bruce's text. He fixed her. She doesn't need to see him again. It was a risk, driving all the way out there, to people who knew the truth, the whole truth. She could find rotten meat on her own. She has a stockpile: She bought fresh meat and added it to the bottom of the box to rot. No more dumpster diving.

Martha carries out beautiful plates of pasta to the dinner table. Enid's, Amy's, and Leon's noses waft up, like cartoon wolves.

Impressed, Amy laughs. "You've outdone yourself!"

"Does this mean we're done with Dad cooking?" Enid asks.

"Hey, I kept you properly nourished"—Leon shakes his head—"but I'm also happy to be having Martha's food again."

"Oh, stop," Martha says as she sits, watching everyone else eat first. Many people find the chorus of slurps and chewing disgusting, but it is a symphony for her. She's missed this so much. Her mother was a terrible cook. Martha would go to bed hungry, barely able to stomach her mom's Midwestern monstrosities, slop-trough casseroles and ungodly abominations bewilderingly labeled "salad." She is determined to be twice the woman her mother was, to make her family feel the love she never felt through her cooking.

She wonders what her child's favorite food will be—probably

steak, given the way she's been eating. She would rather pluck every hair off of her head than allow her child to be a picky eater. She will never let something so juvenile as a chicken nugget or buttered pasta touch his delicate taste buds. He will never eat processed food, no Hostess Cupcake, nary even a Cheerio. Her child will have the refined palate of a middle-aged restaurant critic, wowing other parents as he scarfs down Brussels sprouts.

"This really is incredible. A new high," Leon comments, mouth full, shoveling more into his gullet.

"The food is all organic. All the best for the—" Martha stops herself as he raises an eyebrow. "Family."

"And you're looking great," Amy comments, always quick to notice the slightest change in her daughter-in-law's appearance. "You're feeling better with all your health stuff?"

Martha knocks on the wooden table. "Seems like it."

"Maybe everything in your body is aligned now," Amy says with a smile and a shrug.

Leon tries not to let on too much. "Yes, we're all very happy she's feeling better."

A dampness at Martha's crotch dulls her smile.

He rubs the side of her arm. She looks at her lap, pretending to look at her plate. Has she peed herself the tiniest drop? She rubs her legs together, trying to figure out what exactly is going on down there.

She has. She peed herself.

It was a small amount, a drop really. She's never done that before. Well, she does pee a little when she laughs really hard, but she wasn't laughing. She was just sitting there and a drop leaked.

Martha's about to get up to go to the bathroom, but Leon asks her a question: "Emma said at pickup that she saw you at the Ralphs in South Central. Since when do you shop all the way out there?"

That tumbleweed-haired snitch. She can't get up to go to the bathroom now—it'd be too suspicious. Why did he decide to have this conversation in front of Enid and Amy? He doesn't think about these things. Martha tries to play this off casually, but her breathing becomes slightly raspy. "Oh, I was just in the neighborhood."

"She said you seemed really, uh, frazzled."

"No, no, I was fine." Her breathing gets more and more strained.

"I know I have your location, but you can update me more about your day. So I don't hear from Emma you were across town." As long as Enid was taken care of and dinner was on the table, he'd never showed that much interest in her day before. Now that she's growing a petri dish of his DNA, he suddenly needs updates.

She opens her mouth to respond, but she can barely inhale, like she's breathing through cotton. She can't hide it anymore. She wheezes at the dinner table. They all look to her, concerned.

"You okay?" Leon asks.

"Is she choking? Are you choking?" Amy panics. "Put your hands over your head!"

Martha shakes her head. She's not choking on anything but air. She opens her mouth to respond, but nothing comes out; she's unable to breathe. Leon gets up and stands behind her, putting a firm hand on her back.

Enid asks, "What's wrong with her?"

"Hey, just breathe. Slow, steady. Breathe with me," he commands.

"I'm fine, I—" Martha barely crackles out what little air she can push through her throat. She stops trying to speak, startled by the sound of a rush of water falling on the hardwood floors.

Oh no, oh no.

She looks down, terrified that it's blood gushing out from her, that the baby is gone in a torrent at the dining room table. Enid looks under the table to see the rush of liquid coming from Martha's crotch, waterfalling off the edge of her chair.

Horrified, the girl screams, "SHE'S PEEING!"

Martha is somehow grateful that she's only pissing in front of them, a thin yellow liquid instead of a thick red—it isn't the life inside her dying, only perhaps her dignity.

"She's peeing?" Amy repeats, bewildered.

Leon jumps back at Enid's discovery, looking down to see his wife's skirt completely soaked. "Oh, oh!"

Enid startles back, hitting her head on the bottom of the table. "Ow!"

"Oh dear. I'll get towels," Amy chirps, her judgment palpable.

Martha, completely out of breath, can't stop the deluge; no matter hard she tries, she can't turn it off.

"Give her some space," he stammers.

Enid steps away from the table, horrified, "She's peeing right on the floor like a dog!"

He commands, "Enid! Go to your room."

She happily leaves. Amy returns with the roll of paper towels.

The pee slowly trickles to a stop. The cotton clears from Martha's lungs; she can breathe again. She pants, catching her breath, thankful for every taste of oxygen.

"I'm okay, I'm okay," she repeats softly. Although she's safe in the moment, it dawns on her that no, she is still not okay. Just when she thought she had tamed the beast, her illness has transformed, nearly suffocating her.

"Go lie down," Leon instructs. "We'll clean this up."

Martha nods, going back to their bedroom, still panting, commanded to lie down after she peed on the floor. Enid was right: She is a dog.

Chapter 25

"Incontinence is normal. Don't feel bad about it." Leon nuzzles his chin into her shoulder.

She shouldn't be having pregnancy incontinence yet. The fetus is still tiny; her womb shouldn't be putting pressure on her bladder yet. Maybe he knows that too.

She tries to stay calm, but her mind is racing. It's not so much the embarrassment from peeing herself in front of everyone but knowing that she is still sick. And while losing control of her bladder wasn't fun, being unable to breathe was terrifying. For a moment, she really thought she and the baby might die from asphyxiation. She pushes those thoughts aside. Instead, she says, "I think your mom might be putting the clues together."

"We won't say anything until you're ready."

She nods. "We can talk to Roger about the incontinence tomorrow when we hear the heartbeat." He puts his hand on the left side of her chest, feeling her heartbeat against his hand.

Warmed by his touch, she turns over, facing him. It takes a big man to watch you violently pee yourself at the dinner table and still cuddle with you that same night. She took a shower, of course, but she still appreciates it.

Oh God. She realizes something utterly gut-wrenching: This is the hottest she will ever look.

She's seen mothers' bodies in the locker room at Pilates. Even the ones who try to hide, switching to sweatshirts and loose blouses, she sees them too. Nobody's body really bounces back after giving birth. There's no workout or surgery that really pulls everything back to how it was. Everything sags, droops, bulges, and stretches with the memory of the child. For a woman who's been split open, ripped apart, carved, cracked, and screwed back together again to look the way she wants, this is a mortifying thought. The thought is more painful than all those procedures—at least she got painkillers for that. All her work, her beautiful work, will be torn apart, sullied. While the Imaginary Fertile Woman has been defeated, Martha envisions a new enemy: the Imaginary Fit Young Slut.

She was not afraid of this woman before. Martha's hot, aging well, fucks Leon like she means it. This type of woman didn't seem like a threat. But now her head is filled with rot-fueled visions of varicose veins and a loose blue vagina oozing with mystery discharge.

This Imaginary Fit Young Slut will want one thing from Leon. She will not want his offspring, his love, or even his financial support like the Imaginary Fertile Woman does. The Imaginary Fit Young Slut only wants his hard cock. Why? Because she's bored. Because she has daddy issues. Because she can.

Martha feels confident that he would not leave the mother of his child. No, he's a good man; he wouldn't do that. But perhaps, desperate to once again have the tight insides of a woman grip onto his cock, maybe he'll have a stray night, perhaps even a whole torrid affair.

She reaches out and strokes his face, which is staring back at her. What is she afraid of? He likes to make love, to look in her eyes. He's not the type of man who would cheat. She moves closer to kiss him deeply. His lips are soft, tender. But something is missing, the slow and steady electricity that she usually feels isn't pulsing.

He pulls away with a quick peck. He smiles, ignoring her sexual advance. "Let's get a good night's sleep." He kisses her on the forehead like a grandmother and moves over in the bed, back under his own comforter, leaving her cold.

She can hear scratches at the door—the Imaginary Fit Young Slut claws at her bedroom door with acrylic nails, ruining her fresh set to get to Leon's prick.

* * *

Sitting in total darkness, Martha nibbles on her rotting steak. But it doesn't feel right tonight. It doesn't feel like it's filling her up properly. She knows it isn't, or she wouldn't still be sick. She checks the time: 2:32 a.m.

It's been over a week since she went to the meeting. She ignored Bruce's text, thinking she was cured. But since she now has new issues, perhaps these must be met with a new solution, a new treatment.

She finishes the last bite of the steak. She must return.

Now in a sweatshirt and some sneakers, she quietly walks to the door to the garage.

"Where are you going?"

Martha yelps. She turns around to see Enid in her pajamas looking up at her. "We need to put a bell on you." Martha feels startled by her size. Enid has been growing a lot. In the blink of an eye, she will be taller than Martha. "I'm just taking a drive to clear my head. Go back to bed, sweetie."

"I can't sleep either, I'll go with you."

"No, you need to go to bed."

"You smell funny."

"I've had a rough day. Back to bed." Martha walks up to Enid and guides her back to her room.

The girl takes a step back and balks, suspicious. "What's wrong with you?"

Almost caught, Martha stammers, "Nothing, honey. I'm just, I'm just a little restless."

"You peed at dinner. And Dad wouldn't talk about it. Something is going on."

"When you get older, sometimes you can't keep it in. Don't mean to scare you, but things don't work like they used to." She chuckles quietly, trying to deflect. She puts a hand on Enid's back, trying to lead her back to her room.

"I googled it," Enid says firmly, not budging. "You're pregnant again."

"Enid, I'm just . . ." Martha starts, ready to lie, but she relents when she sees the girl's face. "Yes. Please don't tell your father that you know."

Enid crosses her arms. "You kept it a secret from me."

"No, it's not like that."

"You both knew, and I didn't. That's a secret."

Leon's not going to like this. They really shouldn't tell Enid this early, and she especially shouldn't have told his daughter without him. "It's very early, very. You're not supposed to tell people until at least after twelve weeks. I'm only at eight. And we'll probably wait longer than that. We're really not supposed to tell anyone for at least another month or more."

"If I'm going to have a little brother or sister, you should've told me immediately."

"You're not supposed to tell people in case something happens." Enid's eyes go wide, remembering the scene in the bathroom. Martha nods. "You're not supposed to tell people in case something like that happens because then you have to tell everyone there's no pregnancy anymore."

"That's why you can't sleep."

Martha nods, impressed by Enid's wisdom and maturity in this moment, her actual empathy. Even if the first miscarriage was faked, it's true that she is worried that it'll happen for real. At the dinner table, the split second when she thought the wetness coming from her crotch was blood was her worst nightmare. If she doesn't focus on her health, on healing herself, it could be a miscarriage next time.

"Don't worry about me or the baby." She turns Enid around and pushes her toward her room. "But please, let's pretend we never had this conversation. Your father would be very upset that I told you already. It's really breaking the rules."

Enid enters her room, turning around in the doorway to look back at Martha. "Now we have a secret." The girl's little smile in the dark is sweet and only a little bit ominous.

With her nosy stepdaughter handled, Martha gets in her car, shaking her head. She has to be more careful—it's not only Leon she's dealing with.

She pulls out her phone and opens up his contact—she shares her location with him. He never checks it really. She knows he doesn't constantly check up on her because he'll still ask her where she is, like how he was surprised at dinner about her going to Ralphs. She used to feel annoyed by this—that's the whole point of sharing each other's locations—but now she appreciates it. He only really wants it for emergencies. It's not to keep tabs on her; it's for his peace of mind.

But just in case, she should probably turn off Find My. No, no. That would be too suspicious.

She looks at the directions, memorizes them, then turns off her phone. That way, if he really does wake up and wonder where she is, she can stick with the story she told Enid—she's just going for a drive around the area to clear her head. If he saw her all the way in Boyle Heights, that would be a lot harder to buy. She pulls out of the garage.

Chapter 26

"Pleasure to see you again." Bruce lights up when Martha walks in. "How have the treatments been going?"

"Good. A miracle really. I have my life back," she replies. The tech guy and the hippie woman chat, sitting in the waiting room. They must be eavesdropping.

"You never answered my text, so I got a little worried."

"Oh, sorry. I was . . . busy."

"Do you need more meat? Or just want some company?"

"I'm here because I'm having . . . new issues."

"What are the new issues?"

She looks down meekly, acutely aware of the lull in conversation between the tech guy and the hippie woman. They all ate rancid chicken carcasses in front of each other a week ago, but she still feels embarrassed.

Bruce whispers, "Incontinence?" She nods, relieved. She's not the only one. "That symptom can be quite frustrating. We've got pork tonight. Let's keep you fed."

"I've got the meat covered. But I was thinking that new issues must need new treatment. I remember you said we did treatment Level 1. That must mean there are more levels, right? A Level 2 in Room B? I want the next level."

"We do have multiple levels," he replies tactfully. "But we usually want to remain with the first treatment for at least a few months to gauge your reaction and give your body time to adjust."

"I don't have a few months. I need the next treatment now."

His eyes darken. "I really wouldn't recommend moving so quickly. Even in our most severe cases, we've never had someone progress to Level 2 in only a week."

She leans against the reception desk, looking at him with pleading eyes.

* * *

"It smells like a garage." Martha sniffs curiously as they enter Room B. She and Bruce stand at the entrance.

Angie sits on a low stool, placed on a black tarp that covers the whole floor. "I knew you were tough. Level 2 is not for the weak." Angie gets up to hug Martha. She squints. "Who did your face?"

"Dr. Hirsch in Beverly Hills."

"Masterful. I got all four of my nose jobs in Tijuana. You have a little mustache hair though," Angie says, plucking the stray hair off of Martha's upper lip with her pointed nails.

Martha puts a hand to her face, shocked. "Seriously? If my facial hair comes back, I'd seriously murder someone."

"It's just one, dear. Don't be so melodramatic." Angie blows the hair away and sits back on the stool.

Martha takes a seat, feeling her face for any other hairs. She went through two hundred hours of horribly painful electrolysis. Laser hair removal is neither permanent nor effective against facial hair; the only thing that kills it forever is electrolysis. Nearly two decades ago, Martha paid fifty dollars an hour for an older Eastern European trans woman with a long face to stab a small metal needle into every hair follicle and zap it with electricity until the hair could be tweezed out with ease. Now you can get it covered by insurance, but back then, it was completely out of pocket. Even with Tylenol, Advil, and 10 percent lidocaine cream, the pain was intense, overwhelming. She'd tilt her head back for the electrologist and almost wish the lady would slit her throat instead, end all the pain. The most she could ever do in one sitting was two hours; anything above that was unbearable torture. She tried to find a way to relish the pain, turn it into a little bit of masochism, but that was never her thing.

But perhaps the greatest cruelty of electrolysis wasn't from being electrocuted; it was that you had to grow out your facial hair so that the lady had something to grab onto. Having to grow out the beard to get rid of it—what a twisted joke. And even after the hair was zapped, her skin would pucker with harsh angry red sores. Dermablend full-coverage foundation was her dearest friend.

For the two years it took to complete electrolysis and eliminate the beard, she had to live in the daytime as a boy with patchy facial hair and scarlet welts, even as hormones gave her small budding breasts. That hurt deeply, more than the physical agony. But when it was all done and she touched her face, completely smooth, she knew it had all been worth it.

That is the madness of transsexuality: The physical pain of changing is less than the psychological pain of staying the same.

Thud.

Bruce drops a bright red gas container onto the tarp. Angie rubs her hands together with anticipation. He explains, "You mentioned liquids tasting like gasoline, which is quite common. Just like the rancid meat, our bodies now require certain chemical compounds found in gasoline."

Martha laughs, "What nutrients could we possibly get from gasoline?"

"Every organic compound in your body is made up of carbon and hydrogen, which makes gasoline kind of like a protein shake. It's a no-nonsense dense blend of hydrocarbons—isooctane, butane, paraffins, naphthene."

Angie teases, "He knows a lot of big words, don't he?"

Martha gulps. "So we're having a tea party?"

"It does work, but we've found that ingesting gasoline orally is quite uncomfortable in the stomach."

"So how do we . . . ?"

Angie pulls down her panties and bends over the small stool, hiking up her skirt. "Fill 'er up."

"Oh my." Martha reflexively looks away, shocked to see Angie's butthole and penis staring back up at her.

"A suppository allows the body to absorb the helpful hydrocarbons and then release anything we don't need." Bruce lugs the gas container over to the half-naked woman.

"Feel free to watch," Angie purrs. "You're lucky I'm not charging you."

He lifts the red gas can, the nozzle brushing gently against Angie's well-worn anus. "Ready?"

"Fill up the tank."

He presses the nozzle into her and tilts it, letting it flow into her. She squeals with delight. He explains, "I suggest doing this, at most, once a month. You can overload your body with nutrients." He eases it out of her. A little trickles out, the slick liquid going down her thigh. "Hold it tight."

"I'm doing my best with the old thing. These days, it's more like a hallway than a vault."

Martha asks, "What happens if you do too much?"

"We think it might have adverse emotional and mental effects," Bruce gulps. "Which is why it's important to do in moderation."

Angie snickers, "It'll make you flip your biscuit, send you to the nuthouse."

"That's not necessarily true," he corrects. "We don't have a large enough sample size."

Angie recalls, "One guy came in here talking all crazy, he was butt-chugging diesel every day. He was aggressive, paranoid, on edge, wilder than any junkie I've ever seen. He got sent away."

Bruce clarifies, "His children institutionalized him."

"He was flipping out, didn't even hide the treatment from his kids, and they got him locked up. When he got out, he hadn't done the treatment in months. So he wasn't loco anymore, but he was sick, real sick. We had to go up to the highest level to treat him."

Highest level. Martha already thought she was terribly sick. How bad did you have to get for that?

Noticing the horrified look on her face, Bruce adds, "It's possible that he was already mentally unwell, so we don't know if the gasoline treatment was the cause. But I do notice that if I do the suppositories too frequently or even if I let it sit too long, I get a bit irritable."

Angie agrees, "Yeah, it makes me tweak when I take too much."

He looks to Martha. "So now you've seen the treatment, you've heard the risks, but the choice is yours. You already know my opinion, but you know what's best for your body."

He doesn't know it, but Martha isn't just deciding what's best for her body; she's thinking about the baby's too. For a second, she feels that same fear she felt before she tasted the chicken, only amplified by the life growing inside her—there's no doctor on earth who would prescribe this, especially not to a pregnant woman. But after Bruce was right about the chicken, she trusts him more than any MD.

And maybe this is what her baby wants. Pregnancy cravings are the baby's way of telling the mother what it needs, so fine, maybe her child doesn't need Bugles, peanut butter, and a gas station Cherry Coke slushy, but something uniquely nutritious directly from the pump itself. Could Roger be right after all, that she's creating some demonic thing with scaly skin, horns, and a tail? No, he's another stupid doctor who doesn't understand. She's a miracle, a god, so who cares if she doesn't eat like all the other mortals? She must feed herself like the newfangled deity she is.

But there is one problem: She looks down at her pants. Is she really going to get naked in front of this man? She's a married woman. Nobody besides Leon has seen her naked in years. "I didn't quite dress for this."

"Hey, we're all family here," Angie calls out, bent over.

"I can bring you back to Room A for more of Level 1," Bruce offers.

Martha wonders if this man seeing her naked would be considered cheating. No, she decides. He's a medical professional. Well, not a professional, but he's a serious medical-adjacent person.

She unbuttons her pants, pulling down her jeans and underwear in one quick swoop. Bruce doesn't pretend to give her privacy. He stares directly at her neatly manicured crotch. Martha feels the heat go to her cheeks, a man's eyes on her privates. Feeling both timid and titillated, she asks, "I bend over one of the stools?"

Bruce replies, "You're going to want to get comfortable. It takes a while for it all to absorb."

Angie turns to watch Martha bend over the stool, settling herself in. "And who did your hoohah? It's so chic."

"Dr. Medford with UCLA."

"Spectacular." Angie does a chef's kiss.

"Front or back?" he asks.

Martha does hope Leon will want to fuck her again soon, so it's best not to have gasoline in her vagina. Oh, and probably best for the baby too. "Back. Please."

Bruce lifts up the gas can, the nozzle gently touching her exposed asshole. "Ready?"

"Yes."

He inserts the nozzle into her anus. It brings back memories from before her bottom surgery. An old friend, really, her asshole gave her the gift of penetration, let her fuck without using the genitals she loathed so much. She did like anal. When it felt good, it felt really good. She used to bleed sometimes; when she'd wipe and see a spot of blood on the toilet paper, she'd imagine it was her period.

She gasps as he tilts the gas can, the fluid now filling her anal cavity. She swoons at the peculiar feeling.

Angie giggles, "Tingles, don't it?"

"Like mouthwash almost, or absinthe." Martha used to douche, but this is different, a distinct cool on her anal walls, mentholic. She feels full, filled up. She would've thought that gasoline would burn, but it feels more like drinking orange juice after chewing mint gum. But in a good way, a really good way, tickling something naughty inside her—she still has a prostate, after all.

Involuntarily, she lets out a sensual moan when he pulls out the nozzle.

"Hold it," Bruce commands as a thin stream dribbles down her leg. She squeezes tight, not wanting to waste of drop of her precious panacea.

"Now we let it marinate," Angie says. "Twenty minutes or so."

Bruce sits on one of the stools. He takes out his phone, scrolling absent-mindedly. Martha closes her eyes, trying to settle into the feeling.

"That's a big rock." Angie stares at the diamond on Martha's ring finger.

She gives a coy, polite laugh. "I would've told him to get me something modest, but it was a true surprise proposal."

Angie shakes her head, marveling. "You know I never thought I'd see the day that guys were openly loving on the dolls, marrying the girls. That's like a dream. You're living a dream, girl."

"Leon's something special." Martha feels a tinge of guilt. She's so used to lying, but she doesn't want to lie to these people. She's baring her hole to them, after all.

"What do you do for work?" Bruce asks.

"I run the home," she answers, feeling like a total WASP, a pretentious crock of shit. "I help raise his daughter from his first marriage."

Angie cackles, "That first wife must be murderous knowing her husband left her for a tranny."

"Well . . . she's dead."

"Oh," Angie gulps.

"Sorry," Bruce says.

"Don't be. I didn't even know her," Martha replies. "Sometimes I feel like I have to thank her for dying so I could find my place in their lives. I'm grateful, really."

"Not just a wife but a mother. Do you know how lucky you are?" Angie asks.

She does know how lucky she is. She thinks about it constantly, every waking moment, because she's so terrified of losing it. Guilt overwhelming her, she yelps, "Leon doesn't know."

"Oh, she is carrying!" Angie gasps, impressed.

Bruce looks confused. "He doesn't know? How could he not know?"

Wild about this revelation, Angie cheers, "Keep the tea to yourself and take that designer pussy to the mansion!"

"You raise his daughter, and he doesn't know? How?" Bruce asks again, sounding disturbed.

Martha feels suddenly defensive. She's only ever had to defend herself to Roger before. "I didn't go into it thinking I would never tell him. I always planned on telling him from the start, I did."

Bruce doesn't hide the disapproval in his voice: "But then you just forgot to?"

Angie shakes her head. "You don't know what it's really like for us out here."

"You either get the chasers who only see you as a fuck toy—and even those dry up once you get a pussy," Martha says. "Or you meet a well-meaning guy at the bar, and you spend the entire evening seeing yourself through his eyes, waiting for him to clock you. And while the clock is humiliating, it's almost better than if you have to be the one to disclose, to say the words out loud. Or maybe you met him from an app and you're up-front from the start. If he's fine with it, you still have to deal with all of his panic, all his nervousness, anxiety, fear from a lifetime of society telling him that we are men in disguise or perverts or worse. And let's say maybe he is cool and normal, and you do somehow nab him—you'll still never get over the fear that he's going to leave you for a cis woman one day, someone simpler, someone who would give him an easier life, someone who can have his kids.

"And that's if they're good. That's one of the good ones who still leaves you. There are bad ones, really bad ones." Martha swallows, her eyes hot. "You go home with him, and he's already gotten you absolutely plastered, buying you more and more drinks at the bar, and then you realize you forgot to tell him, so while you're making out on his couch you giggle, 'By the way.' And you think it'll be fine because you're so drunk and he's already felt up your pussy through your underwear, so he knows you've had the surgery, but no."

Tears run down Martha's face, but her voice remains steady. "His whole body gets tense, and he pulls away and asks what the fuck you just said, but he knows exactly what you said, so you try to reel it back in and get out of there, but it's too late. He stands over you and yells at you for tricking him, and only then do you register how much bigger he is, and that you are alone in his house, and that you just met this total stranger at a bar, you don't even know his last name. You apologize under your breath and scramble to put your clothes back on, but he grabs your wrist, hard, and he calls you a dirty lying fucking faggot. He slaps you across the face. You beg for him to let you leave, please just let me leave, and then while he's yelling at you that you're a lying tranny slut, he says if you wanted to fuck him so bad that you had to lie, then you'll get what you want. He holds you down and rips off your underwear and tells you that you'll never be a real girl, no matter what shit you do to your body, you'll never be a real woman. He shoves it in you and covers your mouth, but you already know that there's no point in crying anymore because nobody is going to help you. He fucks you rough, making you bleed—you're worried that he may tear something unfixable inside you, but he doesn't care. You feel thankful that he cums quickly. He pulls his pants up, pushes you over, and tells you to get the fuck out. You race out of his apartment, your heart pounding, and hobble down the street to call an Uber. You feel lucky, so immensely grateful that he didn't murder you and you didn't end up in another one of those Instagram posts about a dead trans woman. So there you are. With your blood and his cum still dribbling out of you, for the first and only time in your life, you're grateful that you can't get pregnant. You finally make it home, look in the mirror, and poke at the bruises on your wrist and face and thighs. You've never felt more like a woman."

Chapter 27

Bruce is transfixed, speechless. Angie purses her lips and shakes her head, reaching out to grab Martha's hand and hold it tight. Martha knows Angie has a story of her own, stories probably.

Martha feels a deep release, finally telling another soul what happened to her. "I didn't go out for a very long time after that. I didn't tell anyone either. Didn't want to relive it. What was the point? So they'd see me as an even more pathetic useless mess of a woman? No. I put makeup on the bruises until they faded. And I forgot about it. Forced myself to. So that I could go back into the world. What was I to do? Let myself waste away? No. I just had to be more careful."

But now there's a new pit in her stomach. Now that she has told this story, she can't erase it, can't truly forget it.

Not long after that, she met Leon. Tall, handsome like an old-fashioned movie star. He bought her a drink at a bar—so nice to meet a guy and for him to see her as only some pretty woman, no other adjectives in front of it. She'd still been wary then, worn out, needing only an uncomplicated fuck. So she didn't tell him when they returned to her apartment, kept it stealth. She only gave him her number because he was so cute when he begged for it. She didn't really think he'd call her, but he wasn't like the other guys; he called her to ask her on a date even after they'd already hooked up.

And then the date was so amazing, just two people having a dinner and they couldn't stop laughing. She waited for the right time to tell him, sure it would present itself soon. If he stared at her for too long, she would panic, thinking he's finally figured out the ruse, but no—he'd just say how lucky he was to find her. She kept thinking he'd break up with her anyway, that she wasn't the type of person to date this wealthy, handsome man with a little kid, so why tell him when she could just wait for it to end? She was sure that there was something undeniably wrong with her, something she could never figure out but that all the other men knew that made them not want to fully be with her.

But he didn't break up with her. She kept passing all of his tests, milestones. Dating, love, it had always felt like pulling teeth, begging some uncaring man to see that she could be something to him, but with Leon, it was easy, effortless, breezy like a beautiful day.

"It all moved so quickly, suddenly with Leon," she continues. "He's a grown man. If someone fits in your life, you make them yours. And when he got on one knee, of course I said yes. How could I tell him then? How could I tell him and ruin my one chance at happiness, at love, at a real life?"

Her speech hangs in the air, waiting for their approval, which she wishes she didn't need, but she does. Roger doesn't really approve and he was the only one who knew. Now that she's told other people, she so desperately wants one other person to sympathize, to tell her she isn't wrong.

Bruce breaks the silence softly: "But literally how do you do it?" Concerned with logistics—such a man.

"I told him my parents are dead and that I have no other family I'm close to because they're all religious right-wing nuts. I never contacted them, so I don't have childhood pictures saved. And that's true enough. They weren't full-on right-wing nuts, but they believed in God enough to think I'm a disgusting embarrassment to the family. Well, my parents might not be dead. I have no idea, we haven't spoken in nearly two decades. I've never thought about looking them up or anything, I don't think about them, ever. My husband never found it weird that I didn't have girlfriends from way back when. He likes that I don't have any social media. My only friend, he owes me his life for taking him in long ago, kicked out by his parents, so he's sworn to secrecy. And I pretend to have a light flow and won't have sex for a few days every month, saying I'm cleaning my DivaCup. It's not that hard. Logistically."

"Isn't that putting yourself through constant stress?" Bruce asks.

"Everyone's life is stressful." She shrugs. "Is it more stressful than being alone? Than living openly as a trans woman? Not really."

He asks, "But how do you love someone who doesn't know who you really are?"

Angie steps in. "You know how many of my sisters have been killed out there? A trans woman who lives past forty is a war hero. So many of us give up on men if we're not getting our rent paid by them. So few of us ever get to have love, real love in the daylight." She purses her lips. "Lord knows I've never had it. I gave up all kinds of love, not just with a man, but with my mom, dad, brother, grandma. I'd still give anything to see my brother again, but he won't speak to me, won't let me see my nieces. All of them, I gave up for this."

"I get that," he says, although he doesn't. "I'm not saying I don't get why you do it, but—"

Angie cuts him off before he can say anything worse. "Why does a man need your complete medical history to love you? Does a man need to know if you have a heart condition? Or a nose job? If you've had your wisdom teeth removed? Does a woman need to tell a man if she's had an abortion?"

He replies, "Of course not."

"Exactly. Because it's private. It doesn't mean there's any less love," Angie asserts. "Bruce, you have a family still. You see your parents every other week and they love you." Martha didn't know that. She'd just assumed they all were in the same situation, but Bruce is young, from a liberal city; things are different now. She feels a flood of jealousy. "And you might even have a kid of your own one day."

"I can't afford a kid," he corrects, defensive.

"But one day, you can have one," Angie emphasizes. "I've been on my own since I was fourteen, out on the streets. No matter how badly I wanted it, I never in a million years thought someone like me would have a family, a proper family. This girl is living a fucking dream. Let her dream."

Martha feels touched by Angie's defense. Someone who knows, who really knows, approves of her. That means more than any skepticism from a man, cis or trans.

Bruce dials back. "Sorry, I didn't mean to criticize you or anything. I was curious, that's all. I'm happy you have everything you want."

"Thanks." Martha's not entirely convinced by his apology. She can't tell if his judgment of her has made him less attractive or more. She notices that in her confession, she might have loosened a bit, some fluid leaking down her thigh. "I think I need a refill."

Chapter 28

Roger moves the wand around in Martha's vagina. She didn't realize this would be a transvaginal ultrasound, but apparently that's the best for hearing the heartbeat.

He is well acquainted with her vagina. He was there when it was forged. He took care of her after her vaginoplasty, brought her ice packs, fed her, changed her bed pads, and dosed her pain medication, a dutiful nurse on his one and only summer vacation in med school. He kept her to her grueling dilation schedule. It was exhausting, painful, stretching herself out so many times a day. He was by her side while she was wearing diapers, learning to walk again, learning to pee again with her new organ. She felt like she had to become a baby to become a grown woman.

The first guy she fucked after her vaginoplasty was an old fuck-buddy. She wanted someone she was comfortable with, and she felt like she owed him some pussy after all the times he used the back door. It was fumbling, awkward, learning how to feel pleasure with her new parts, but toward the end, it started to feel good, started to feel amazing. She'll never forget the orgasm, how it went through her body like waves. It was nothing like what she had felt before. She called Roger before the guy even left her bed.

And now he is by her side once again, unsensually sticking something up her canal.

Leon and Martha watch the screen expectantly. She feels even better than she did before. It was clear that she really was missing those nutrients from the gasoline. She knew she wasn't moving too quickly. She worried that her hole might burn the next day, but it feels normal. She took her morning shit with nothing out of the ordinary besides perhaps the faintest Arco scent left over from the night before.

Roger moves the ultrasound to the correct position, and there it is again: the black hole inside her, now with a slightly larger almond with some of the definition of a real creature enveloped within, almost like the liver she flushed down the toilet crawled back inside her after all. He turns to the nurse. "Now, if you click for me . . ." The nurse manning the computer clicks a button on the screen. From the tinny speakers on the computer, they hear it.

Whoosh. Whoosh. Whoosh.

"The heartbeat." Leon smiles.

"148 bpm," the nurse reports.

Whoosh. Whoosh. Whoosh.

"Is that good?" Martha asks.

"That's totally normal," Roger reports, hiding his surprise.

Leon clenches his fist with excitement. Martha's eyes widen, staring into the black hole, now accompanied by the droning beat.

Whoosh. Whoosh. Whoosh.

* * *

The weeks pass quickly by. Martha can't believe how fast they're going. She feels amazing, incredible. Better than before even. Has she ever felt this good in her entire life? Not only has all her health stuff completely cleared, but every single moment she feels as if she is doing the most important thing in the world: bringing a new life into existence.

Everywhere she goes, she has her constant companion. She speaks to him. Although they don't know the sex, she imagines her unborn child as a boy, a little boy who will love his mommy wholly, unconditionally. She never knew how alone she was. Now there is a closeness, a true closeness, that can only come from a thing growing inside her.

Whoosh. Whoosh. Whoosh.

Martha continues her treatments, eating rancid meat in the dark or in the middle of the day when nobody's home and she's extra hungry. She's good about keeping on top of her supply, making sure she always has something rotting. No more trips to the dumpster.

She feels a new jealousy of her SUV, an erotic charge added to her previously mundane Chevron routine. She's titillated, pressing the button to unlock the fuel door, like unclasping her bra. Turning the fuel cap open becomes foreplay, a finger twisted around her clitoris. And then the main event: She slides the thick heavy silver nozzle into the greedy wet tunnel of the tank, her crotch slickening, wishing it were her. She always selects premium now—all the best for the baby.

In the middle of the day when everyone's out, Martha uses a tube she purchased from an AutoZone to siphon gasoline from her car. Like a low-life criminal, she sucks on the tube, getting the slightest burning bit in her mouth. Not wanting to hide a large gas can in her home, she lets the transparent yellow liquid flow into a mason jar. She holds it up to the light—it looks like a jar of piss.

At CVS, she purchases her old companion, a douche. In the office bathroom, she sticks the nozzle into the mason jar of gasoline and squeezes on the bulb, the air bubbling through the yellow liquid with little *blubs*. Naked, she bends over in the bathtub and gently inserts the douche. She squeezes the bulb, the liquid filling her. She's gotten good at clenching tight for twenty minutes, not spilling a drop when she pulls out the douche. She's grown to love the tingly sensation, refreshing like a Glacier Freeze Gatorade Frost. Since she and Leon still aren't having sex, it's the closest she gets to that deep pelvic fullness.

She knows she's far exceeding the recommend dosage, but she feels great, better than ever. She's definitely not going crazy, or not any crazier than before. She's paranoid, incredibly anxious, but anyone would be in her situation, lying to so many different people, hiding the vulgar things she does in secret. Even with her overconsumption, she promises herself she won't let herself end up like that man Bruce and Angie warned about, sent to a padded cell and returning to get the highest treatment. She doesn't even want to know what that dreadful final treatment must be.

Once she's satisfied with all the nutrients absorbed from her suppository, Martha releases the gasoline, watching as the corn silk liquid snakes toward the drain. She always takes a shower, rinsing off herself and the bathtub, and puts the towel immediately in the laundry.

Whoosh. Whoosh. Whoosh.

The doctors keep testing her, scanning her every which way. Martha smiles with her arms crossed when the doctors go over the results, always positive, always normal. A not-so-Virgin Mary, she feels prodigious. Even if the doctors are skeptical, she knows she's a miracle, a saint even. Roger has given up trying to convince her to tell Leon. For the moment, at least.

Whoosh. Whoosh. Whoosh.

Although she has become self-sufficient for her treatments, Martha still goes to the meetings a couple times a week. She likes the company, the solidarity.

It's a risk, leaving in the middle of the night, but she has her cover story, a drive to clear her head. And she's still only sleeping a few hours every night. What else should she do with all this extra time?

So Martha turns off her phone and drives to the warehouse by memory.

Bruce is always so happy to see her. Angie too. Martha likes the others as well—Eric the tech guy, Lacey the hippie girl, Ted and Fred the bears.

Martha missed being with trans people, even if it's only two of them now.

Cutting off everyone you knew was how it used to work in the '60s and '70s, decades before she transitioned. You were only allowed to get bottom surgery if you'd been living as a woman, passing; they weren't giving it to the bricks. And your psychiatrist would instruct that once you got your sex reassignment surgery, you move towns, cut off everyone you once knew, and start a new life. If you wanted the real experience of womanhood, you had to go stealth; otherwise you only had a foot in the door. So the girls packed their things and left town, starting new lives, quiet ones. She did think about relocating to some sleepy third-tier city, but she couldn't give up LA's autumnal warmth, impossibly specific Erewhon goods, and unfortunately attractive men. When Martha met Leon and went stealth, she told herself she was following in the tradition of many trans women before her.

She used to go to meetings, used to know other trans women. You had to, to get all the information, figure out the best surgeons, navigate the law. She transitioned with only a burgeoning internet in the aughts. There was Susan's Place online, but the best information was found in person with real live girls, in the flesh.

Martha never quite emotionally connected with the other trans women at the meetings. She used them mostly to gather information. She had a college degree, did boring corporate jobs. And while she lived as a boy for the first couple years of her transition, once she made the jump, she passed. She felt bad, but she found it hard to connect with other trans women who lived so differently from her. The bricks were living as bricks. She was living as a woman. It's harsh to put it so bluntly, but that's how she saw it.

There were some girls she'd get drinks with, the prettier ones. They'd complain about the men they were dating, the wait times and cost of surgeries, the ugly women at the meetings. Martha did feel like she should've had some solidarity with the other girls, but they didn't make it easy for themselves, always saying something off-putting and self-pitying at the meetings in their deep voices, wearing spaghetti straps that only emphasized their hulking shoulders. She knew that she was sipping vodka sodas and criticizing those who didn't meet the strict specifications of womanhood, but she didn't feel the need to hold herself to a higher standard; the cis women at the next table were doing the exact same thing, sipping their cosmos while detailing the many sartorial offenses of their frumpy coworker.

And God, the hard front wigs those other girls wore were terrible—it was hard not to comment. Martha shuddered to think that some of them, stubble poking through even the thickest foundation, fucked the same men that she did. Chasers weren't that discerning. She tried to steer clear of those men, but finding a considerate straight man who was only the right amount of accepting and not utterly obsessed with trans women was incredibly difficult.

Martha admired the trans lesbians who passed very well, not by being hot but by being real, so real. They weren't necessarily sexy, but they looked like sweet women you'd see at a grocery store who you'd never take a second glance at. While she pitied the bricks, she knew that the grocery store fish lesbians must pity her. Because Martha didn't just need to pass; she needed to be hot, so hot that no man could deny her. She had to diet and work out and carve herself up for the attention of men who still didn't care if she lived or died. Martha knew that cis lesbians could be cruel toward trans women, but she often overheard the women in the meeting talking about girlfriends. They always seemed to have girlfriends. She knew they dated each other too. And they seemed happy, deeply happy, in a way that felt utterly foreign to Martha, impossible even. They must have cringed at her, so obviously begging for the affection of men who would never claim her, while they were baking sourdough bread in cozy Eagle Rock one-bedrooms.

One of the prettier ones she got drinks with didn't show up to one of the meetings, then missed another one and wasn't answering anyone's calls. One of the girls who was closer to her went to her apartment, noticed a strange smell from outside the door. She got the police to open it, finding the girl's throat slit, face nearly unrecognizable, lying on the floor with half-crusted blood and flies feasting on her corpse, presumably brutalized and slain by some disgruntled boyfriend or client, never caught. Martha went to the burial, sitting in the back with the other women from the meeting. The dead girl's parents buried her in a suit. Martha did not want to go to any more funerals.

All of those people felt very specific to that time; they didn't make it out of there. Nobody went looking for Martha when she disappeared. She felt more comfortable with the motherly friendship she had with Roger. They both knew they lived very different lives; that's what made it work.

Before she went stealth, back when she went to these meetings, trans people were rarely discussed publicly. Before the tipping point, before all the memes, the conservative pundits, the celebrities, political scare advertisements, all the laws, the average person didn't really know what a trans woman was, let alone thought about what rights they should have. Sure, people knew of trans women as synonymous with drag queens, as the punch line for a joke or a segment on raunchy talk shows, or maybe if you lived in a city, you'd pass by them late at night, laughing as you discovered these women had a little something extra. But nobody really thought that some of these freaks were living in regular society right under everyone's noses.

Only after Martha went stealth did it all explode. Trans people are now a constant topic of discussion, of litigation. Enid even has a nonbinary classmate, and she promptly corrected Martha when she referred to the kid with the wrong pronoun. Martha can't believe this new age, a trans child who is supported by the community. Trans kids are certainly still not accepted where she's from, but now everyone in her hometown actually knows what being trans is, even if it's known as the enemy.

The dolls who barely used to pass are probably getting clocked a lot more now. Before, nobody was looking for it—you could get through by being feminine with no glaringly obvious tells. But now people are trained, hungry to sniff one out, even wrongly accusing cis women of trannyhood. And they aren't only looking for hints of masculinity. Overt beauty is suspect now, with crazed people on the internet accusing the most gorgeous celebrities of gender trickery. Thankfully, Martha isn't just beautiful, but right as rain. She survived the crossover without a stray eye on her, and now that she's pregnant, her identity is completely impenetrable.

But being with Angie, and even Bruce, is refreshing. They understand Martha, her transness and her sickness. They share something few else do. She feels comforted by Angie's raspy laugh and Bruce's low-effort flirtations. She feels a connection with them that she hadn't even felt with other trans people before.

While Angie has all these wild stories about being a working girl on the streets when she was younger—disgruntled johns, even more disgruntled wives—she says she's a boring old nail tech now. In her twenties, she once only made it out alive by stabbing her stiletto claws into a man's eyes, so she finds her profession of the last twenty years apt, manicures saving her from life on the streets once again. Her nails are always impeccable, intricate—nothing Martha would ever wear, but she respects the artistry.

Angie says she has totally given up on love, despite her neighbor's constant advances. She feels like she's been through it all and there's nothing out there that she wants. She can satisfy what little sex drive she still has with her left hand and Shemar Moore on reruns of *The Young and the Restless.* She claims Shemar once held the door open for her at Musso & Frank and wanted her desperately even though he walked in with Halle Berry. They all laugh as she insists, wagging her talons at them, "If times had been different back then, trust I would have been Mrs. Angelica Moore."

Angie stresses constantly about the antics of her four daughters, young trans women from nineteen to thirty-one. "I worry these kids are gonna get themselves in trouble, always playing in men's faces," Angie chastises. A proper mother, Angie helped the girls get on hormones, taught them how to do makeup and hair, how to dress, how to protect themselves, how to navigate insurance for surgery, always making sure they have food in their bellies and their nails are slayed for the gods. "And I can't really blame them. When they play in your face, play them right back."

Martha laughs, "Amen."

Bruce normally patters on with complaints about his "anchor

partner," as he calls her. He explains that they're "relationship anarchists," so calling the woman that he lives with and has sex with his primary partner—or, even worse, his girlfriend—is giving in to hierarchical structures. Martha could not handle even the remote thought of Leon sleeping with other women; it's a haunting nightmare for her, the Imaginary Fit Young Slut.

Bruce seems to struggle with any type of rules or restrictions, working odd hours as a waiter at what seems like a new restaurant every other week after endless complaints about new managers, each one a bigger jerk than the last. He and his partner seem to be in constant arguments negotiating their "boundaries," which really amounts to Bruce spending too much time with his side chicks, "chicks" being a gender-neutral term here, as he'll fuck anything that moves, regardless of gender presentation or genitalia. He uses condoms religiously, terrified of pregnancy even though he's on testosterone. It takes Martha a second to process until she realizes that Bruce could actually get pregnant if he had sex with a cis man. He says that would be a fate worse than death for him, his body ballooning, obviously marked by his vestiges of femaleness; he'd hoover the sucker immediately.

The anchor partner only dates cis men apart from him. Since she doesn't use birth control as it "makes her crazy," he admits that he worries about her getting pregnant too. She claims she also always uses condoms, but since he's not there to verify, he worries that if she gets pregnant with some cis man's sperm, she may cut Bruce as her anchor, instead tying the ship to the father of her child. And, as he keeps telling her, she knows Bruce can't handle adding an STD from some freak on Feeld to his list of ailments.

"She knows about all this?" Martha asks, surprised, gesturing to the rotting meat.

"Of course. It takes up a lot of time," he replies. "And we have a total-transparency policy with each other. That's the only way our arrangement works, complete honesty. She was skeptical at first, but she can't deny that I'm healthy now. Obviously nothing I'm doing is hurting me. And she loves me, she wants what's best for me."

Leon, bless his heart, would never accept this, right? Her life would get a whole lot easier if she could tell him about this. She can prove that she's healthy—she has countless tests to prove it—and he loves her and wants what's best for her, same as Bruce's partner. Maybe Leon would support her after all.

"Do you tell the other people you see?" Martha asks.

Bruce looks ashamed. "No. It's a medical treatment, they don't need to know what medicine I take. And the more people we tell, it does add some risk that someone might report us."

"We're all consenting adults. What can they report?"

"I mean I am sort of the de facto ringleader of this whole thing. I imagine I could get sued, arrested even. I was afraid of telling other people at first, but I knew that I had a duty to help those who were suffering like I was suffering."

No, she can't tell Leon. She's his pregnant wife, after all. He's worried enough about her health already. She can't risk him taking this whole operation down if she told him. It wouldn't be fair to the others.

Whoosh. Whoosh. Whoosh.

For Thanksgiving, Martha spends all day in a kitchen whirlwind, basting the turkey with extra care, feeling a kinship with the bird as she squeezes the baster bulb full of delicious golden liquid over the browning skin. But at dinner with Leon's extended family—Amy, the brothers, their wives, and her niece and nephew—Martha only picks at her plate, making small talk with Leon's brother's wife, relishing the compliments at her creations, trying to move her food around enough so that nobody will notice.

But in the dead of night, Martha sneaks off to the warehouse to share a moldy, putrid turkey with her sick brethren. They all agree that it's not as good as chicken, but it's the only way to celebrate the holiday.

She's risking everything by sneaking out, but seeing these people is worth the anxiety she feels when she returns to her garage, always fearful that Leon will be waiting up for her. But he is always asleep.

And fine, maybe she likes it when Bruce shoves something up her ass—is that such a crime?

Whoosh. Whoosh. Whoosh.

Autumn rolls through without fanfare. The Santa Ana winds breeze through November, palm trees whipping wildly in the wind.

Back at Power Sculpt, Christine razzes Martha for not pushing herself as hard as she used to. This is Christine's playful and only somewhat discreet way of telling Martha that she notices that she's gotten a little softness in the stomach. And it's hard to avoid drinking with Christine; their friendship can be rather liquid. Martha's been declining any obviously alcoholic invitation, coming up with some excuse every time. Christine is starting to notice, commenting that Martha's been quite the busy bee lately, but thankfully, she's still distracted enough by the new boyfriend that her mind is occupied.

Since running into her at the Ralphs, Martha's been avoiding Emma like the plague. Emma still manages to sneak up behind her at pickup. She has the gall to say that Martha is looking "healthy." Seeing the furious look in Martha's eyes and realizing the faux pas, she tries to backtrack, noting how full of life Martha's skin looks. "Full of life"—another euphemism for weight gain. In any other context, these comments would have wrecked her for weeks, impelling her to punish herself even more at the gym and in her calorie intake, but she brushes it off now. She is healthy, full of life, a precious little life.

Whoosh. Whoosh. Whoosh.

At the December recital, Martha and Leon brace themselves to listen to an hour of off-key warbling. As they get in line to enter the auditorium, Kent pats Leon on the back.

"Try to nap through it," the old man laughs.

Leon chuckles politely. Martha's surprised to see that Kent even made it to the recital, but she's more surprised when she sees Kayla, tired in a Brandy Melville sweatshirt, her roots grown out; Kent and Grover must already be sucking every last bit of youth out of her.

"Hi, Kayla, is this your first one of these?" Martha offers kindly, ambling into the auditorium.

"Yup," Kayla replies weakly.

"Must be nice to leave Grover with the babysitter for an evening."

Kayla nods. "I get so worried leaving him alone, but I'm trying to relax."

"I told her she'll drive herself crazy if she can't be away from the kid," Kent adds.

Kayla confesses, "He's been a little sick recently, so my mommy brain has been kinda fried."

"Those baby colds are gnarly," Leon says. "They'll keep you up at night, but he'll get better quick." Martha feels left out of the parenting-an-infant discussion, but she knows she'll be able to complain just the same soon enough.

Kayla mutters, "We're not really sure what's wrong exactly."

"The doctors all say the kid's totally fine," Kent insists. "This lady's getting herself worked up because Grover stays up all night. He's a baby, they don't sleep through the night."

"He used to make it through the night though. And he'll cry and cry and nothing will help him. He's so fussy with the bottle too, like he hates it now. It's this whole big regression." Kayla sighs, defeated. "I wish he could talk to us and tell us what's wrong."

A lump fills Martha's throat, stopping her in her tracks for a moment. Leon gently tugs her along. Her mouth dry, she says softly, "I hope Grover gets better soon."

Whoosh. Whoosh. Whoosh.

Enid keeps her secret, not telling Leon that she knows that Martha is pregnant. But Martha can feel the girl watching her. Thankfully, he hasn't seemed to notice that his daughter has been gentler with his wife recently, taking a bit of her usual bite out of her tweenage tone. Enid is probably worried that if she stresses Martha, she'll become a bloody mess on the bathroom floor again.

Whoosh. Whoosh. Whoosh.

Leon treats Martha like a princess, his prized doll. He checks in with her constantly. He holds her any chance he gets. He kisses and rubs her stomach, helping the baby grow with his love. He makes sure they all eat healthy. He won't eat sushi, out of solidarity.

But he won't fuck her. He touches her more than ever, always wanting to be close to her, but he never wants to ravage her. They haven't had sex since she got pregnant, and it's already December, frigid despite an average temperature of sixty-eight. She rubs against his crotch when they cuddle, but it does nothing. She's too embarrassed to keep trying with him, her self-esteem unable to take another "I'm tired."

She masturbates vigorously, horny from the pregnancy hormones. She hadn't masturbated since before she met Leon. She closes her eyes and thinks of him, which seems like the right thing to do. But this only makes her feel worse, having to imagine a sex life with her husband after it's dried up.

She scrolls through various mental sexual fantasies, trying to find something less depressing, and somehow ends up on Bruce. At first, she's surprised by his sudden entrance into her erotic imagination, but she welcomes him with open labia. She's never been with anyone without a penis. So when she imagines them fucking, Bruce has one. No ordinary penis but a schlong, a feral hog, a third leg, a massive one-eyed purple-headed wonder worm. And it's hard, diamond hard for her. He fucks her roughly in her asshole. She wonders if it's bad to imagine him with a body part that he doesn't have, but she pushes that thought aside as she masturbates to completion.

Satisfied post-orgasm, Martha's fear subsides. The internet says it's normal for men to be freaked out by intimacy when their wives get pregnant. Leon will have to get horny enough one of these days and get back to her. That's what she tells herself to keep the Imaginary Fit Young Slut at bay, whose talons are beginning to wrench open the door to their bedroom.

Whoosh. Whoosh. Whoosh.

Chapter 29

"Over a fucking text message. Sixty-one," Christine scoffs, standing on Martha's doorstep in a sweater. It is a cool mid-December day. "He'll qualify for social security at the end of this year, and he broke up me with via text message."

"I wish him nothing less than a heart attack."

Christine smiles. "I'm sorry this was so last minute. You don't have to drop everything for me."

"Please, I needed a break."

The woman enters and gives a devilish grin. "And I didn't want to drink alone while the sun is still up on a weekday."

"Ooh!" Martha smiles, trying to figure out how to get out of drinking this time.

"That's the only thing I like about winter. The sun sets early, so you can drink sooner. But I'm not gonna make it to five today." Christine can tell her usual drinking buddy is hesitating. "One drink with me please. I hope I didn't interrupt anything."

"Oh, I was just starting on dinner."

"It's not even two in the afternoon and you're already preparing a fabulous dinner," Christine scoffs, shaking her Ozempic-induced bobblehead, almost too big for her now thin body. "And I had to cancel all my meetings for the rest of the day because some guy I've been seeing for a few months broke up with me. God, I'm a total mess. I'm too old to be a mess."

"Let's go to the backyard. I set up a little something."

"Perfect little housewife, you."

Martha notes some contempt on the way she hits "housewife" but chooses to ignore it. "You need to gorge yourself after a breakup. Eat all those calories you'd been avoiding for him."

They walk through the kitchen to the backyard, the rosemary bushes fragrant, the air cool. Martha's set up a little charcuterie spread, picture-perfect, like everything she does. "Leon's been sprucing up the backyard. We're going to be throwing a little holiday party in a bit, so we want all the plants and flowers settled."

"Ooh, a holiday party? Lovely." Christine rightfully raises an eyebrow as she pulls out the wine. Martha's already planning the little party they're going to host to announce that she's pregnant. She can tell that Leon gets nervous when she talks about the future, but only because he doesn't know the miscarriage was merely a theatrical work.

"Let me get a corkscrew," she offers.

"Screw top." Christine rips off the cap and pours two cups. She quickly downs her glass and pours herself another, which she now sips more politely. "I didn't cry when I got divorced. Kent told me he was leaving me for his assistant, and I didn't cry. It made my blood boil, but not a single tear. I was sad for Quinton, his father tearing our family apart so he could stick his old, withered cock in some young slag-bag, but I wasn't sad for myself. All I thought about was my warpath, how to get everything in the divorce. But now some guy, some schmuck with no hair on his head who I've only even known for a few months, is making me cry. How pathetic is that?"

"It's not pathetic at all. You're losing the whole future you imagined."

"I don't know." Christine shrugs, taking a big puff of a vape. "I liked him, I did feel that spark, but was I totally in love with him already? No." Martha leans back slightly, avoiding the puff of vape smoke. "We broke up because I wanted him to meet Quinton. It's been months. I thought we could do something cute before Christmas. Not even on actual Christmas, just something with the holiday spirit. And it's not like Quinton is some little kid. He's eleven, I'm not looking for a man to change diapers with me."

"Maybe that's still a little fast? Meeting the kids can be tricky, especially for men."

"I don't think there would have been a good time for him to meet Quinton. That man is a bald child. No wife, no children. At first, I thought, wow—I hit the jackpot! This man has no baggage. Turns out that we all should have baggage at this point, it makes you a man-child if you don't. I have baggage on baggage, over the weight limit for Pathetic Hag Airlines—"

"Christine, you're a beautiful and successful woman. You're a catch! You are." Martha knows very well why Christine can't find or keep a man. As a friend, she's fun, but as a girlfriend, she'd be snarky, gruff, cold, even downright rude—always quick to tell you the restaurant you picked was awful. It's impossible to imagine Christine having sex, like getting into a dogfight with a snarling pit bull, all tooth and dank breath. Well, if the hound could criticize you too.

"But there's nobody to catch me. Guys my age don't even have me in their radar on dating apps. I'm fine with a little older, but anyone who's single at sixty is either a total weirdo who no sane woman would ever marry or an asshole who destroyed his last marriage. I know I'm supposed to feel satisfied with my life, but when Quinton's at his father's, I'm all alone in my big house that used to have my whole family. It's empty. Makes me want to blow my brains out."

Christine is the friend who makes Martha feel like she's made all the right choices, that everything she had to do to get here was right, and everything she does to stay here is completely correct, justified, if it means not ending up like her dog-faced euthanasia-craving friend.

Martha feels her phone buzzing in her pocket. She figures it's probably her husband, and it would be incredibly rude to answer while the woman before her is lamenting the misery of men and contemplating suicide. "I should reach out more. I've been a little occupied."

"Spare me the pity. It's not that I don't have enough friends. But some spaces can only be filled by a man. I want to wake up next to someone hairy every day. Is that so wrong? Maybe I should give up on the whole thing. Accept my spinsterhood. I could stop working out, eat whatever the hell I want, stop doing my hair, stop with the injections. Say to hell with it. It would be easy, wouldn't it?"

"You don't know how close I was to joining you." Martha's making the exact same face with the exact same voice of all of those women that she used to detest who would try to give her a pep talk when she was single. The sympathy face, what a cruelty.

"I told you spare me the pity."

"Sorry, sorry. But I do know how hard it is. I really do."

"I find that a little hard to believe."

"It's true."

"Look at you. Don't tell me this shit was ever that hard for you."

Martha was perpetually single when she was dating as an openly trans woman. There was never anybody who fully claimed her. She was merely a reliquary for men's sexual attention, not intimate affection. Anytime she talked to a stray cis woman, a coworker, or some gay man who was curious enough to ask about her dating life, her skin crawled at the way they looked at her, that sympathy face.

"I didn't have a boyfriend, a real proper boyfriend, before Leon." She's never told Christine that before because it's a bit clocky.

"Bullshit."

"It's true," Martha insists, feeling a few more buzzes from her phone in her pocket.

"You never had a boyfriend until you were in your thirties? There's no way."

"I don't like to tell people because it's kind of embarrassing, but I really didn't."

"Were you religious or something?"

"My parents were, but I'm not. That wasn't the reason."

"Then what the hell was wrong with you?" Christine cackles.

"Oh, stop it," Martha laughs, secretly worried that her friend will sniff her out. "I had flings, believe me, I had truly historic flings—Big and Carrie–level flings. But I never got past them. Right when I thought we were about to become real partners, they'd leave—they'd find Natasha." And these Natashas were always cis women.

"Oh, come on! You had to have one boyfriend somewhere along the road."

"Seriously. I never got to properly say 'This is my boyfriend' until Leon."

"Wow," Christine concedes, finishing her second generous glass of wine. She looks at Martha's untouched alcohol. "Don't make me drink alone, come on."

"Sorry, I should've said, but I haven't really been drinking lately. For my health. You remember how sick I was. I'm still trying to really not push it."

"Did you ever figure out what was wrong with you?"

"Not really. Just got my body back aligned and feeling a lot better now."

"Weird," Christine says, taking Martha's glass and sipping from it. "And you're sober now?"

"I'm not *sober* sober, just not drinking at the moment."

Christine raises her eyebrows as far as the Dysport will allow and grabs Martha's hands. "I know you're not supposed to tell me what I think you're not telling me, but blink twice if there is a thing you're not telling me."

Martha knew that someone would catch on sooner or later. She thinks about lying, but . . . she blinks twice.

"Martha!" Christine gets out of her chair and pulls the expecting mother up with her, jumping with excitement.

"Please don't tell anyone! We want to wait until we're sure everything is okay."

"Mommy! Mother! Mama!"

"We're getting the amnio tomorrow, and if that all goes well, we're telling everyone. Please, please pretend that you don't know." At fifteen weeks, Martha has passed the first trimester, when most people tell everyone, but she wants to wait for an amniocentesis to confirm that her baby is in tip-top shape.

Christine pulls her into a big hug. "I'm so happy for you."

"Thank you." She hasn't had anyone besides Leon give her the whole fanfare. Roger is too panicked about the science of it all to really congratulate her, and Enid had no excitement. It feels great, jumping up and down with another woman, like a scene from a movie that she's seen a thousand times, never thinking she'd be the lead.

Once Martha's new kid goes to school, there will be a whole new crop of mothers to establish a pecking order with. Enid and Quinton will both be in college—will her and Christine's friendship survive without the school connection? She hopes yes, she does like Christine genuinely, but she'll be much busier with a new child.

"You're going to be the best mommy ever. And I'm more than happy to drink alone now! Hell, I'll drink for two. Or should I say three."

Martha smiles demurely and puts a hand on her stomach. Oh, it comes so naturally to her—the soft smile and gentle hand on the stomach is the most cunt thing ever.

Christine says, "Your mind must be racing with everything, but one mother to another, I promise it will all work out. It might not work out like you think it will, but you're the best mother this kid could have."

Martha feels moved by her friend, not usually one to be this corny. Martha is already confident that her child will be sparklingly perfect, but it feels good for someone besides the father to recognize her immense motherhood potential. "Thank you. But promise me that not a word of this gets out. Not a soul until we tell everyone. Leon would be upset with me."

Christine mimes locking her lips.

Martha's phone keeps buzzing in her pocket and she finally gives in. She pulls her phone out slightly and takes a peek—Leon. "Speak of the devil. Give me a moment."

"Go ahead."

"Hi, honey," she answers.

"I've been calling you," his voice cracks.

She's caught off guard by the tremor in his voice. "I'm sorry, Christine came over. Are you okay? You sound a little . . ." She hears the sound of his sniffles getting caught in his throat. "Leon, where are you? What's going on?" For a moment, she thinks the worst: Roger's told him. She's finally living her dream, and a scornful gay man has decided to take it away from her.

Leon whimpers, "I've been calling you."

Christine asks, "Is everything all right?"

"Give me a sec," Martha replies to her, walking back into the house.

"You weren't answering," Leon whispers.

"Honey, I told you I'm with Christine." She closes the door for privacy. "She got broken up with and came over, it was a last-minute thing. Is everything okay? Why did you call me?"

No, it's Enid, Martha decides. Something happened with Enid. Right when she's about to get her perfect family, the universe will take it from her. She was so arrogant to think it really could be hers.

"You're okay?" he asks. She can hear his focused deep breaths over the phone.

"I'm totally fine. I'm asking if you're okay."

"She's okay, she's okay," he repeats like a mantra.

"I'm totally fine. Is something wrong with Enid?"

"Everything's fine," he replies, finally sounding like himself again. "I've been texting you and calling and your location is at home, so when you didn't answer . . ."

"Oh, honey, you shouldn't get all worked up because I didn't respond immediately."

"I know, but I couldn't . . ." he admits, surely imagining her dead on the bathroom floor.

"I'm fine. I'm great actually. Everything's great."

She doesn't hear anything on the other side for a moment. Finally, he chuckles a little at himself, "I miss you. I miss you a lot right now."

"Are you at the office still? What are you even doing right now?"

"I went straight to the parking lot. I'm in the car right now."

"Oh, Leon, you're so sweet," she softly sighs, nervous for her now fearful husband. "There's nothing to worry about."

Chapter 30

By now, Martha knows that Leon holding her will not lead to sex. She doesn't even get her hopes up. The night before her amniocentesis, they both vibrate with anxiety, which neither wants to show. He rubs the side of her arm; she's his worry stone now.

She turns over to speak to him. "Do you think you should start seeing somebody again? Or taking something?"

"Why?"

"Earlier today, when you called me, you didn't sound so good."

"I was just a little anxious. It was one bad moment."

"You sounded like you were crying."

"I was a little worried, given your history," he replies, unusually defensive. She puts a hand on his face, holding his strong chin. He softens with her touch. "Maybe I should see someone again."

"Being a father to a new child, to a baby again, that's a lot of stress. I'm here to support you."

"I'm the one who's supposed to support you through this."

"We're supposed to support each other. We're a team. Always."

"Always." He kisses her gently. She hates that she resents this, but his kisses are all sweetness, no fire, no lust. "I never wanted you to see me like that. I thought that side of me was gone."

"Baby, I want you to feel your best. But there's no side of you that I wouldn't love." She won't put her foot down just yet, but she will not let him be a nervous Nellie once the kid is born. She will not raise the kid in a bubble of Leon's anxiety. She wants her child to be confident, sure, magnetic—qualities she thought Leon had.

He pulls her in, holding her head against his chest, and kisses the top of her head. She feels a fluttering in her belly, little pops of fizz bursting gently. She wonders at first if she's just really horny, like how she felt when she first dated Leon, until she realizes. "Feel my stomach."

He moves his hand to her abdomen, moving it around for the patter of something alive. She feels like a genie lamp, him rubbing her for his deepest wishes. He shrugs, not feeling anything. "I think it's too early for me to feel it. Fifteen weeks. I think we need to wait another month or so."

"Oh." She deflates. "You can't feel it?"

"I don't think so."

She focuses, trying to get the feeling to the surface, the quickening. She becomes frustrated and then titillated; there's something in her body that is a whole other nervous system with its own will.

He asks, "You think that's his way of telling us everything's all right?"

"It won't take too long to get the results of the amnio back. And Squilod's been doing well so far, I know he'll keep up the straight A's."

"It's getting hard avoiding talking about it in front of everyone, Enid especially."

Enid's managed to keep the secret so far, but still Martha wants to get off the subject. "And your mother keeps making her little comments about my weight."

He does not offer any proper husbandly response to the weight comment. Instead, he asks, "Have you noticed anything funny with your car?"

"With my car? You were using my car?"

"Sometimes I use yours for little trips. I didn't know that you were so possessive of it."

She tries to reel back her panic. "I just, I didn't know you did that."

"It seems like it's leaking fuel. Like I'll know that nobody's used it, but the next time I get in, the fuel gauge says there's fewer miles left. It's not like hundreds of miles or anything, but like five or ten."

She feels violated. She thought her car was a safe space, but he has kept tabs on that too. This whole thing doesn't work if he becomes controlling, vigilant; this all worked so well because he was her kind, bumbling husband who never interrogated her too much about what she did when he wasn't around.

She deflects: "Sounds like the gauge is broken. Is it even that accurate?"

"No, I took it to the shop, and they said it was working perfectly."

"Took it to the shop? When did you take my car to the shop?"

"You were taking a little nap; I didn't want to bother you. It was a quick trip," he replies, confused by her annoyance. "I always take your car to the shop for you."

"I know, and thank you, by the way, I just didn't know you did it again."

"Well, they said it was working perfectly. It's so weird, it's like—"

She rolls over to turn off the light, trying to end this conversation. "We have a big morning, let's get some sleep."

"Oh, okay," he grumbles. "If it's leaking gas into our home, that's obviously not safe."

"I think we would know if gas was leaking into our home."

"Most likely, but—"

Martha laughs. "Honey, I think you might be letting your anxiety spill over a little bit. Let's go to bed."

He sighs, annoyed. "Good night."

She shuts her eyes, though she won't sleep for much longer. She has to be more careful. She needs to refill the tank whenever she siphons it. She probably needs to stay away from the warehouse for a while, just to be safe.

* * *

Roger paints Martha's stomach with yellow-brown iodine, a nauseating color, to prepare her for the needle. He presses the ultrasound wand on her stomach, looking at the fetus. The expecting parents look at the screen. No longer an almond, the fetus looks truly human; they can really see the head, the fingers.

The nurse pulls out a comically long needle. Leon looks concerned.

"Don't worry," Roger assures. "It's not going near the baby. That's what the ultrasound is for. We'll watch the needle go in very carefully."

"And we'll give you a lidocaine injection first," the nurse says to Martha. Roger didn't say anything about the pain—maybe he wants it to hurt her, just a little bit.

Martha winces slightly as they inject her with lidocaine. She feels the numbing sensation quickly. Roger carefully sticks the long needle into her. She watches with a sick fascination as it disappears inside her abdomen. Leon stares at the screen, making sure the needle stays away from his precious fragile child. Roger replaces the top of the needle with a syringe to collect the sample. He draws back the syringe, sucking up her amniotic fluid.

She's surprised to see that the fluid is basically clear, with a faint hint of yellow, almost like gasoline. She thought it would be red—isn't the baby swimming around in her blood?—but no, it looks more like saliva. Or like an egg white, which is exactly what it is to her fertilized yolk.

Roger seals the syringe and pulls out the needle. "And we're done."

"That wasn't so bad." She smiles.

Taking off his gloves, Roger gets serious, going full doctor mode. "The amniocentesis tests for things like Down, Edwards, or Patau syndrome. It can confirm genetic disorders like sickle cell or cystic fibrosis. Anencephaly, where the brain and skull don't develop, and the babies die within a few hours of birth." Martha's mouth dries, imagining going through all this, only for her baby to die within the length of a film. Would she even get to hold him? "There's a lot more that I don't have to mention, but it doesn't test for everything. Blindness, deafness, cleft palate, cognitive impairments. We can't entirely cross those out, no matter how much testing we do in utero. This is the best information we can get, but that doesn't mean it's entirely comprehensive."

Leon nods. "We hope for the best, prepare for the worst. I've been through this before."

"Yes, of course I know that." Roger looks to Martha. "I want you both to be fully informed. Or rather informed of all that we won't know."

She looks at the vial, her precious fluid that holds the fate of her child. Everything rests on the egg white.

Chapter 31

Wait, you really didn't know I knew?" Enid laughs.

"Shush," Martha huffs. They made it all this way only for her to admit it—not everyone's a good liar.

Leon raises an eyebrow. "You knew? How did you know?" Enid sits on her bed, while Martha sits in the desk chair. Leon crouches to be on his daughter's level.

The results of the amnio were perfect, healthy, normal. Roger did a full anatomy scan as well—also perfect. Martha knew it would all be flawless. Roger and the other doctors were bewildered, but she laughed in their faces at their disbelief. She's the real deal, honey. Roger warned again, incessantly really, that the amino doesn't test for everything, like scales instead of skin or congenital heart defects, but she ignored him. Why should she worry more than any cis woman?

"She told me, like a long time ago." Enid shrugs.

"Hey, I didn't tell you. You figured it out yourself." Martha turns to Leon. "She put together the clues and I didn't want to lie."

"Oh, you just wanted to lie to me?" he laughs. "When was this?"

"In the middle of the night, when Martha was—" Enid starts before Martha cuts her off.

"She couldn't sleep. And she asked me directly. She's a smart kid. With internet access."

"Does this mean everything is okay? With the baby?" Enid asks timidly, one of the moments where she seems very small again. Martha looks to him to answer it.

"Uh, we never know for certain," he says. "But all the test results have been nothing but healthy. Pregnancy, birth, it does have risks. But that's why we need to take good care of Martha these next five months. Make sure she's relaxed, calm, happy, healthy." He pats Martha's thigh. "Do you have any other questions?"

Enid thinks about it for a moment, looking away from them. Her room is the only place in the house where there are still pictures of her birth mother on the walls. Martha glances at a picture of them all at a zoo. Enid is a toddler there; Leon is the only one still alive to remember that sunny day, but the girl gets to keep the picture of a memory she can't even recall.

She looks to him and asks, "Can I start calling Martha 'Mom'?"

"Oh." She wasn't expecting that. She leaps out of her chair to sit next to her daughter on the bed and pulls her into a hug.

Enid seems overwhelmed by the emotion even though she was the one who started it. She pats Martha on the back and explains, "The baby will call you Mom, so it would be weird if I didn't too."

"Yes, I would love that."

Leon beams, hugging them all together tightly. No longer Dad and Martha, just Dad and Mom. Martha feels a touch of guilt toward Enid's birth mother; she carried this child in her womb until it tore out of her, only for Enid to now call another woman Mom, another woman who didn't suffer like she suffered.

"Mom," Enid says for the first time. Martha's so delighted to hear that word from the little voice of a child, of *her* child. "Can I talk to Dad? Alone."

Pained to already be pushed away, right after they truly became a family, Martha pulls herself out of the embrace. She gets up, pretending to not be hurt by the girl's request. "Of course."

She may be Mom now, but that doesn't mean she isn't still an interloper in Enid's life. Or maybe girls just like their dads more. Martha hopes she has a boy—that's what she always imagines. Leon had requested not to learn the sex of the baby—he wants to be surprised, he likes the speculation, that's what humans did for centuries. She agreed, not caring one way or another, making sure that all of the doctors were careful not to mention it to her.

She exits the room, leaving Leon with his daughter. She thinks about putting her ear up to the door, but that's a bit too obviously crazy, even for her. Maybe she needs to get used to boundaries. Isn't that what a mature parent would do? She walks away.

* * *

Leon enters the bedroom, cautious like he's entering a lion's den; the lion relaxes in bed, scrolling through nursery-decoration videos on TikTok.

"What did Enid need to talk to you about?" Martha asks, nosy, putting her phone away. "Or am I not supposed to ask? Are we supposed to let her have a separate relationship with each of us? Or are we both supposed to know everything?"

He makes a face like he's being really emotional. "She wanted to talk about her mother."

"Oh." Something feels off. "What did she say?"

He gets into bed. "She thinks her mom would be happy that our family is growing."

"That's so sweet." She puts a hand to her heart, although she wonders if he really might be lying to her, though he never has before. "I really didn't see the 'Mom' stuff coming. I thought if that was ever going to happen, that it would've happened a long time ago."

"Well, you are her mother. But she's right. If this baby was calling me Dad and you Mom, I think Enid would feel like we were making this new family without her. She wants to stay in our family."

Martha doesn't like that answer. She preferred when she thought it came from pure acceptance, that Enid finally fully saw her as her mother.

He turns to her with a peculiar expression, one that makes her feel uneasy. "How are you doing?" he asks, with the pathos of a third-rate therapist.

"Great, the baby is the picture of health."

"No, like, emotionally. Are you feeling good? Excited?"

She can sense something is wrong. What did Enid really say to him? Martha senses she's not getting the whole story. "Obviously I'm excited. Now that Enid knows, we can start looking at nursery decorations. I sent you some stuff on Instagram."

"Do you wish I were home more? I could try to work from home some days."

"No, I'm good. Save that for taking care of the baby. You don't need to stay home with my pregnant butt."

She can tell he doesn't seem convinced by that. Throwing out a Hail Mary, she goes back to one of her age-old tricks: She kisses him and reaches for his crotch.

"Oh, uh," he replies. He's distracted for a moment by the sheer randomness of the kiss, then returns on his previous thought. "I just want to make sure you're good, inside and out."

"Got it. Thanks," she says, trying to use his penis to clear his head. "I'm great."

His member remains utterly flaccid. "This, uh, isn't your best ramp-up."

Ouch.

He adjusts: "I mean, I don't think we set the mood."

She rolls over. She should have known that distraction sex doesn't work anymore. The Imaginary Fit Young Slut claps, her head rolling back with laughter, watching Martha fail to seduce her husband. "It's been months," she yelps. "I don't have to tell you that you're not going to hurt the baby, right?"

"Hey, hey," he says, reaching out to her, trying to turn her back toward him. "I didn't, I didn't realize it had been that long."

Oof. Wrong again. Watching this catastrophe with glee, the Imaginary Fit Young Slut digs her hand into the bucket of popcorn.

"You didn't even notice we weren't having sex?" Martha gasps as she gets out of bed, standing over him with her arms crossed. "Our sex life evaporates and you don't even notice?"

"I didn't say that. But I'm respectful of the fact that we're in this period of change and adjustment."

"I'm in a period of change! You don't have shit happening to you. You should be the same!"

"We're both changing."

She can't hold it in anymore: "So I'm unfuckable now?"

She has never had to ask something like this before. Since transitioning, she's had a lot of insecurity about men's interest in her, but she's never doubted her attractiveness. It's a crazy thing to ask, a coerced confession. It won't result in a truthful answer, but she can't help it.

"I think you're sexy and hot and beautiful and gorgeous and—"

"You can use all the synonyms you want, but I don't make your dick hard anymore."

"You do! You make my dick hard, very hard," Leon, still in bed, reaches to his crotch, desperate to conjure a stiffy to end the argument.

She scoffs, throwing a pillow at him. "Don't start jerking off under duress."

"You questioned my dick getting hard for you, so I'm getting it hard for you. This is what you asked for."

He isn't usually such a stereotypical man in arguments with her. Usually he listens to her to solve the problem, not just to concoct a defense as she speaks. That's how she knows that this is bad, seriously bad.

"I'm sleeping on the couch." She grabs the pillow that she didn't throw at him. He starts to get up. "Don't," she barks as she looks to his crotch—still flaccid.

"Honey, I think you might be a little hormo—"

"Don't you dare finish that sentence."

He puts his hands up, backing off.

She storms out of the room, pillow and blanket in hand. Maybe it's the extra doses of gasoline making her irritable, or maybe she hasn't been properly fucked in ages—the Imaginary Fit Young Slut can have him.

Chapter 32

Martha tosses and turns on the couch. It's only 2:30, she can never sleep this early anyway, but tonight she is particularly stirred. They fight so rarely, if ever. Maybe she is hormonal. And horny.

She needs a release, badly.

She hasn't gone back to the warehouse since Leon questioned her about the gas, but she needs something right now to calm her, and all she can think of is Bruce's hairy hands.

* * *

"I'm great, Bruce," Martha replies. She hasn't flirted, properly flirted, in so long. She walks up to the reception desk. Her sense of smell is surely heightened, Bruce's smoky, musky, slightly tangy aroma more appetizing than ever. "How's the old anchor-and-chain?"

"She's great. On a business trip for the past week actually. So it's been me all alone at home. But I don't mind. It gives me more time for other things, other people."

Martha's breasts, now leaning over the reception desk, have already gotten bigger. She hasn't told Bruce and Angie that she's pregnant. They may know a lot about her, but that's simply too insane, too preposterous to tell them. At this point, she does have a clear bump if she's fully naked, but it's small enough to hide with the right outfit. And never in a million years would they assume that Martha's pregnant when they know she's trans. She'll have to stop going at some point soon.

"The beard is looking good, Bruce," she says, drawing out his name. Flirting is too easy. You say someone's name really slowly at the end of your sentence, and they're putty in your hands.

He smirks. "Thanks."

She bites her lip. She hasn't done something like this in ages, but it's thrilling already. She's still not going to do anything out of the ordinary, at least she doesn't think she is.

"What are you in for today?" he asks. "For Room B? Angie isn't here, already in Tijuana for the holidays, so I think it would be only us tonight."

Is Bruce really going along with this so easily? That slut. One compliment on his facial hair and he's invited Martha to go into a room alone with him.

"Perfect," she chirps, following him to Room B. The garage smell disgusted her at first, but now it excites her, revs her engine.

She quickly takes off her pants and panties in one fell swoop. She tosses them aside. She would've put on something sexier, but she couldn't go back into her room to change and risk waking Leon, especially not for him to see her put on her sexiest skirt and panties for another man.

She bends over. She doesn't need to actually have sex with him.

No matter what she's feeling, she's not going to cheat on her husband, not really. Unable to help herself, she says, "I think I need a big load tonight."

"You've got it." Bruce lifts the red gas can to her asshole. He sticks it in. She openly gasps with pleasure at him entering her, feeling her hole stretch.

"Deeper," she commands. There is no real need for him to put it in deeper. He must know this, but he obliges, watching the nozzle go deeper inside her puckered pink hole.

She moans louder, feeling the thick plastic go deep into her, tickling parts of her long untouched. She doesn't try to soften or stifle her moan at all. She moans like she hasn't been fucked in ages, her prostate already screaming, *Yes, yes, yes.*

He smirks, pulling the nozzle back a little before pressing it back in. She gasps. She knew he would play along. He pulls it back out, in and out, the gasoline pouring into her. She moans from the tingly feeling, getting filled and fucked at the same time. She feels full of him, of this fire roaring inside of her.

He growls, "You like that?"

"Yes, please, please. Fill me up. Fill me up." She loves his stiff plastic nozzle cock, hitting all the right spots. It's so hard, so impossibly hard—it would never go soft on her.

Her pleasure crescendos quickly. It's never been this easy before.

Her voice crackles as she swiftly cums, a desperately needed orgasm. Her hole clenches, clamping onto the hard plastic, and then relaxes, completely leaking all of the gasoline, dribbling it onto the tarp.

She pants, reality setting back in. Did she cheat on Leon? No, not really. No penis entered her. They didn't kiss. Bruce didn't even really touch her, not with his hands.

"Fuck," he says, impressed.

Flustered, she reaches for the packet of wet wipes on the ground. She wipes at the gasoline streaming down her thigh.

"This is a new one." He smirks. "Even for me."

She doesn't know what to say. "I've got to go" is all she can muster, out of breath. After wiping off her petroleum ejaculate, she pulls up her underwear and pants.

"A hit-and-run," he laughs, a lot calmer than she is about this unconventional one-night stand.

She feels insane. She has never had a one-sided sexual experience where she's been purely serviced by a man. She's given out countless unreciprocated blowjobs, but nobody's ever made her cum without her even remotely touching them back. But she can't possibly return the favor. She can't really cheat on Leon. This doesn't count. An orgasm during a medical procedure isn't cheating, even if it wasn't so accidental.

"Thanks," she mutters, leaving the room and walking down the hallway, not even waiting for Bruce to reply. She decides the gasoline must be making her insane because she would never do something like this. It must be the diesel making her irritable, horny, deviant—it has to be. Maybe she should reel back her usage, she doesn't want to end up in the psych ward, but no. She wants more.

She worries that Bruce will follow after her, but he doesn't. He probably has to clean up the rest of her mess. She feels like such a man.

Chapter 33

Martha drives home with post-nut clarity and terror. This was stupid, a huge mistake, but it's one that she'll take to her grave. With no traffic at night, she'll be home soon. She'll quietly shower in the guest room to make sure she has no smell on her, and she'll crawl back into bed with her husband, who, she reminds herself, does love her very much.

She pulls up to their garage. She's never felt gross about coming home so late in the middle of the night like some common adulterer, but now she feels vile. The garage door opens slowly.

Her stomach lurches when the garage light spills out, already on. As the door rises, her headlights shine on Leon.

It's over. It's over.

She thinks about turning the car around, driving to Mexico and starting a new life, never turning back. But no. She's planned for this. She's rehearsed this confrontation a million times. She can face it.

She pulls in, puts on a smile, and waves. He does not wave back.

She parks and gets out of the car. "What are you doing up, honey?" she asks, like he is the weird one in this scenario.

He whisper-yells, "Where were you?"

She answers calmly, "I just went for a drive around the neighborhood."

"Tell me where the fuck you were." He never curses. This is bad. She needs to sell this, really cinch that Best Actress win. Not even just win some pity award like Zellweger's ham-fisted *Judy*, but for the performance of a lifetime that would make Meryl quiver in her boots.

"Just a drive to clear my head." She reaches out to grab his hands, but he pulls away. "I couldn't sleep after how we left things, so I needed to drive around."

"But no, it's not just tonight. I know you've been doing this." He knows? How could he have known this whole time? "You lied to me about the gas. You knew why the gas was lower and you lied right to my face."

Enid. Her stepdaughter tattled on her—how unfortunately cliché. That's what she had to talk to him about, and that's how he now suddenly knows. Martha will not soon be forgetting this betrayal.

"I'm sorry, I didn't want to worry you that I'm going nocturnal again. I'm not doing it all the time. Only when I really can't sleep, it helps me sleep."

"Why did you turn off your location?" He isn't going to be won over so easily.

"I didn't turn off my location."

"You turned off your phone so it wouldn't update your location. It still said you were here, but when I came to the garage, your car was gone."

"Oh, it's the middle of the night and my phone wasn't charged because I wasn't sleeping in our bed. I didn't need it to navigate. I told you I was just driving around here."

"That's bullshit, bullshit!" He really yells that one, forgetting about his sleeping daughter. He pulls his voice back to a reasonable volume, keeping the anger. "That's why Emma saw you in South Central too."

Oh no. Did he follow her? Has he figured it all out? It's all going to come tumbling down.

He grits his teeth. "Tell me who he is." She bursts out laughing. Even when butchers and other school dads flirted with her, Leon had never been jealous. "This isn't fucking funny."

"You think I'm having an affair?" she laughs. Even after her little incident with Bruce, she's not having an actual affair. She feels grateful for him jumping to a woefully incorrect conclusion. "I am pregnant. Not having an affair."

"We're about to announce to the world that we're having a baby and now I'm wondering if the kid is even mine and you're laughing at me."

She stops herself from laughing, hurt by the accusation that this baby could be anyone's but his. The only person she arguably had an affair with has no capacity to get her pregnant. "Leon, the kid is one thousand percent yours. I am not having an affair."

"YOU'RE SNEAKING OFF AT NIGHT! WHAT ELSE AM I SUPPOSED TO THINK?"

"Don't yell, you'll wake Enid."

"The truth, Martha. Tell me the fucking truth."

"Leon, baby, I'm sorry. I should have told you from the start."

She hugs him. His body is tense, but he accepts her touch this time. He growls, "Tell me who he is. Now."

"There's nobody, Leon. I'm telling you the truth. Calm down."

He pulls back so he can look at her face but stays in her arms. "I can handle it. Whatever you're doing, just tell me. It'll be okay, but I need to know." Pleading for the truth, he looks so kind, so filled with genuine care and love for her, that she almost can't help herself from telling him everything. Maybe he would support her like Bruce's partner?

But she sticks to her story: "A drive to calm my nerves. I'm sorry. I know I should have told you from the start. I think maybe I wanted something just for myself."

"Just a drive?" he asks, finally starting to believe her.

"I drive places I loved before I met you. Like Ralphs and the park I used to eat lunch in and stuff like that. With the baby, this new chapter, I want to remind myself of me. I have a piece of you growing inside of me. Everything in my life, in our life, feels like it's all about this big, huge change. Which I couldn't be more excited for, but I think I needed a thing to have to myself. My body isn't mine anymore."

"I can understand that." He reaches his arms out to squeeze her, clearly moved. She's got him now. Every other nominee shouldn't even bother writing an acceptance speech. "We're still going to be our own people. You're not just a baby incubator to me. I see you. I still see you."

"That's all I needed to hear." She's relieved but annoyed. He's invaded her privacy; he has made her into a liar. Well, a bigger liar. He's made this all about his anxiety, even though this really has nothing to do with him.

They look at each other in the harsh garage light. While Martha hides so much from him, this is the first time he's learned that she might be capable of lying to him. Even though she thinks he's satisfied with her story, there's now a tiny thing growing inside of him too: a seed of doubt.

Chapter 34

"My mom's gonna cause a scene." Leon nods, smiling, sipping a beer. "You've gotta be ready for it. There'll be a lot of gesticulation in every direction and an unfortunate amount of spittle too."

"Let's try to keep her contained. Not to be a pregnancy-zilla, but let's remember that it's our moment." Martha takes a sip of the tonic water she desperately wishes were mixed with gin. They're telling the world tomorrow night, everyone invited to the house under the guise of an innocuous holiday party.

"You could never be a 'pregnancy-zilla.'" Leon takes her hand off her drink, pulling it closer to him across the white tablecloth of the far too expensive Marina del Rey steakhouse. He rubs his thumb across her knuckle, flecks of amber in the center of his green eyes twinkling in the light of the sunset. "You really are glowing. I thought that was just a saying, but you really just have this, this vitality to you. You're always beautiful, but this is just, wow, so gorgeous."

A date, a proper date, that was all they needed. It was his suggestion. They've been so disconnected lately, so busy with everything, they just needed to put on something nice, get out of the house together, let Amy watch Enid for a night; then everything would be better.

This morning, it seemed like a desperate last-ditch attempt at reconnection, but now, sitting across from each other, it feels right. Even without alcohol, Martha feels tipsy, loose. Last night's fight, the whole thing with Bruce, it all seems so ridiculous now. Maybe she and Leon have been out of the loop with each other, but they know how to loop back together.

He speaks softly: "How do we make sure there's always room for you? With everything going on, I don't want you to get lost in there."

So what if they haven't had sex in a while? That happens to every couple. Before him, she never had a relationship where a man wanted anything from her *besides* sex. A man who truly wants to be with her, whether or not she gives him an orgasm, that isn't distance; it's growth.

She smells him before she sees him—smoky, musky, slightly tangy. He interrupts: "Hi, I'm Bruce, and I'll be taking over for your server today."

Her skin turns icy. She pulls her hand out of Leon's, holding it to her chest, instinctively protecting her vital organs from attack. She's never seen him in the light of the sun before. He's even handsomer now, all scruff and smirk, wearing a black button-down shirt, an apron around his waist. Her sphincter puckers with the memory of the night before.

Bruce looks back and forth between the couple, an impish grin. "Can I take your order?" That bastard. He's toying with her.

Leon replies, "I think we still need a moment to look at the menu, sorry."

"Take your time," he teases. "I highly recommend the beef carpaccio." He walks away, returning to the back of the restaurant.

Leon nods, looking down at the menu. "I was already thinking of getting the carpaccio. If you don't mind." He looks up, smiling at first, then concerned at the terror on Martha's face. "You okay? I don't have to get it."

She hesitates for a moment, but she can't just sit there and let Bruce trifle with her. She pushes her chair back with a screech and gets up quickly before her husband can say anything. "Bathroom."

"Oh, okay," he mutters, confused, watching his wife quickly charge to the back, her wedges clacking with each step.

She weaves through the tables, turning a corner at the back of the restaurant toward the kitchen and bathroom. There he is, leaning over the counter to speak to someone in the kitchen, that simpering gremlin.

She quietly growls, "You can't do this to me, you sneering little shit."

Bruce turns around, unfazed, and steps toward her. "Didn't expect to see you here." He reaches out to touch the side of her elbow, but she takes a sharp step back.

"Don't you, don't you touch me. That is my husband out there."

"He seems like a great guy."

She wags her finger in his face. "I don't know what you think this is, what we are, but this is not some horny little game to me. This is my life. And I will do anything, I will end you, to protect it."

He holds his hands up, almost laughing at her panic. "Babe, you came into my restaurant. I'm not, like, stalking you." Her anxiety's so spiked that she didn't quite realize that, but yes, he is right; she came into his place of work. "You knew I'm a waiter."

"I didn't know it was here. I would've never come."

"I just started this gig. And I won't say a peep, don't worry. You're the one running back here, being all sus. You really went ghostly white out there."

"Why did you take my table? You shouldn't have come up, you should've gotten any other idiot waiter to take it, not you."

"You left so abruptly last night, maybe I wanted to talk to you." His voice goes deep, gravelly. "Or maybe I wanted to see you squirm for me. Again."

She scoffs, incredulous, pinching her nose in fury, though the wetness in her panties betrays her anger. "I will not let some greasy beverage monkey threaten me. If you do, I'll tell the police about you, what you're doing."

"What *we're* doing."

She wants to slap him across his smug face, but she can't cause a total scene. "I never want to see your pathetic loser ass ever again."

She turns around sharply, huffing back into the room, not wanting to look at him for another moment.

"That isn't very nice," he calls after her, proud to have gotten under her skin. "He's handsome, like you said. Old movie star."

When Leon sees her return, he looks up, concerned. "What's wrong?"

She takes a quick breath to redirect herself. "I'm really not feeling well. Let's go."

"You want to leave? Go home?" He deflates, disappointed.

"I need to get out of here. I feel hot, very hot."

"Oh no. What do you need? Should we call Roger?" He stands abruptly, reaching toward her to grab her forearm.

"I'll be fine. I just need to leave."

He glances at his half-drunk beer. "Should I tell the waiter?"

"No!" she hisses, pulling out of his grasp and walking away without him.

He walks quickly to catch up to her. She pushes open the door, the breeze outside cooling the sweat off her face.

The valet approaches them, confused. "Leaving already?"

"She's not feeling well," Leon answers.

"Ticket, please."

As the valet takes the ticket, the door opens again.

"The bill, sir," Bruce stands halfway in the door. "For the beer and the tonic water."

"Oh, so sorry, we didn't mean to dine and dash," Leon apologizes, embarrassed. Martha stands there, frozen, mortified. "This should cover it." He hands Bruce thirty in cash. "Sorry, we had to step out fast. The wife, she's pregnant, she isn't feeling well."

"Pregnant?!" Bruce gapes, crumpling the bills in his hand.

Her eyes go wide, eyebrows practically reaching her hairline. She wants to explode Bruce's stupid little skull with her brain, she wants to run him over with her SUV.

Leon looks befuddled. Confused, he says, "Yeah, she really is pregnant. And keep the change."

"Pregnant! Wow. She's pregnant," Bruce chuckles, turning to look right at her. She turns her head away, looking for the valet, needing her getaway.

"Yup." Leon nods, proud.

"Well, that really is such a miracle, an impossible blessing." Bruce grins. "I'm so happy for you. Congrats!"

The valet pulls the car up and steps out. Leon thanks him and hands him a five. Bruce stands in the doorway, dumbstruck, waiting for her to look at him, but she won't. She stares ahead and gets into the passenger seat.

She finally starts to feel safe again as Leon puts his foot on the pedal. She wonders if she was perhaps mean to someone who had only been kind to her, but something just came over her. She didn't know what Bruce might do; she had to shut it down. And maybe she was yelling at herself too, knowing how badly she still wants it—his rough hands all over her, his stubble scratching her soft sensitive skin, her tight hole taking whatever he has to shove inside her.

For so long, it was only Roger who knew the truth, who held the keys to her thumping heart under the floorboard, but it hasn't been just him for a long time now. Bruce may have saved her life only a handful of months ago, but now her existence is forever in his hands. And it's not even just Bruce: Everyone in the treatment group knows about her, knows what she does in the dark when she thinks her husband's sleeping. It isn't just that she can't return to the warehouse; she has to be more careful, more vigilant, everywhere she goes.

Leon clears his throat. "That guy was a little weird, huh? Who talks like that? 'Impossible blessing'? Sounds like, like . . . I don't know what it sounds like. But it's weird."

Martha nods, wiping the sweat off her forehead. "Yeah."

"How're you doing now, babe? Still hot?" He fiddles with the air conditioner, putting it on high.

"I'll be fine now. Thanks."

Only because Bruce can't hurt her now, and because she can't help it, she turns to look at him through the back window of the car. He's still staring at her, amused. She takes one last look at him. She can't go back to the warehouse; she will never let herself see him again.

Buzzing with anxiety, she will wait until Leon's sleeping, and she will gorge herself in the guest room. The rotten juices dribbling down her chin will calm her, put her to sleep like a baby with a belly full of mother's milk. And tomorrow she will be all smiles, all warmth, all pink blush and white teeth, and it will all be perfect. She will be a good girl now.

Chapter 35

Leon pounds on Enid's door and yells, "People are starting to arrive. We need you out here." No response from the other side. Martha walks up behind him.

"Go finish stocking the bar." She shoos him away and speaks through the door. "Dad is gone. I'm not going to make you come out if you don't want to, but just open the door."

She waits a moment until she hears little footsteps. The door unlocks. Martha opens it, and Enid, still in her pajamas, has already scrambled back to her bed, sitting with her arms crossed, refusing to face her.

Martha enters and closes the door gently. "Honey, what's wrong? Why aren't you wearing the dress we picked? I thought you liked it." She notices all of Enid's clothes strewn across the ground, a feminine scene she knows all too well.

"I look disgusting in it." Ah, welcome to womanhood.

"Don't say that. You looked gorgeous."

"You say that because you have to. I looked like a fat pig."

"Don't say that about my daughter." Martha sits next to Enid on the bed. She'd hoped they could have had a little bit longer before having to tackle LA private-school-induced body dysmorphia. Martha is prepared, having talked Roger through a similar meltdown in Palm Springs when the Speedo he bought at nineteen no longer fit at twenty-eight.

"I'm not wearing it. Everyone's gonna be looking at my stomach."

"Honey, they'll be looking at my stomach. That's kind of what this is all about," Martha teases. "You looked so pretty in it, I promise."

"I'm not wearing it."

"Fine, you don't have to wear it." Martha gets up and searches through the clothes on the floor. "But you do have to wear something."

"I look fat in all my clothes. I need all new clothes." Enid finally turns around, staring poison-tipped daggers at her. "You'd never get it. You look . . . you look like you."

"I've said the exact same thing! Those words exactly, my clothes scattered on the floor just like yours," Martha kneels in front of Enid, her hands on the girl's knees. "Every single woman on this planet has said that. I bet cavewomen were saying it with their loincloths thrown across the cave. I know Taylor Swift has said it too." She manages to get a smile from Enid. "I don't like telling people this, but . . . I didn't always look like this."

"What do you mean?"

"For a long time, I hated how I looked. People on the street, I'd feel like they were looking at me, thinking how ugly I was, how disgusting I was."

"Nobody would ever think that about you."

"They did, I promise you they did. But one day, I just stopped caring."

"How did you stop caring?"

Martha can't admit that she had just about every surgery under the sun, so she goes with: "I realized my body is meant for far more important things than fitting in last year's jeans. It will take you to fabulous places, help you meet new people, hug the people you love, carry that big brain of yours. Your body is the home of my favorite person in the world." Martha pokes Enid's nose. She seems to soften slightly.

"I still look fat in it."

"Fine, I'll tell you the truth." Martha stands up. "But if I tell you this, what I really did to get over it, you have to get ready right now."

"What did you do?"

She reaches out her pinky to make a deal. "I'll tell you the truth, the real truth if you promise me that you'll put something on." Enid, curious for the secrets of grown-womanhood, curls her pinky around her stepmother's. "I do my makeup better than any influencer or celebrity. And I got a boob job." Enid gasps, titillated. "Since you're not getting implants at eleven, why don't I let you try a little mascara? L'Oréal Voluminous Original in carbon black. You don't need anything expensive. Waterproof drugstore mascara is all a girl really needs."

* * *

Ice clinks in glasses as flushed faces talk at each other in the twinkling lights of the backyard, bougainvillea climbing up the back wall, the tight white and orange-brown flowers of the loquat tree in full bloom. Martha loves this backyard, especially when it's filled with light and people and laughter and alcohol.

Enid, attitude changed by a little glam, talks with Quinton and another kid from school. She wears a baby-doll dress Martha picked out for her and looks so much older than the six-year-old Martha first met.

The mother of the hour wears a floral-print halter dress with a flouncy skirt, perfect for showing off her flourishing bosom while hiding her bump. She chats with Roger and the twenty-six-year-old boy who he's been seeing for a few weeks. Just by the smell of him, it won't last. She hopes Roger will vet the boys a little better when there's a baby around. She imagines birthdays in this backyard, a petting zoo for the first and a clown for the second.

"Sparkling water with a lime wedge," Roger whispers, nudging Martha. "Very subtle."

"Only you can smell that there's no vodka in it. But it won't be our secret much longer."

She looks over to Leon, talking with his brother and his wife. He looks back to her, a drunken smirk on his face. He's so adorable when he's a little tipsy. That's how Martha knew he was a good man. Only two months into their relationship, he got far too drunk at a dinner where the hostess kept refilling their wineglasses. Martha had known many good men who were bad drunks. She'd put up with them when she shouldn't have. But Leon, drunk in the Uber on the way home, just wanted to pet her head and kiss her face and tell her how happy he was that she was there, that they were together. He didn't try to have sex with her when she put him to bed. He dutifully drank the glass of water she handed him, looking at her with big moon eyes, cheeks flushed.

When she turned off the lights, he told her that he loved her, casually, like they'd said it a thousand times before, but it was their first time. The next morning, he had a pounding headache. She fed him Advil and toast and eggs and bacon and coffee, nursing him back to health, while she made sure Enid got to her Sunday swim meet on time. She was wife material; there was no more denying it. Leon told her he loved her again that night, sober, and Martha acted pleasantly surprised, saying it back.

Now he raises his eyebrows at her—*Ready, partner?*

She nods and turns to Roger: "It's time."

Leon and Martha stand next to each other at the top of the patio, looking out at the rest of their party. His coworkers, his old friends, some of the families from school, ladies from her gym classes that she's gotten drinks with, Amy, his extended family. She smiles, thinking this will be the village that will help raise this child. She notices Christine, already shaking with excitement. Martha can't wait for the rush of the cheers, the celebrations, the congratulations, and especially the offers to help her in any way they can.

"While you know we don't need an excuse to throw a party"—he smiles, and everyone can already tell where this is going—"there is a reason we wanted all of you people who we love so much to gather with us tonight."

"Enid," she remembers. "Get up here."

"Yes, Enid get up here," he agrees, trying to cover up the fact that he was about to announce their new family without her. The kid, standing at the front of the crowd, shakes her head, squinting her blackened eyelashes. "Oh, come on," he urges. She shakes her head again. "Let's do this together."

Perhaps annoyed by her initial omission, Enid does it herself: "Martha's pregnant."

Everybody gasps, pretending to be totally surprised.

"Enid," he snips.

"You heard her!" Martha laughs, far better at powering through awkwardness. She puts a hand on her stomach, feeling like she's in a commercial as everyone yells out congratulations.

"Finally! Finally!" Amy cries out, rushing toward them, making sure she's the first to hug them. "My baseball team!"

Leon and Martha laugh as Amy pulls them into a big hug, jumping up and down.

"I knew you were glowing! A mother knows!" she says, victorious, gesticulation and spittle as predicted. "Martha, you're a mother now too!" She kisses Martha on the cheek, leaving a creamy lipstick stain.

ZAP.

A sharp electric pain shoots through the side of Martha's mouth. She pushes Amy away, putting a hand to her mouth.

Amy asks, "Dear, you all right?"

For a moment, Martha thinks that her mother-in-law must have shocked her, but no, it's far too painful, still buzzing like she was struck by a Taser.

"I don't know. Fuck." She winces, really pained, like nothing she's ever felt before. "Something, something zapped me?" She feels ridiculous saying it out loud.

Leon asks, "Zapped you?"

Everyone looks concerned. She feels terribly embarrassed as her tongue explores the sudden injury.

Oh God. She finds something solid floating around her mouth. She moves the hard chunk with her tongue and spits it out into her hand.

"Oh Jesus," Amy gasps.

"Ew," Enid gags, covering her eyes.

The whole crowd looks at a bloody wet tooth sitting in the palm of Martha's hand.

Chapter 36

Pregnancy-induced gingivitis," Dr. Folstein explains, a gloved finger poking around Martha's mouth. "Swelling and inflammation of the gums. Pregnancy can make your gums swell, like any other part of your body. That leads to a rapid increase in decay and gum disease. Combined with the fact that your bones and ligaments get a little weaker, it resulted in the loss of your tooth. It's not common, but I've seen it before. You should see a dentist to prevent further loss, but there's no specific treatment besides heightened dental care."

Martha waits for Dr. Folstein to pull her fingers out of her mouth so she can ask a question. She had to wait until the new year for the specialty doctors to return. She may be Dr. Folstein's prized patient, but not quite important enough to deal with over the holidays.

Martha, Leon, Enid, and Amy celebrated Christmas together, making it extra special, knowing that it'll be Enid's last one as an only child. After they opened their presents, Leon told Martha that he has a special present for her in their room. Amy watched Enid as she tried out the skincare products Martha got her. The couple snuck off into their bedroom. She felt guilty that she didn't get him anything special. He reached into his drawer and pulled out a small box, about the size of his hand. He handed it to her, a smile on his face. She gently tore off the wrapping paper and opened it, touched when she saw a green baby rattle. "It's perfect," she said, shaking the rattle. They kissed with their mouths closed, neither wanting his tongue to poke the gap in her teeth.

She was thinking that the doctors at Cedars-Sinai would be more surprised by her tooth loss, but Folstein is an abnormal pregnancy specialist, after all—one measly missing tooth is nothing.

She raises her eyebrows and starts to make a noise. Folstein finally pulls her finger out of her mouth. She licks her teeth to get rid of the latex taste, her tongue investigating the hole where her tooth once was. "Pregnancy makes your bones weaker?"

"Your body has to expend a lot of nutrients to feed the fetus. You should make sure you're getting enough calcium because the body is investing its resources into the fetus and diverting them from you."

A lack of nutrients. She knows how to fix that. She's been a bit lax on her routine. Fearing that the gasoline was making her crazy, she hasn't been douching. And with Enid and Leon home for the holidays, the house felt a little claustrophobic anyway. Since he's already suspicious, she'd even avoided eating the meat, worried he might stir in the night and look for her, not having to wake up for work in the morning. She needs a good session, a long one. She will not let herself go toothless.

"Martha, Dr. Folstein and I are going to perform a vaginal exam? Do we have your consent?" Roger asks, already putting his gloves on before she answers.

"Yes," she replies, staring at the other doctors in the room, all men.

The doctors adjust their glasses. Everyone wants an up-close-and-personal look at the designer pussy.

"Lean back, we'll put you in the stirrups," Folstein commands. Martha does as she's told, hoisting her legs up.

"I'm going to perform an exam with my finger. Do I have your consent?" Folstein asks.

"Sure," Martha replies, and the doctor wastes no time sticking a lubed-up gloved finger right inside of her. Folstein pokes around. It hurts. She realizes she hasn't been dilating. It's been so long since her vaginoplasty that she doesn't think about it anymore. Having sex with Leon was more than enough dilation, but now she's gone months without anything going in there. She shouldn't have done that, but she threw out her dilators years ago when she moved in with Leon.

Folstein pulls her finger out again. She almost expects fanfare but gets none. "Now we're going to use a speculum so we can take a look."

"All right." She shudders as the cold speculum presses inside her. She winces as Folstein expands it, her gaping vagina open for all who wish to see.

"It doesn't have much elasticity," Folstein reports. Martha crinkles her nose. She hasn't gotten that review from any man who tried it before. "I'm incredibly skeptical that a baby would be able to safely pass through the vaginal canal."

"As expected," Roger agrees. Dickhead. Martha simmers, feeling like his medical mystery ticket to success—*The Case of the Pregnant Male.*

"You think I need to have C-section?" she asks, disappointed.

"Certainly," Folstein says as she closes the speculum and removes it. Martha feels offended that the doctor determined that in mere moments. "You may put your feet down."

"I want to give birth vaginally."

"Your neovagina was not designed to give birth, to stretch to accommodate the size of a baby," Folstein replies coldly.

"What if I dilate? I could use larger and larger until it's the size of a baby," she offers. She wants the real deal. Why come this far to have a doctor cut it out of her like any other boring old surgery? This is going to special, spectacular. She's a miracle of a woman. And she doesn't need an ugly scar on her stomach. No, she wants to push and push, Leon holding her hand. She wants to be drenched in sweat as they gently lay the baby on her chest. She'll have to figure out a sweatproof makeup look; if Beyoncé uses the One/Size waterproof setting spray on tour, it should work for childbirth.

"The average circumference of a newborn's head is thirteen and a half inches. Do you understand how big that is?" Roger scoffs, holding up his hands to form a large circle. Martha narrows her eyes, offended he would question her vaginal capabilities in front of the doctors. "You think you can take this?"

"Honey, just give me a couple margaritas and some elbow grease." Roger turns red in the face. Nobody laughs. Martha clears her throat. "But you don't think it's possible that my vagina might increase in elasticity? I still have like five months." She remembers distinctly the pain from dilating those first few months. Lying naked, taking deep breaths to fit even the smallest of the medical dildos into her. She was a diligent student, getting to the biggest dilator, but it's true that it's nothing compared to a baby's head.

"We have no idea what we're dealing with here, so sure, that is possible, but it's highly unlikely," Folstein replies. "Your body wasn't designed for this. It would put not only your life but the baby's life at risk."

"Well, it doesn't take a fancy degree to see that my body wasn't designed for any of this and it's still very much happening." Martha crosses her arms. Folstein gives a soft humph, not dignifying her comment with a response. "Are we done for today?"

"Yes. But I would like to have a word," Roger says, turning to the other doctors: "Alone."

They nod and file out. Martha adjusts her gown, wondering what Roger needs to tell her. She feels anxious, eager to get home. Even the doctor said it: She's low on nutrients. She needs to feed herself.

She shrugs. "I'm not apologizing to them."

Roger sits on a chair, staring at her. "The baby is reaching viability. Soon, very soon."

"And why don't you sound excited about that?"

"When the baby reaches viability, it means that if you gave birth, it would be premature, but we'd try to save the child rather than consider it a miscarriage. Right now, you're almost at twenty weeks. Generally, at around twenty-four weeks, the fetus is considered viable. It seems like yours will be in line with that benchmark."

"You're saying if it was born now, it would actually live?"

"Not saying that. In a couple weeks, it would be considered extremely preterm, at that point it would be periviable. If you gave birth now, there's a very slim chance that the baby would live, and that's assuming it's the same rates as cis women. But as the weeks go on, the chances go up."

"So the baby could die, but you'd try to save it?"

"At a hospital like this, there's a chance of survival. But that's not why this is important. In the state of California, viability means the end of abortion," he says gravely. "In a month, you may not legally elect to get an abortion anymore."

She has absolutely no desire to get an abortion. This is her dream. She's already planned out the child's entire life in her head. But still it rattles her. A true point of no return.

"What about if it's threatening my life?" she asks.

"Even then, they would induce and try to resuscitate the baby." He looks right at her, making sure she comprehends the gravity. "It's possible, given the nature of your case, that you could get some special exception, but it would be fiercely and publicly litigated. So this is your last chance to make another choice."

"I have no other choice."

"You don't know what I've seen, Martha. It's dark, really dark. Neonatal encephalopathy, the baby doesn't get enough oxygen, and it turns dark purple, a dead infant in your arms. Congenital heart failure, we can't always diagnose it in utero. The baby has a hole in its heart and—"

"We've been over this."

"You know these things, but you haven't really sat with them. You say you want this baby so badly, but consider how it would feel, truly how it would feel in your bones, for this baby to die. For you to look at the corpse. It'll haunt you forever."

"Come on, would you really say this to a cis woman?"

"And living isn't always a good thing. Have you seen the NICU? These tiny little things, barely holding on to life. Or maybe your kid, this baby you say you've dreamed of, will live to twenty, needing round-the-clock care, unable to function, unable to survive on its own. You'll spend the next two decades solely dedicated to this little human who'll never be old enough to buy a drink. You haven't seriously considered what might really happen, what horrible new disorder you might birth into the world."

"You're not gonna scare me."

"And that's just the baby. Hemorrhaging—that's what could happen to you. Maybe you don't care if you live or die, but I don't want to watch your body bleed out for this unborn creature."

"Child, not creature, Roger. Look who's giving all the dramatic speeches now."

"Eclampsia. Do you know what that is?"

"I didn't go to med school, but that doesn't make me some idiot who can't make her own decisions."

"Seizures in pregnant women that can kill you. Sure, we can monitor preeclampsia, but there's no telling if it'll pop up during birth and shake you to death. And it's not just during birth. Sixty-four percent of maternal mortality happens between a week and a year after birth. You're bringing a human into the world—this is a decision for the rest of both of your lives."

"That's true for every woman," she repeats, although perhaps he is starting to wear on her.

"I know how this whole experience has made you feel, but promise me, promise me you will seriously consider what it means to take this child to term. You have just a few weeks before there's no turning back."

* * *

Martha exits her car, a flurry of emotions, her tongue still poking around the crater in her gums. Everything was under control; she had it under control. This shouldn't be happening.

She googled eclampsia. Fine, Roger scared her. His grubby words finally got under her skin. The symptoms of eclampsia are severe headaches, blurred vision, difficulty breathing, and urinary issues—all of which she's had. Those are the same ROND symptoms that others at the warehouse have, but nobody else is pregnant. She needs to be even more careful to keep it all under control so that she doesn't seize up as she's giving birth, widowing Leon a second time.

She's tempted to return to the warehouse. There are more treatments past Level 2, but she never asked what they are. She had no need for them when it was working. But it's too risky to go back after

Leon caught her. And she'd have to wait until the dead of night. She doesn't want to wait that long. She wants this fixed now.

She has a month to back out. A month before it's out of her hands. But she stood in front of everyone she knows, the whole world, and announced her pregnancy—she can't back out now. And she's already been forever changed by this child growing inside her, the immense warmth of love pumping throughout her abdomen. No, she will not even consider it.

She marches herself to the guest room. She and the baby will be healthy. Maybe she needs a double dose. She puts her phone on the desk, ready to relax. She needs peace, privacy. She has a few hours until she has to pick up Enid from school, and Leon won't be home until much later. She dives in, unpacking the boxes, tearing through the trash bag to get her supplies.

She grabs a chicken carcass, the douche, and the mason jar of gasoline. Usually she's not so greedy, doing them all at once, but she needs a big dose now. She heads into the bathroom, determined to cure herself. She'll let the gasoline marinate for an hour if she has to. So what if it makes her a little crazy? She'll do whatever it takes.

* * *

She doesn't know how long she's been in the bathroom for, deep in a meditative state, not even realizing she's moaning loudly as she nibbles on the chicken, clenching on the gasoline bubbling inside her. She does not hear the footsteps nearing the door, her moans fluttering out of the room.

Leon barges in, flinging the bathroom door open, whimpering: "Martha, are you—"

He looks down at her, completely naked, on her back in the bathtub, gasping in pleasure as she devours a raw chicken.

Her jaw drops, flabby chicken skin still stuck in her back teeth. "What are you doing home?"

"You weren't answering your phone, I kept calling you and I was getting worried and, and," he stammers, a look of complete and utter disgust on his face. "What is that smell?" He gags as it really hits him. "What the fuck are you doing?"

She must keep him; she must. He's a good man who loves her.

"It's just some pregnancy thing one of my friends recommended," she says nonchalantly, looking up at him with a pleasant grin. Even filled with panic, realizing that the very foundation of her life is cracking, Martha will not give up the Best Actress win—this is the scene they'll play at the Academy Awards when they call her name.

He bends over, inspecting closer. The chicken is not only raw but rancid, yellow and gray, covered in black and white spots of mold. The carcass barely holds together anymore. Martha has chewed through the meat, the tendons. He looks at her mouth, the mouth that has kissed him countless times, still swallowing her last bite.

She gulps, "I can explain."

Chapter 37

She's suddenly aware of her nakedness. She knows she's not going to convince him that what she's doing is normal while she's still in the buff. She lets go of the chicken remains and puts her arms on the sides of the tub to hoist herself up. Trying to get up, she accidentally relaxes, the gasoline squirting out of her anus in a big wet sloppy shart.

"What the fuck," he gasps, choking as his eyes well with tears from the fumes. He stumbles back, now completely terrified. "Martha, it looks like—"

"Let's not jump to conclusions," she laughs, trying to push herself back to standing.

"It smells like, like gasoline. Like you had gasoline up your asshole. But it can't be that because that would be insane, that would be so fucking insane."

"Let me tell you—" she starts, but she loses her balance and slips on the feces-infused diesel, slick on the cold porcelain.

Out of instinct, he reaches out to catch her. He grabs her wrist and keeps her upright for a moment before he lets go, his hand recoiling. He turns away, dropping to his knees, kneeling before the toilet, retching bile, straining his throat.

She steps out of the tub and quickly slips on the robe hanging on the door. She crouches next to him, patting his back like a toddler with an upset stomach. "I know, I know," she coos. "Get it all out."

Still looking into the toilet, stringy spit dribbling out of his mouth, he mumbles, "I wish you were cheating on me." He leans up and puts his back to the wall, still sitting on the floor, worn out.

She has to make him understand: "You remember how sick I was. My whole life, our whole life, was fucked up. I tried everything. Every doctor, every recommendation, none of it did anything for me. I saw the life we built together slipping away because I was so sick, and nobody could help me. I didn't want to lose our life together. I love our life together." She inches closer to him. "I came across these people online. They'd done this themselves and I obviously thought there were totally insane. I felt exactly how you feel right now. And then it was the most delicious piece of chicken I ever had. And I felt better, finally. And now I have to keep myself healthy for the baby and I know it seems insane, but this is the only thing that works. I love you, baby. Leon, you love me. You know me. You have to trust me. Please, please trust me that this is what I need."

She watches for a sign of life as he takes it all in.

"Baby," he speaks softly and for a split second, she thinks everything is really going to be okay. "We're going to get you help."

"No, no. I'm good! I don't need help. I'm great, fantastic even."

"We're going to make sure everything is good with you and the baby, and we're going to get you help." He lifts himself back to standing.

She stands quickly, blocking him from leaving. "We already know the baby is good! Roger did every test imaginable, and the baby is doing amazing. The amnio was fantastic. Because of what I'm doing, this keeps the baby safe."

He holds his hands out, taming a wild animal. "I know with your history, this must all be very stressful—"

"I've been doing this the whole pregnancy. The baby is healthy. Now you know that I've been doing this, and the baby is still healthy."

He pushes past her, slinking out of the bathroom, reaching into his pocket. She follows him back into the office. His phone is a threat.

Her voice now stern, she commands, "You can't tell anyone."

"I have to. You know I have to. Because I love you."

"If you trusted me, if you really loved me, you wouldn't have to tell anyone."

He shakes his head. He holds the phone away from her, his other arm stretched out to block her, and starts to dial. "We're going to find people who can help you through this."

She grows angry. "You'll kill me. If I stop, it'll kill me and the baby." She tries to grab the phone from him, but he stops her.

His voice cracks. "You can't say that."

"It's the truth. You will kill us." Why can't he be like Bruce's partner? Why can't he be the man who stands by her no matter what? In sickness and in health, he said—no, he swore—in front of God and Enid and the state of California. He's breaking their vows. She must make him believe. "You have to understa—"

He grabs her by the shoulders: "You're crazy! You've gone totally fucking insane. I need to put your crazy ass in the psych ward to protect you and the baby."

He has never spoken to her like this before. She never thought he'd ever threaten her, red in the face like her father. Maybe she's just been so wretched, so nasty, that she's broken him, forced him to act like this.

She shakes her head, refusing. "No, no, no. I won't go"

"I'll tell a judge you're shoving diesel up your ass and they'll put you away."

She breaks into a sob: "No, no. Don't do that to me. I'll die in there. I will die."

"You won't. You will live, safely. They'll help you." She can hear the terror in his voice. He isn't angry because he hates her, but because he loves her; he still does. He's still the sweet man she knows him to be, the one who cares for her, the one with the countless morning kisses. But he won't listen, he won't understand, refuses to.

She pulls away from him. He has left her no choice. She doesn't want to say it, it feels horrible to even put the words into the air, but it's the only thing she has in her power. "If you do that, I'll . . . I'll . . ."

"There's nothing you can do. This is what we have to do. It's final."

"I'll get rid of the baby. If you send me there, I'll do it."

He deflates, his lip quivering, this butcher threatening to murder his child. "How can you say that?"

"I don't want to. You know it's the last thing I want to do. But I can't go in there. I can't."

"You wouldn't. You wouldn't." She wipes her tears and looks at him—she would. "Martha, what am I supposed to do with you?"

"You can't send me away."

"But I can't let you keep doing this."

Chapter 38

Martha sits on the couch with Amy, her new full-time warden. The old woman knits, watching TV, while Martha spends every waking moment thinking about how to get her fill. She'd been full for so long that she forgot what it feels like to be hungry, and now she is starving once again. The house arrest will be as deadly as the sanitarium if she can't treat herself soon.

Martha can tell by the way her in-law sneaks glances at her that she thinks that her son is making a grave mistake, building a family with a psychotic woman. Leon didn't tell his mother the whole truth, nothing specific about rotten meat or gasoline, only warned that Martha is a danger to herself and the child, with unspecified strange predilections. Amy agreed to stay in the guest room indefinitely—anything for her future baseball team.

"That sounds like a prison," Enid scoffed at the dinner table after her father explained the new house rules. Martha was proud of her daughter for understanding that the new alarm on the front door and big silver lock on the garage are not safety protocols but barbed wire for the inmate.

The only thing they immediately agreed on was not telling Enid. Martha negotiated staying out of the psych ward by letting Leon turn their home into one—her freedom supervised, her phone and computer controlled by him, and definitely finding a new doctor, as Roger must surely be incompetent to not notice this.

Martha has no idea how to tell Roger he's been fired while Leon supervises her phone. Even contacting him at all could be risky if he texts something incriminating to her in response and Leon reads it. Roger will be furious when she doesn't show. He'll want answers. But his anger is the least of her worries right now.

She has to stop the nightmares Roger warned about. Every pang of hunger she imagines as a cry from the baby: *Save me, Mama. Don't let me die.*

Leon had suggested that maybe she was doing this as a way to keep control over her changing body, her changing life. He read reports of other women swallowing buttons, rocks, even thumbtacks. But for all his intelligence, he doesn't know everything about her.

For a moment, she had even thought about telling him the whole truth. Maybe he would let her continue her treatment if he knew everything. The words had touched her lips, but they wouldn't come out. She couldn't do it, images of bloodied trans women, left to rot in motel rooms and rivers, flashing across her mind. Even if he didn't kill her, he would leave her. No, she'll never tell him. They can still be a family after this, still have the future she imagined with her child. To keep herself and the baby safe, she'll just have to find a way to secretly continue her treatments, outwit her captors, successfully Jerry the foolish Toms.

And they don't even really know who they're up against. Game on.

Leon enters with bags of groceries. "Mom, would you mind putting these away for me?" He puts the bags on the floor. Martha glares at him as he uses one hand to cover the keypad he installed next to the door. He inputs a code that he pointedly does not let her see, despite her craned neck to gather any hint to the numbers.

"Alarm engaged," the robotic female voice announces. A security system is really meant to warn you of intruders, but Leon has turned it into the watchdog for his kept woman.

"I got it." Amy gets up to get the groceries.

Leon approaches his wife, cautious. He kisses the top of her head. Even after everything he saw, he still has a tenderness for her, this injured bird he must believe he's nursing back to health. "Christine texted you asking why you weren't at school, but I told her that you haven't been feeling well again and need some space. I said not to worry."

"I thought we were replying to my texts together?" He's already shifting the rules.

"It was easier for me to reply."

Martha calls out: "Amy, I can help you."

A challenge. Leon looks to her, wary. For a moment, she worries if he won't allow it, but he says nothing.

In the kitchen, Amy puts the groceries away. Martha watches her, tantalized as Amy sticks steaks into the fridge. Martha's mouth waters. The steaks are fresh; they wouldn't feed her properly yet—she imagines them rotting and melting in her mouth like cotton candy.

Amy hands Martha peanut butter and rice cakes. She silently puts them away.

"Mom, why don't you make the pork tonight and the steaks tomorrow?" Leon calls out, walking to his bedroom.

Starving, Martha spots the raw pork cutlets at the bottom of the grocery bag. She moves toward the knife block and pulls out a large cutting knife. "Leon loves caramelized onions with pork cutlets." She pulls an onion out of the grocery bag. "I'll get started."

"Thank you, dear," Amy replies.

Martha pulls out the wooden cutting board and slices the onion in half. On her second cut, she purposefully nicks her finger. "Ow," she yelps. She holds up her finger, a slice of ruby droplets at the tip—the distraction for her sleight of hand.

Amy looks nervous. "Oh, honey. Are you—"

"I'm fine. Just get me a Band-Aid. From the bathroom."

"Go wash it." Amy races out of the room.

Martha quickly uses her non-bleeding hand to reach into the grocery bag. She grabs one of the packages of pork and shoves it into her pants, securing it into her waistband. She covers it with her shirt. Trying to keep the pork in place, she waddles over to the kitchen sink. She turns on the water and sticks her bleeding finger under the stream, the blood running down the drain.

Martha looks at her hand, curious, as her fingers seem to inflate. The swelling starts with her cut finger, but quickly spreads to her whole hand, growing pink and swollen. She holds out her other hand to compare them, but both hands are now swelling, throbbing, the veins under her skin flush.

"Let's see that finger." Amy holds up the Band-Aid and grabs the bleeding hand. "Were your hands already so swollen?"

"It just, it just happened," Martha stammers, a peculiar pressure on her extremities.

"Pregnancy did swell my hands and feet a bit." Amy dries Martha's finger with a paper towel. She deftly puts on a line of Neosporin and secures it with the Band-Aid. "This is a bit much though. You should ice them."

Martha pulls back her hand and waddles away. She pretends to cough, trying to hide the crinkling sound from her pants. "I'm gonna go lie down."

"You go do that. I've got dinner."

Martha stomps loudly to cover the crinkles as she goes to her bedroom. She finds Leon putting on a T-shirt. He asks, "You good?"

"I need to lie down."

Amy yells from the other room, "Leon, you only got one package of pork cutlets. We need two!"

He yells back, "It's at the bottom of the bag!"

"I emptied both bags! You must have forgotten it."

"I didn't forget it!"

"If you didn't forget it, then come show me where it is!"

He sighs. He looks at his wife, determining if he should leave her unwatched for a moment.

"You're the one who wanted to live with her," Martha teases. "Another five months of that voice."

He relents. He'll return quickly. "I'll be right back," he says to her like he's reassuring her, when they both know it's a threat.

With him out of the room, she races into the bathroom. She quickly locks the door and pulls the package of pork out from her pants. She tears open the plastic and takes a bite.

She gags—not rancid yet. Damn it. She'll need to let it rot without him finding it.

She opens the cabinet under the bathroom sink, but no, that's too obvious. She looks across the room for a better spot, needing this desperately.

He calls out, "Where are you?"

"Bathroom!" She looks to the toilet, her throne. Bingo. She lifts the cover off the tank and places the package of pork inside, positioned above the water.

"We agreed you'd keep the door open."

She goes to put the cover back on the toilet, but struggles to grip it with her swollen fingers. "You really need to watch me crap?"

She stretches her fingers just enough to grab the cover and put it back on the toilet tank. She pulls down her pants and sits on the toilet right as he swings the door open.

He stares at her. He speaks softly but firmly: "What did you do with the pork?"

"Do with what?" He enters the bathroom and flings open the sink cabinet. "Please let me shit in peace." He ignores her, rifling through the sink cabinet. "You haven't grocery shopped in years since I've been dutifully doing it for you." He opens the medicine cabinet, still finding no pork. "You really think you couldn't have forgotten an item?"

He flings open the shower curtain, frustrated. He crouches to be on eye level with her. "What did you do with it?"

She rolls her eyes and shrugs as she flushes the toilet.

He purses his lips. "We're having steak tonight."

* * *

In the dead of night, Martha monitors Leon's breathing, making sure he's fully asleep. She slowly gets out of bed and walks to the bathroom.

Not even turning on a light, she quietly closes the door. Her hidden treasure—she carefully lifts the tank cover to reach in and pull out a cutlet. It will smell soon. This can't be its final resting place, but it'll work for now.

She hunches over and takes a huge bite—not sufficiently spoiled, still tough, but better than before. Her teeth gnash the muscle fibers; it tastes slightly off, not processed enough by the bacteria, but hunger is the greatest spice. She hopes this will tide her over until it can rot more.

She imagines her baby cooing, *Thank you, Mama. This is delicious.*

The door flings open. Leon flicks on the light.

She shrinks from the sudden glare, Saturn devouring his son, the swine still dangling from her maw.

He scolds her like he's punishing a dog, "Martha, no! No!"

She hisses, trying to shovel the entire thing into her gullet like a boa constrictor. He lunges toward her. She turns away, but he grabs the end of the pork chop and yanks the slimy thing. She tries to hold on with her teeth, but a powerful jolt of electricity bursts through her incisors. She gasps, letting him take the half-masticated chop.

She winces, groaning, at the steady current running through her entire mouth. She didn't feed herself enough. Her whole jaw seizes, chattering in excruciating pain.

He mutters, "You, you okay?"

She falls off the toilet, down onto her knees, shuddering in misery as she sputters up blood and a gleaming tooth onto the mint green bath mat.

Bending down, disgusted, he yelps, "Jesus Christ."

Lightning storm raging, she spits out more and more teeth, smooth gory pearls, tasting hot iron. She looks up at him, her face dewy with a grisly half-empty smile. Her voice garbles through the gaps in her teeth: "Look what you did to me."

Chapter 39

Martha wriggles her lips into a grin, new dentures shining in the passenger seat of Amy's car, driving back from the dentist, late January sky gray. She licks her lifeless false teeth, feeling truly geriatric now, like she should start filling her purse with loose Werther's Originals.

What will her kid think of having the mommy with no teeth? It'll be a lot harder to pull off boho meets '90s Hollywood glamour without pearly whites. She'll be the old witch all the other kids snicker about. And how will any man ever want to fuck her again? Nobody wants to kiss a dentured mouth. She has no desire to have sex at the moment, still too hungry to think about her other needs, but her vanity has taken a serious blow. She's well aware that the showstopping kind of womanhood she's worked so hard for has an expiration date, after which she'll spoil to middle-aged wallpaper, unnoticed, no more heads turning. Leon's imprisonment is only quickening her unfuckability.

Maybe it's just the pregnancy hormones talking, still giving her hope for an increasingly unlikely future, but she does still want Leon, wants him to want to fuck her, wants him to get outrageously hard for her. The Imaginary Fit Young Slut gets a Brazilian wax while she laughs at Martha's hideousness—it's almost too easy now.

They pass an old peeling billboard for *S.W.A.T.*, with Shemar Moore looking handsome in a black LAPD uniform. Martha sighs, missing Angie, wondering if the old bat misses her too. She thinks for a moment about what it would be like if, instead of Amy, Angie was taking care of her, cooking her dinner, doing her nails. She seethes with jealousy, imagining watching reruns of *The Young and the Restless,* freely boofing diesel.

Martha stomach grumbles with bottomless hunger. The baby pleads, *Mama, don't forget about me.*

She cannot let herself get sicker. Not for her own vanity and not for the baby. It's clear to her now just how quickly things will get dire if she doesn't get her precious nutrients. She'll have to be smarter, finding a way to sneak her rotten meat even with the bathroom door now removed by Leon.

Martha looks out the window longingly, when suddenly she spots the sign for the gas station ahead. *Do it!* the baby urges.

Martha blurts out, "I need to pee."

"Can you wait?" Amy asks. "We're almost home."

"No, I need to shit. I'm gonna shit my pants if you don't go to that gas station."

"Got it." Amy pulls into the Speedway Express. Normally, Martha wouldn't dare step foot in anything less than a Chevron or Shell, let alone put it in her body, but desperate times. Martha feels incredibly grateful that Leon was too embarrassed to give his mother all of the gory details—the old woman doesn't suspect a thing.

Amy pulls the car up to a gas pump. "I'll fill up the tank while you're in there." That won't work. Martha hesitates. "Go on."

"I need you to come inside."

"Oh, I should be going with you to the bathroom, right?"

She needs the old woman away from the gas, but if Amy came into the bathroom with her, Martha wouldn't get a chance to sneak to the pump. "No, I need you to get snacks while I use the bathroom."

"You don't want to just get them yourself after you go?"

"Chex Mix. A banana. Two Nacho Slim Jims. A sleeve of Double Stuf Oreos. Ranch sunflower seeds. Nerds Gummy Clusters—rainbow, not very berry. And a carton of Hostess Snoballs."

"I need to write that all down. But why don't you just get yourself whatever you want?"

Martha gets out of the car, trying to take advantage of Amy's fear of her daughter-in-law's psychopathy. "Get it for me immediately, or I will lose it. I'm pregnant and about to crap my pants!" She slams the door behind her. "And a Sweet Lady Vidalia Pickle-in-a-Pouch."

"Okay, okay." Amy pulls the car forward to park.

Martha struts into the station, the bell dinging. She makes a beeline to the fridge, swiping a Lemon Lime Gatorade, holding it low as she marches to the women's bathroom. She turns the handle door, but it's locked. The door dings again as Amy enters, frazzled, going to rifle through the shelves.

Martha doesn't have much time. She turns the handle on men's bathroom—unlocked. She hasn't set foot in the men's room in nearly two decades but, once again, desperate measures.

She swiftly locks the door behind her, wincing at the stale-piss scent, thankful to see a window high above the toilet. She rips open the stolen Gatorade and dumps it into the sink. She closes the urine-glazed toilet lid with her foot, clacking it shut. She shoves the empty Gatorade bottle into the pocket of her sweatshirt and stands on the toilet, climbing up onto the tank, almost slipping as she steps up. "Shit."

She grabs the grimy wall to stay upright. Steady, she reaches up to unlatch the rusted lock on the window. Stuck, she slams the heel of her palms into it, popping it out the other side, hoping that Amy's perusing the pickle section for the elusive Sweet Lady Vidalia that Martha entirely made up.

She puts one foot on top of the urinal and then grips the edge of the window, hoisting with all her might. She pulls her torso up, her sweatshirt probably the first thing to clean the wall in years. Grunting, she heaves half her body outside of the window, her stomach pressing against the windowsill. Flopping in the air, she realizes she has no plan for the other side.

A tall muscular man on the street turns to her, shocked.

Martha pulls her arms out, waving for help. "The bathroom door was jammed."

"I got you." The man runs over, grabbing her hands to pull her out.

"You're so strong," she purrs, wildly attracted to this kind, athletic stranger, who steadily brings her down to the ground, frees her legs from the window, and guides her to her feet. "Wow, thank you."

"No problem. You're okay?"

No time to flirt. "I've got to run, thanks!"

"No problem," the man says as Martha races toward the pump, her hood over her head.

She sneaks one glance to see Amy still searching through the shelves. Martha goes to one of the pumps on the other side, hidden. She slides her credit card into the slot, then pulls the empty Gatorade bottle out of her sweatshirt and opens it, using one hand to hold the bottle and the cap. After making sure nobody's watching, she sticks the gas pump in the plastic bottle. When she squeezes the trigger, the golden liquid fills the container quickly, her butthole salivating with anticipation. She puts the nozzle back, carefully keeping the Gatorade upright to reseal it.

Clutching the bottle tight, she walks back to the store, the bell dinging once again. She spots Amy, "You ready?"

"I didn't notice you get out of the bathroom," Amy startles, her arms filled with snacks. "I don't think I got everything." She makes a concerned face when she sees Martha's now dirty sweatshirt. "You okay?"

"I'm lovely. Let's go."

Amy nods and goes to pay as Martha returns to the car with her amber medicine. It's not as high quality as her usual Chevron fare, but she's finally going to feed herself and the baby again.

"I hope this will do." Amy enters the car, handing Martha two bags heavy with snacks. For a moment, she worries the old woman will notice that it's not actually Gatorade in the bottle, but Amy starts the car to pull back up to a pump, then gets out to pump the gas.

Martha looks down at the diesel in her hand. She won't be able to boof it. Not only did Leon throw away her douche, but without a bathroom door, she'd never have the privacy to let it sit. She remembers Bruce did say it would work if ingested orally, but it's less comfortable.

She doesn't have the luxury of comfort anymore.

She opens the bottle and takes a big swig, her eyes watering as it burns her mouth and throat, a silky blaze with a hint of a sweetness, like a really good peated scotch. She imagines her baby, now flushed with health, chirping in utero, *Yum! This is just what I needed.*

As her mother-in-law reenters the car, Martha quickly closes the bottle, trying to minimize the intense odor. As they return to the road, she opens the window to let the air in as she takes another quick sip, feeling every sizzling drop go down her esophagus.

Hunched over the wheel, Amy clears her throat. "I had my kids a long time ago, but I still remember how it all felt. I know how you're feeling. Maybe not exactly what you're feeling, but I've been through it."

Martha hears something new in her mother-in-law's voice—a hint of genuine care. "Was it difficult for you?"

Amy laughs. "You bet your ass it was! I blew up like a goddamn Macy's Thanksgiving Day Parade balloon and never went back. The bigger they are, the harder they fall; same goes with tits." With one hand, Amy scoops up her sagging breasts dramatically. "That stomach, that behind, those bosoms, thighs, jowls, everything, it never recovers."

"Jeez."

"This is a time of change, good change and really scary change." Amy grips the wheel tightly. "And Leon, he's a good man, but that's it. He's a man. They don't understand what it means to have your body betray you." Martha's body betrayed her long before the pregnancy, long before the sickness. Her body has betrayed her for her whole life, really. "Sure, they have the hairline receding and the paunch growing larger, but we still love our men, bald, fat, and hair out of their ears. And Leon's father, he loved me, still desired me, even after four kids. But I never felt comfortable again. I missed the way I felt when I walked into a room, when I wore a bikini, when I took my clothes off. I hope this is okay to say to you."

"Yes, of course." Martha takes a big gulp of the gasoline, finishing it off with a straight face, urging the nutrients to go straight to the umbilical cord.

"And that's just the vanity of it all, but we know it's more than that. The aches and pains that our men, the people we love most in this world, will never feel. We've been carrying that ache with us since we were twelve. And to be pregnant, you're finally fulfilling that dream you were told about for your entire life, and no matter what anyone said to you before, no matter what I'm saying now, nothing will ever really prepare you for it happening to you."

"No, nothing could have prepared me for this." Martha's never gotten a period, but she's had an ache inside of her for as long as she can remember.

And now she feels a sharp pang in her stomach, gurgling loudly.

The old woman sniffs curiously. "Still smells like gas, I hope I don't have a leak."

Martha puts a hand to her abdomen, a queasy stabbing pain. Bruce did say it was uncomfortable. But it's all worth it for the baby.

"I don't think Leon would have told you this, but he nearly killed me," Amy confesses. "He tore me open, and I just kept bleeding. Not during the birth, postpartum hemorrhaging. After we were back home, I was holding him in my arms, my first night in my own home as a mother. All of a sudden, my stomach hurts like hell, I'm light-headed, dizzy, I can't see straight. It happens so fast, blood pours out of me, bright red on my nice linen sheets. I don't even have the energy to scream before I pass out. Ed comes back into our bedroom and finds his wife and his newborn in a puddle of blood."

"Jesus." Martha grimaces, her insides now caustic. She takes a deep breath, trying to not let it show.

"I wake up in the hospital and they tell me that I almost died. They said that if Ed came back even five minutes later, I would've been dead. They told me I was lucky. Lucky! Can you believe that? Everything still hurt, we were worried it would happen again, and they had the audacity to tell me that I was lucky? Obviously the doctor was a man."

"Wow. Leon never told me that." Martha swallows her spit to try to keep everything down, fighting a nuclear holocaust in her digestive tract. She knows this is just the price she has to pay to feed the baby.

"Of course not! He was a couple days old, he doesn't remember it. I've told him the story before, but I don't like thinking about it," she says softly as she pulls into the garage. Amy shuts off the car and turns to Martha, green eyes kind like Leon's, the light dimming as the garage door closes. "We die for this. We die to keep the world going. And we're supposed to be all cheery while we're pregnant? We're supposed to laugh about the pain, giggling while we think of baby names? We're supposed to act like we're lucky to still be alive? No. Fuck that. You get to be crazy if you need to. You get to feel however the hell you want because you're doing something that no man could ever do."

Amy leans over and squeezes Martha's knee. Soothed by a mother's touch, Martha's stomach seems to calm.

Martha has not had a mother in a very long time. She never had a mother who truly cared about her, about the woman that she is. She's been so focused on becoming a mother herself that she'd almost forgotten that she's orphaned, motherless. It was just another line on the long list of things that she'd go without, that she told herself she would never have, that she didn't even think she missed.

But this woman next to her, who Martha had previously only seen as a mild annoyance, was right in front of her the whole time, ready to love Martha with wide-open arms, sagging pterodactyl skin. Martha wipes a tear with her finger, feeling guilty that she ever compared the woman to a scrotum. "Sorry, sorry."

"No, baby, let it out. Mama's here," Amy coos, pulling Martha into a hug over the center console, both of their seat belts still on. For the first time in a very long time, Martha feels that snickerdoodle warmth of maternal love enveloping her in a cozy womb of a hug. "I get it. I do."

"Thank you. Thank you for saying all that."

"I know how lonely this can be, and I want you to know that you're not alone. There is someone here who does get it."

Martha lets herself get lost in the moment. "Thank you."

Amy pulls out of the hug to look at Martha right in the eyes, her eyebrows knit expectantly. "And I had to get professional help, psychotherapy. When I was pregnant with Leon's brother. I couldn't stop replaying it in my head. I would see myself from above, like I was looking down on little Leon, me, and the bloody linens. I obsessed over it. Ed, he tried his best, but he couldn't help me alone. I thought about ending it, the pregnancy, but I saw a professional, and it really helped."

This was Amy's bargain with her vulnerability all along: get her crazy daughter-in-law a shrink.

All at once, the full force of Martha's stomach pain returns. Her abdomen squeezes like a tube of toothpaste, vomit bursting forth, acidic, pungent.

Amy yelps, "Oh God!" Neon-green puke splashes all over Amy's pants and the front of her car.

Martha recoils, gagging. She opens her mouth to apologize, but another pump of barf squirts out of her gullet, toxic fluorescent splatter all over her sweatshirt and tights.

Amy groans, "Oh, honey, not on the leather seats."

"I'm sorry, I'm sorry."

"It's okay. I raised four kids, this isn't the first time I've had spit-up in my car, although this might smell the worst," the old woman sighs. "Let's get us both cleaned up and I'll figure out the car. Maybe you won't need all those snacks after all."

Martha exits the car, dripping sickness onto the garage floor, eyes hot with tears, not from embarrassment but because she just threw up her life-saving medicine. She must have drunk too much too quickly. Hopefully she was able to absorb some of the nutrients.

Amy opens the garage door and lets them both in. "Run to your bathroom. Try not to drip." Once inside, Amy quickly locks the big silver padlock with a key she pulls out of her pocket as Martha walks away. Amy tails after her. "I should change too, but let's get you in the shower first."

Martha walks right into her bathroom, the door removed. Amy enters after her, not allowing a second of privacy. Martha carefully takes off her vomit-soaked sweatshirt and throws it into the trash. She lifts her shirt off over her head and unclasps her bra, surprised to look in the mirror and find her left breast taut, heaving, angry, like when she first came out of surgery.

Leaning against the sink, Amy asks, "I know it's none of my business, but your breasts are fake, right?"

"Yes," Martha replies, too distracted to be bothered by the intrusive question.

"I always thought so. They look great, of course."

Martha squints at her left breast, covered in tender red bruises around her protruding areola. She pokes curiously at the contusion—it stings.

"You know you might need to take special precautions with feeding and pumping."

Martha presses on her left bosom, wincing. Little pink drops of milky blood squeeze out of her nipple, glistening.

"Your first milk." Amy bends down to examine the inflamed mammary. "That looks like a clogged duct." Martha taps her finger onto the strawberry droplets, sticky, creamy. "Light strokes only. You need Tylenol, a warm compress, and a breast pump. You shouldn't massage a clog too hard. Don't want to pop an implant."

Chapter 40

Leon and Martha watch television, sitting on opposite ends of the couch, her new breast pump suckling under her shirt. She feels like a factory cow, getting milked by a contraption instead of feeding a tender calf. Amy went out with Enid to get a little treat, and Leon offered to watch the inmate for a bit.

Still terrified that she hasn't fed herself and the baby properly in weeks now, Martha's mind races, trying to figure out how to get her next fill.

Someone pounds on the door, too aggressive to be a delivery person.

"I'll get it," Leon says like he's being polite, when Martha can't even open the door without an alarm going off. He inputs the code with his hand covering the keypad, as usual. He opens the door. "What are you doing here?"

She wonders who it could be, eager for some contact with the outside world.

"Hi, Leon," Roger says like he's speaking to the manager of a crappy hotel that he's on the verge of berating. Martha knew this would come, sure that he had been blowing up her phone, although Leon never told her. "Can I talk to Martha?"

"Sorry, she's too tired."

"She missed an appointment. I called her a million times, but she didn't answer. It was kind of an important one."

"We're actually seeing a new doctor."

"A new doctor?" Roger laughs, incredulous. "Martha is my patient."

"We both decided it would be best to see a new doctor for the rest of her pregnancy." They went to the doctor Leon selected, Dr. Cabrera, an ugly old man with ancient hands. She shuddered thinking that those knotty hands will deliver her baby. He confirmed the baby was still healthy but noticed some scarring by Martha's labia and "unusual vaginal tissue." She panicked for a moment, but there was no world where they were going to jump to the conclusion that she's a pregnant trans woman with a vaginoplasty. She just muttered vaguely that she had a "hard childhood," and both men never mentioned it again.

Leon nods. "I'll tell her you came."

"I need to talk to her," Roger insists, sounding catty. "I'm not leaving until I talk to her."

"She'll talk to you when she's up to it, all right? Thanks for stopping by." Leon goes to close the door.

"Thanks for getting the door, but I'm up for it," she chirps, reaching under her shirt to remove the breast pump. She can tell from the stiffness in Leon's back and his grip on the door that he's furious at her for speaking up.

"Are you sure?" he replies, faking calm. "You don't have to get up."

"I've got it." She stands, knowing he won't cause a scene in front of Roger.

"All right." Leon gets out of the way and lets Martha stand in the doorway.

Roger shakes his head. "Can I come inside?"

"She's pretty tired, it's best to keep this a short visit," Leon calls out, sitting on the arm of the couch, thirteen feet away, far enough to act like he's giving her privacy while watching her every move.

"If she's tired, that's important for me to know." Roger makes a face. He's never seen Leon like this, controlling his wife, telling her what she can and can't do. Roger must know something is wrong. He whispers, "You missed your appointment. What the hell, you know how important those are. The doctors are furious, hounding my ass that you're derailing their research."

"I know, I'm sorry, but we decided it was best to see a new doctor." Martha shrugs, not sure how to play this.

"You can't see a new doctor, are you mental?"

She can feel her husband's eyes piercing through the back of her skull. "I'm sorry. We'll work this out."

"Girl," Roger says firmly, getting angrier. "You're a week away from viability." The first week of February, the last seven days she'll be able to get an abortion. Then there will be nothing stopping Leon from sending her to the psych ward.

So then this is her chance. She can run off with Roger. She can leave her husband behind and escape. She could raise the baby with Roger. He could support her. Maybe that was the answer right in front of her nose the whole time: raising a baby with her gay best friend. She loves him, not the same as she loves Leon, but he is already her family; maybe they could be a proper family together.

But would Roger let her do the treatments? He's a doctor—he would be afraid of something so seemingly dangerous, damaging, downright toxic. But he, at least, actually knows the whole truth. If he can believe in a transsexual pregnancy, maybe he could believe that rotting meat and gasoline heals her?

But even if Roger accepted her treatments, Leon would surely go to the police if she ran away. He would tell them that she's self-harming, a danger to herself and his unborn child, and they'd put her in protective custody.

And if it got to that point, it would be the end of their marriage. She knows they have passed many points of no return, but some part of her still hopes that once she has the baby, they can work things out, so hopped up on oxytocin from the beautiful newborn. Leon still is the best man she's ever had. He's doing all of this because he cares about her. He's protecting her, not trying to punish her—he thinks she's gone mad, and he has good reason to.

But it would be two gambles if she tried to run off right now: that Roger will let her do the treatments and that she won't be institutionalized after Leon tells the authorities. She's not sure of the odds.

"You're going to get yourself and the baby killed without me." Roger clearly wants something out of her, something real instead of the lies she's trying to sell him. When Martha was properly feeding herself, she wasn't worried about Roger's warnings. But now that she hasn't fed in weeks, she knows her body's falling apart—she doesn't want to think what could be happening to the baby now.

Leon calls out, "She's had a long day, I think it's best if you head out."

She looks to Roger, her brain scrambling, trying to calculate all the possibilities and decide. Freedom—the door is open for her if she'll only take a step forward and run.

Roger, impatient, leans in close and whispers sharply: "I'll tell him."

No, there is no freedom on the other side of the door. Only

another man who wants to control her, to steal her power and take her truth away from her. After everything she's done for him, put a roof over his head, fed, bathed, and clothed him. She put all her love into him, as any mother does, all for him to stab her in the back. No, she can't trust him either. She can't trust anybody but herself.

She whispers, "You wouldn't dare, you conniving little faggot."

He rolls his eyes. "Watch me."

Even with Leon keeping her momentarily captive, she still believes that once the baby is born, she has a shot at a normal life. If Roger tells Leon, she has no chance of a happy ending, not even a glimmer of it. Leon will either kill her, refusing to allow his unholy mutant spawn to be born, or perhaps mercifully leave her disgusting freak ass all alone to unemployed, unfuckable transsexual single motherhood—she doesn't know which is worse.

And she still wants Leon.

"You've always just been jealous of me," she snarls quietly so that her husband won't hear. "That I'm happily married while you drunkenly piss yourself to sleep, chasing after brain-dead twinks who never like you for more than a season, the skin on your neck getting looser every year like a sunburnt turkey."

He rolls his eyes, trying to take a step forward. "Excuse me, but—"

"I'll tell the medical board about the vodka you sneak in the office, you alcoholic imbecile." She blocks him from entering.

Leon stands nervously. "Everything good?"

She whispers, dead serious. "And I'll slit your cock-sucking throat with my freshly sharpened kitchen knife. For my baby, I will actually fucking kill you."

Roger gasps. He knows her well enough to know she's crazy enough to really mean it.

"Thanks for stopping by," she chirps loudly. With the slam of the door, she abandons her firstborn for the hope of a new child. She turns to her husband: "Block him right now."

Heart pounding with adrenaline, she walks back to the couch.

"Everything okay?" Leon asks.

"He's a shit friend and a shit doctor," she huffs, rejoining him. "Block him right now. We're never speaking to him again."

Wary, he nods. "All right."

Martha sits for a moment, still worried Roger might pound on the door and tell Leon the truth. She finally calms when she hears his car start and drive off.

Threat averted for now, she grabs the breast pump to put it under her shirt, but before she can, she gasps with sudden pain. She puts her hand to her left breast as the electricity returns, now coursing through her nipple.

"What, what?" he stammers. "Do we need a doctor? Should I run and get Roger?"

"No! Do not!" She writhes, shaking with pain.

"Let me just get him."

"NO!"

He reaches toward her. "Should I massage it? What do you need?"

She swats him away, growling: "Don't touch me." She squeezes her aching breast. "It hurts, it fucking hurts." She pulls her shirt off over her head, body contorted on their white modular sofa.

Blood and milk dribbling out. Bloodier this time, dark red.

"How can I help you?"

She looks him dead in the eye, fake teeth gritted in agony: "You know what I need."

A thick red blob oozes out of her breast, but it won't fully come out, stuck in her duct. She feels like she's already giving birth, her body tearing open to release some horrible creature.

He repeats, "Tell me how to help you."

In too much anguish to contain herself, she pleads, "I'm starving. I need to feed. You need to let me eat, or you're gonna kill me and my baby."

He looks at her with horror, but she doesn't care anymore. All of the pain she's felt is because of him. She feels all of it as fiery anger toward him.

"You're sick, Martha. I'm calling the hospital."

"Don't call them," she hisses, the blob pushing out of her.

"You need help. I won't say anything, I just want you to be—"

"It's here. It's here," she gasps as the red-and-white coagulated blob falls out of her breast onto the couch, staining it with a maroon udder booger.

She lies back down, out of breath. He moves closer to look at the angry red thing. He grimaces. "Dear Lord."

He will never fuck her again. She is no injured bird to him; she's a disgusting monster that he's only keeping around long enough to give birth to his spawn before he exiles her. Now she's sure he'll send her to the psych ward once she has the baby. He'll easily get custody after recounting her peculiar behavior. The Imaginary Fit Young Slut waits patiently at her door. She doesn't even need to fight anymore. She just needs to be standing at the ready with her waxed pussy to replace Martha once she's produced Leon's heir.

She puts her hand over her chest, still ringing with sharp pain, the ducts torn open by the blob. It's clear now that there's no chance of them having a happy life together.

The baby whimpers, *I'm gonna die in here.*

Right there, Martha makes a decision.

The pain snapped something inside of her. She does not want an abortion. She loves this baby too much, loves the life she's imagined for the two of them. It will be gruesome, but all the pain will be worth it when she holds her very own child. But still, in a week, Leon can throw her in the psych ward. She does not want this man. She doesn't want him raising her progeny. No. He is useless, cruel. Roger will not save her either. This leaves her with one option. She must go to the warehouse, to Bruce and Angie.

She must escape.

Chapter 41

Thursday afternoon, Amy knits while Martha pretends to watch reality television—the home renovation show she used to love, now a mockery when her home has become a penitentiary. Martha is drained, weary, wearing a big sweatshirt, ice packs on her chest. She's in no condition to leave, but with Leon working late and Enid having swim practice, she's sure she'll be sent to the psych ward—or die—if she doesn't make her escape now.

Amy takes a sip from her mug of coffee and checks the time. "We're gonna pump in twenty minutes. Don't want another clog."

"Bathroom." Martha pulls off the ice packs and gets up. Amy puts her cup down and follows her.

Amy sits on the chair of the vanity, looking into the bathroom. Martha flushes the toilet. She pulls her pants up and stands, breasts aching with her every movement. She hates looking at herself in the mirror, her tired swollen face, her fake teeth. She opens the medicine cabinet. Thankfully, the cabinet swings outward so that it blocks Amy's view.

Martha quickly locates the melatonin drops that Leon takes every night.

"What are you getting, dear?"

With one hand, Martha slyly grabs the melatonin drops and puts them in her sweatshirt pockets. Like a magician, she distracts Amy by holding up the Tylenol with the other hand: "It's kosher."

She opens the Tylenol and pops two out. She puts them in her mouth, bends over the sink, and takes a sip of water to swallow.

They return to the couch. Martha eyes the coffee. Amy notices her staring. "I'd miss caffeine too."

In her pocket, Martha unscrews the melatonin but keeps it upright so it doesn't spill. "Let's pump now." She points to the machine, sitting on the credenza under the television.

"I've got it." Amy puts her knitting down and walks over to grab it. Martha dumps all of the melatonin into the coffee. She doesn't think melatonin can kill you, but it's a risk she's willing to take.

Martha shoves the empty bottle back into her sweatshirt pocket as Amy turns around, holding up the pump. Martha smiles. "And would you mind turning the heat up?"

* * *

Half an hour later, the room is cozy, warm, perfect for an old lady to take a nap. The breast pump on, Martha grows impatient, but she can tell that Amy is fading.

Amy yawns, struggling to stay awake. She stretches, knitting resting on her lap. As the home renovation host yammers on about paint swatches, Amy can barely keep her eyes open. Finally, her head falls back, her mouth open. Martha waits until the old woman starts fully snoring to take off the pump.

Martha needs to get as far away as possible. She needs to get to the warehouse. The only safe place, she knows how to get there by heart. Bruce and Angie won't be there until the dead of night, but Martha will wait. It's her only option.

With no time to waste, she races into the office, the couch now pulled out for Amy. Martha's swollen feet already ache, but she ignores it. She finds the woman's purse and rifles through it. She finds the keys to Amy's car. Overjoyed, she kisses them. She just needs to find the keys to the garage. She can't go through the front door, or the alarm will go off and wake Amy.

Martha goes through the desk and boxes, getting more and more frustrated. Where did they hide this key?

She rifles through Leon's dresser, not caring about messing up his clothes. She'll be gone by the time he finds them; he'll have to fold his own clothes now. But she finds no keys. She grips the dresser, digging her nails into the wood, furious. She's gone through everything in Amy's room and now everything in her bedroom. But she doesn't know how long her prison guard will be asleep. Time is running out.

Martha returns to the sleeping woman. She very slowly puts her hands on Amy's pockets, feeling for a key—but still nothing. She decides that she has to go for it. Once Amy wakes up, she'll find the house ransacked and realize she'd been drugged. Martha will not get another chance to run.

She walks to the shoe rack next to the door. She tries to put on her sneakers, but her feet are too swollen. She slides into flip-flops instead.

With a pang, she realizes she may never see her home again. She may never see Leon or Enid or Amy again. She may never see this house, her kitchen, her beloved toilet again. She'll never see her clothes again, her beautiful clothes.

She inputs a number into the alarm, Enid's birthday. It buzzes—wrong. She looks to Amy, stirring slightly. Martha can't risk guessing again. She has to go now. And be fast. Faster than the old twat.

Martha takes a deep breath.

The alarm blares as she swings open the door.

As she races outside, the daylight blinds her for a moment. Heart pounding with a freedom that she hasn't known in a long time, she runs down the entrance steps and toward the garage.

"Martha, no!" Amy screams from the doorway, barefoot and bleary-eyed, alarm blaring.

Martha ignores her, trying to pry open the garage from the outside. But she's too weak, her fingers still too swollen.

Running at her, Amy yells, "No, Martha!"

Martha gives up on opening the garage and runs down the street toward a parked car, crazed, desperate, not really sure what her plan is now.

"Stop running! I'll drive you." Amy chases after her. "I'll drive you wherever you want."

Martha reaches the parked car. She tries to open it, but it's obviously locked. Desperate, her swollen fingers scratch against the opening to the gas tank, but she can't pry it open.

"Leave the car alone!" Amy barks, catching up to her.

Martha gives up on the parked car and runs into the street. She has no idea what her next move is. Her brain isn't thinking anymore, only her body.

A car drives toward Martha. She waves at it. "Help me! Help me!"

"No!" Amy yells. "Do not help her. She's insane!"

The car slows as it nears Martha. Amy pants, catching up, shaking her head.

Martha runs forward, wondering if the car really is stopping to help her.

Her flip-flop folds under her foot, tripping her.

Her ankle twists with the distinctive snap of a tendon tearing.

She falls. Her hands aren't quick enough to cushion her fall, so her face smashes against the rough asphalt of the road. Her jaw hits the ground, dentures popping out of her mouth, skidding across the pavement with the clatter of fake teeth. "Fuck," she yelps, toothless, ankle searing in pain.

Honking, the car brakes, stopping just before the tires crush her.

Amy nears her. "Are you hurt, are you—"

Martha cries out as her ankle swells, quickly, far too quickly. Like nothing she's ever felt before, her blood feels hot, magma boiling inside of her. Something is wrong, very wrong.

Panicked, Amy shrieks, "What's happening?"

Martha looks down to see the veins in her ankle throb, furious, overwhelming, torturous. Her whole foot looks inflated. She contorts, closing her eyes, unable to look as the fiery red swelling creeps up from her ankle, up her whole leg. All her veins filling with molten lava.

The blazing swell crawls farther up, the blood vessels bulging on her thighs and stomach, her whole lower body on fire, boiled from the inside out. Writhing in agony, Martha wonders if she'll die right there. If her arteries will burst and she'll bleed out right in the middle of the street, her baby broiled to death inside her. She winces, an enraged vein bulging on her neck, throbbing, throbbing.

Chapter 42

Leon, now haggard with some light stubble, enters, pushing Enid into the bedroom. The girl, incredibly uncomfortable, like her father has a gun to her head, holds a large slice of chocolate cake with two candles.

"We couldn't forget your birthday," Leon says half-heartedly over the whir of the air conditioner, struggling to fight off the late May heat wave.

For the past few months, Martha has done nothing but lie in bed, go to her doctor's appointments, and struggle through any movement that Amy forces her to do. She hates the way they look at her. She doesn't even need a constant watch anymore, unable to do much at all on her own. Leon did discuss putting her in a mental institution, but she promised, pleaded that she'd be good. He had no reason to believe her except that it seemed physically impossible for her to do anything. Might as well save the embarrassment of telling everyone that his wife's in the loony bin. And now she's so close to the end she can feel the baby aching to leave her decrepit carcass behind.

Leon pushes Enid forward, close enough to hear Martha's strained slow raspy breath. Enid avoids looking at her directly.

Martha glares at the "40" candle on top of the cake, mocking her. Forty has officially hit her like an eighteen-wheeler.

Her feet are swollen and pink. Leon has not kissed them, let alone massaged them, even once, afraid to touch her, like she might infect him. A bright red rash brands her ankles, crawling up to her knees. Her thighs are mottled with cottage cheese cellulite and varicose veins, eager to burst. She wears only loose granny panties, stained with pink-and-brown discharge from her flabby, fat-lipped, purple-blue twat. Her stomach, carrying a supposedly healthy life, is massive, bulging. It rises and falls with her raggedy breathing, a big shiny taut mound of flesh, striped by rivers of stretch marks. Her hands, just as swollen as her feet, rest on her stomach. Her bruised breasts sag toward her armpits, nipples wet with leaking milk.

Finally, her face, her gorgeous face. She's nearly unrecognizable, so puffy, disfigured. The eyelid of her left eye is so inflamed that she cannot open it. Rimmed by crusting, oozing sores, her lips bulge out, unable to fully close, her throat always dry. Without her dentures, her gums are crimson, sickly, hanging on to a few straggling teeth. A trail of dribble slips out of her mouth onto her chin.

She gave up her vanity months ago, avoiding mirrors, too distraught to really accept that this is what she looks like now, that this may be what she looks like forever. Unable to even lie on her stomach, she spends her days staring at the ceiling through the slits of her eyes, some trash TV playing in the background that she can never focus on. Though Leon does sleep next to her, a girthy pregnancy pillow always stands between them. He bought it as a gift, supposedly for her comfort, but she knows it's for his—a wall to keep the monster outside the gates.

Enid does not do well with hiding the disgust on her face. Pushed by her father, she creeps near Martha and drops the plate of cake next to her stepmother.

He urges, "Blow out the candle."

Martha refuses. Of all the cruel things he's done, this is the worst—reminding her that she's forty. She wants to beat him to a pulp, but she can barely lift her head off the pillow. Her youth is officially gone, wasted, drained. She's middle-aged.

Seeing that she won't blow out the candles, he does it for her. Before the flame has even fully extinguished, Enid asks, "Can I go now?"

"Fine."

She races out of the room.

He sighs, "Your due date is twelve days from now. We've gone on vacations much longer than that." He sits on the side of the bed, looking down at the cake. "All the tests say the baby is a beacon of health. None of the stuff you're going through is life-threatening to you or the baby."

She doesn't forget Roger's warning of lifeless purple babies and mothers seizing, foaming at the mouth as they orphan their newborn. There's no guarantees in any of this, no matter the tests. With how she's been feeling, with how she's been looking, she wouldn't be surprised if this baby does have horns, scales, and a tail after all.

Leon continues, "I've seen stuff online of people with similar issues. The crazy swelling. There's even a thing called 'pregnancy nose' from how much your nose swells. It seems to clear up after, a lot of it, at least. We're going to get through this. We're close, so close."

"'We'?" she groans, her voice deep and mean after months locked up in this room. Nothing has been what she dreamed of: nobody getting up on the bus for her, no doors held open, no skipping lines, no women telling her she's glowing. She's been alone, so totally alone, whether or not Leon decides to sit next to her for a moment. For the first time in a long time, she starts laughing, a chuckle at first, until it grows to uproarious raspy laughter. Her whole upper body heaves with each deep belly laugh. He looks nervous, almost trying to laugh with her for a moment, but it's uncomfortable, too weird.

She doesn't know what he plans to do with her once she has the baby; she doesn't want to know. Leon and Amy went and picked out the crib. They've set up the nursery next to Amy's bed. Martha wasn't even consulted on the color. They both know the truth: There is no "we."

* * *

The wind howls outside the window, air lapping at the glass. Martha wakes in the dead of night as the baby stirs. The skin on her stomach stretches from the inside. She puts her hand on her abdomen, feeling the creature move around. The flesh presses out, a baby's foot begging to leave its cage. The baby cries, *Get me out, get me out.*

She reaches to her face to pull off her sleep mask. As she pulls it off, clumps of hair tear off with it, falling onto her shoulder. She runs her fingers through her scalp, more long locks falling out between her fingers, easily gliding off her head.

She panics, throwing off the blanket and hauling her huge body out of bed. Wearing only loose, soiled panties, she trudges to the bathroom.

In the dead of night, she sees herself in the light from outside. Not only has the hair on her head sloughed off, but her face, her once beautiful face, is littered with dark stubble. She puts her hand to her neck, rubbing her cheeks, feeling the prickles of a five o'clock shadow.

All those torturous hours spent burning off each follicle, now totally wasted by her mutant biology. Her hands go farther up her head, long strands tumbling off with each swipe. Like a tortured Barbie doll, clumps of sweaty matted hair stick up next to patches of splotchy bald scalp.

She shakes her head, grief boiling to rage. She's come this far, done so much, just to end up like this. No, no. This can't be it. She could put up with all of it—pain, discomfort, humiliation—but fuck this. In the mirror, she sees something staring back at her that she hasn't seen in a long, long time: a man.

That's the last straw. No, she won't let this be her fate.

She slowly creeps back into the bedroom, Leon still sleeping soundly. She walks quietly to the kitchen, making sure each footstep is silent. She opens a drawer and pulls out the duct tape.

She starts with Enid. No, she's not going to hurt the girl. But she doesn't want Enid getting in the way, so she seals her in, slowly taping the edges of her door. Even maneuvering the tape is difficult with her swollen fingers, but she strains through it, determined. She's not sure how well it will actually hold. Hopefully Enid won't even wake up.

Next Martha goes to seal in Amy. She doesn't want her intervening either. She puts the duct tape on the top corner of the office door.

Opening the door, Amy says, "Dear, are you—"

Martha's hand shoots out. She slaps the duct tape across the old woman's mouth. Her eyes wide, Amy screams, but nothing comes out of her taped mouth. Amy tries to push Martha back, but she's too big. She uses all her might to push Amy hard against the wall, knocking the wind out of her. Martha has been weak for weeks, but she feels strong now—a mother suddenly lifting a car to save her baby.

Martha looks across the room, now partially prepped for the baby's arrival, the pull-out bed sandwiched between the crib and the changing table, and grabs the first thing she can reach: Amy's thick knitting yarn. She grabs Amy's wrists and tries to tie them together with the yarn, but the crone struggles too much.

Amy manages to punch Martha right in the nose. Blood squirts out, gushing over her open mouth; she tastes her own blood. Furious, she jabs Amy right in her stomach. The old bag wheezes from the impact. With Amy stunned from the pain, Martha quickly ties her wrists together. Using the yarn, Martha pulls her to the ground and sits on her stomach. The woman can barely breathe under her weight. She ties Amy's wrist to the foot of the crib.

Amy desperately tries to scream through the duct tape, but nothing gets through. Martha puts her hand to her nose and leans her head back, the nosebleed slowing. Martha looks down at her mother-in-law, hogtied, squirming, absolute terror on her face. She reaches to remove Amy's duct tape from her mouth.

"Scream and I piledrive you into your grave," Martha growls. "Tell me where the garage key is."

* * *

Martha enters the bedroom, an imposing silhouette in the doorway. She creeps toward Leon, slow, quiet. She looks over him, menacing.

Her bloody drool accidentally falls right onto his face.

He wakes up, startled. "Jesus Christ," he groans, still in his chemically induced slumber. She jumps into action, quickly wrapping the duct tape around his hands. "What the fuck?!"

But before he can even process what's happening, she tapes his wrists to the bedpost. He tries to sit up, but his tied hands keep him down.

"Don't do this, don't do this. Not to the baby," he whimpers. "You know it's bad."

She ignores him. She quickly reaches under his pillow, feeling for the key. He tries to whack her with his hands and free himself from the tape, but he can't reach. He launches his face at her arm, biting her as she pulls the key from underneath him. She yelps.

He uses her momentary distraction to move his legs out from under the blankets. He kicks at her, trying to get her off her him. She groans as his foot collides with her stomach.

The wind knocked out of her, she stumbles back, hitting the wall. "Fuck, fuck." She rubs her stomach, trying to feel that the baby is okay, terrified that her husband has ruined everything.

He looks horrified at his actions—after all this, he was the one who hurt the baby. "I didn't mean to. You know I would never."

"But you did." She holds her stomach as she brings herself back up to fully standing. The key is cold and hard in her hand.

Helpless, squirming, he pleads, "Please. I'll do whatever you want, you can do whatever you want, just let me go."

She ignores his cries, galumphing out of the room. His unheard pleas echo off the walls. She marches through the hallway, past the kitchen, and reaches the lock to the garage door. She unlocks it, heart pounding with the promise of freedom. She walks down the two steps and sees her car, her gleaming chariot.

She opens the car door, expecting the keys to be inside.

"No, no, no," she mutters, searching for the keys in the glove compartment and not finding them. She must find them quickly before Leon can wriggle free or everything will be lost.

A little voice speaks out: "Martha."

She turns around to see Enid standing in the doorway to the garage. The duct tape wasn't enough to keep her door shut for long. She can't let the girl stop her. This is her only chance.

Martha stumbles toward her, pleading. "Me and the baby will die, we'll die if we stay here. You have to let me leave. I need to go back in and find the car keys."

They can both hear Leon's shouting from his bedroom: "Help! Help me!"

Enid remains still, standing in the doorway, blocking Martha from reentering the house. Martha steps forward. "I need to go inside and find the car keys." She doesn't want to hurt her, but she doesn't know what she'll do if the girl won't comply.

Enid holds out her hand: The car keys glimmer in her palm.

Martha snatches them quickly, touched that one person in this house would actually help her. She puts her hands on Enid's shoulders and crouches. "I need to have this baby and then I'm coming back, okay? I'll be back once everything's okay. And we'll be a family. A big happy family."

Martha first met Enid on a playground when she was six. She was so cute then, all pudge and sass, eyes wide like saucers, knees covered in dirt, barely making it up to Martha's belly button. Enid was wary of this new woman whose hand her father held instead of hers. But with every freshly baked chocolate chip cookie, finger painting, homework help, bath time, school pickup, Band-Aid applied, good night kiss, and Taylor Swift song belted in the car, Enid warmed up to Martha.

"I will always, always be your mother. Raising you, getting to be a part of your life, it's been the most precious gift. But I need to go now. I will be back. I'll be back for you."

No longer with the saucer eyes and dirty knees, but on the precipice of her own womanhood, Enid presses her face against Martha's chest, wraps her arms around her. They both know she can't come back. In the silence of their embrace, they still hear Leon crying for help in the bedroom. Enid lets go, pulling away. "I love you, Mom."

Martha clenches the car keys tightly—she still knows the way to the warehouse.

Chapter 43

Bruce looks up from behind the reception desk and turns pale, terrified at the mostly naked monster that just walked through the door. "What the hell?!"

"It's me, it's me," Martha wheezes, her speech slurred without her dentures. Wearing only stained stretched-out panties, she lifts her arm to cover her nipples with her hand, as if that were his issue with this whole display.

"Stay over there. I can help, I can help you. Just stay over there," he stammers, stumbling backward against the wall.

"Martha, it's Martha," she repeats, trying to look him in the eye and get him to see what was once there.

He shakes his head. "Wait . . . Martha? Like *Martha* Martha?"

She nods, her swollen lips curling into a smile.

"What, what happened to you?"

"What the hell is going on out here?" Angie asks, pushing open the door from the hallway. She yelps when she sees the beast, "Baby Jesus!"

"It's Martha," he says softly, still in disbelief.

"Help me, help me," Martha whimpers. A sudden pain shoots into her stomach, she stumbles back. "Fuck."

Bruce and Angie quickly go to catch her and guide her into a chair. She sits, hand on her belly, still wincing from the turmoil inside her. She knows it's bad; she knows it's the baby.

He asks, "You stopped your treatments?"

She nods. "Husband caught me."

"But, but we've never seen this shit," Angie stutters, really examining Martha now. "You look like the fucking thing from the fucking lagoon, but with . . ." Angie cocks her head, looking at the creature's engorged stomach, veins bulging and throbbing. "Whatever the fuck is going on there."

"I'm pregnant."

"You're what?"

"Pregnant. I'm pregnant."

"You really are pregnant like he said?" he whispers, confused. "You lied about being trans?"

"No, I swear to God. I am a pregnant trans woman. Believe me, you have to believe me."

Bruce shakes his head in disbelief, while Angie sucks on her teeth, impressed: "Biiiiitch."

"But that's, that's not possible," he says like it's any use pointing that out.

"We medically require gasoline shot up our assholes," Angie says. "Impossible is just a lack of imagination."

"And I need your help," Martha says gravely.

"You're going to need more than the meat and gasoline," Angie warns. "This is, this is far past that."

A cold look falls over Bruce. "She needs our most advanced treatment."

"Are you sure? That's a lot, that's a lot for anyone," Angie says, nervous. "And she's pregnant."

He sighs, "And she's sicker than anyone we've ever seen."

She shudders. "The last guy who did this was fresh out of the psych ward. Are you really sure about this, Bruce?"

"It's not my choice." He looks down at Martha. "It's hers."

* * *

Bruce flicks on the light in the room at the very end of the hallway. Angie helps Martha in. Martha sees a doctor's examination table in the center. On the doctor's stand where you'd normally see a scalpel or the like, there's a large battery and jumper cables.

She puts a hand to her toothless mouth. "The electricity."

"I figured you must've felt some shocks before you became, uh, in this condition," he says, fiddling with the device. "The body runs on electrical signals, action potentials. But those signals only function properly given the right nutrients, electrolytes, and you haven't been feeding yourself in what seems like a very long time. Right now, you lack the right signals and then get these huge shocks when they build up. We need those electrical signals to work again. We need to give you the electricity, as a nutrient of sorts." Bruce turns to look at Martha, seeming unsure. "It's rare, but we have used this before. Although never to a pregnant lady."

"I need it."

"We're going to start low and go as high as you can take. The higher we go, the better the results," he says cautiously. "You're completely sure you want to do this?"

"Yes."

"I don't have a single clue what it could do to a baby."

"We need it."

"Help her onto the table."

Angie leads the patient to the table, heaving her into position. "Let's get you tied down so you don't start swinging everywhere like one of those inflatable-arm people." Angie takes Martha's limbs and tethers them.

Bruce grabs the clamps of the jumper cables. "You're going to feel a pinch." He clamps one of the cables onto her nipples—Martha yelps, the cold metal biting onto her tender breast. He grabs the battery and readies it for the treatment. "We're going to start you off slow, in pulses."

She takes a deep breath, nodding. She's terrified, knowing that she might end up electrocuting herself and the baby to death, but she's more afraid of what happens if she doesn't try it. "Light me up."

He turns a dial. The machine hums and buzzes as it gives her a quick pulse of electricity. Her whole body bucks, back arching as the jolt courses through her.

He turns it off. "How was that?"

She pants for a moment, her muscles settling. But she feels recharged, ecstatic, eager for more, like she just got fucked for the first time in months, like Bruce pulled out and she needs his electric cock back inside her to take her over the edge to a lightning orgasm. She begs, "Higher, give it to me higher."

He turns it back on, the buzzing louder as he increases the voltage.

She moans, shaking, muscles spasming. While the electricity that struck her from the inside felt like it was tearing her body apart, this feels like it's turning her on, giving her energy. She can feel the baby moving inside her, her whole body a battery, powering this new life.

The current courses through her, and she can feel her whole body relaxing, even though she's violently shaking on the table, pulling up against the restraints.

"YES! GOD, YES!" she moans loudly, wildly, her voice shaking. "GIVE IT TO ME! MORE! MORE! MORE!"

Leon rips open the door.

Chapter 44

Leon's pregnant wife convulses on a table with cables clamped onto her nipples like some perverted Frankenstein's monster coming to life, yelling at the top of her lungs, "FUCK YES! GIVE IT TO ME!"

He charges full force at Bruce, smashing him against the wall. Leon, a good ten inches taller than Bruce, easily tackles him.

"Dude, what the fuck?!" Bruce yelps, dropping the device as he hits the wall.

The electricity stops. Martha opens her eyes to see Leon pinning Bruce against the wall.

Angie screams, "Simmer down, dickhead!"

"WHAT THE FUCK ARE YOU DOING TO HER?!" Leon yells in Bruce's face. "You're the asshole who made her crazy!"

Bruce yelps, "She asked for this, dude, I'm helping her!"

"Leave him alone," Martha wails, still tied to the table.

Leon grits his teeth. "You fucking asshole." He punches Bruce hard in the face. Bruce falls to the ground, blood sputtering out of his mouth.

"No, no," Martha wails. "Leon, please."

"Hands off, fucker!" Angie barks, pouncing on Leon from behind. But Leon easily shoves her off, her head hitting the wall with a hard smack. She collapses onto the floor.

"I am sending every one of you nasty perverts to prison," Leon barks, ripping Martha out of her restraints one by one. "This woman is fucking pregnant! You're sick. You're all sick."

"Don't do this," she begs. "I need this." He pulls her off the table, making her stand next to him. "I need to finish the treatment," she howls. He grabs her by the arm, digging into her skin, and drags her out of the room. "I need that, or I will die, the baby will die."

He drags her down the hallway as she struggles to wriggle out of his grasp. She feels stronger, much stronger than before, but still far weaker than him.

"Don't you see how sick I am?" she pleads. Her speech is clearer, her lips less swollen. "I stopped this, doing what I needed to do. You made me stop and look what happened."

"You are really fucked up," he says, angry tears streaming down his face. "How could you? How could you? If you didn't want this baby—"

"You know I want the baby, it's all I want."

He pushes the door open to the waiting room and drags her away.

She gets another shooting pain in her stomach. Her legs give out, but he holds her up by the wrist. He shakes his head, whimpering, "Look what you did."

Leon drags her out into the parking lot, the hot dry wind lashing against her bare skin, wicking up the sweat on her thighs. She can barely stand from the pain in her stomach, but he keeps pushing her forward.

She looks between her legs to see a puddle of liquid wetting the parking lot. She falls to the damp ground, wriggling out of his grasp. "My, my water broke. My water broke!"

"Your water actually broke?"

"The baby's coming, I need—"

"I'll take you to the hospital. Come with me."

"I can't go to the hospital. I'll die there. They don't know what I need."

"This isn't your decision. Let's go."

"They can't help me. I'm not going. You can't make me." She uses her hands to push herself off the ground and stand in front of him, determined.

"Yes, I can." He tries to grab her arm, but she swats him away.

"You don't even know me. You don't know what I need. You should've trusted me from the start, but you don't even know me."

"To the car. Let's go."

She hisses, "You're nothing, nothing but a stupid man. You can leave me, try to kill me, I don't give a fuck anymore. No, you'll never see me as your wife, as a woman ever again, but I'm not afraid of you. I'm not afraid of life without you. The only thing that matters is me and my child."

"Martha, enough! I'm trying to save our fucking baby. We're going to the hospital."

This man who once looked at her with such immense love now looks at her like she's a demonic monstrosity. She never wanted to change, to become this person who disgusts her husband, but she's a desperate beast now. She will do anything to save herself and her child. And she knows she's completely changed—she's about to become a fucking mother.

The few strands of hair she still has flutter wildly in the slicing wind. Martha stares him right in the eye, her voice crystal clear: "I'm a transsexual."

He laughs incredulously. "See? You are fully off the deep end."

The words taste so delicious in her mouth, she could practically sing them: "I have XY chromosomes. I was born Michael Ian Paisley. I've been taking some combination of estrogen, progesterone, and spironolactone for the last seventeen years."

"That is impossible, you fucking psycho."

"I've had a brow shave, rhinoplasty, chin reduction, jaw contour, tracheal shave, fat transfer to my lips and cheeks, breast implants, countless hours of hair removal, and, of course, a masterful vaginoplasty."

"You are pregnant, Martha. PREGNANT!"

"It's a miracle. I'm a miracle. I'm a motherfucking goddess, and you are a puny sniveling mortal."

He gets red in the face. "YOU ARE PREGNANT, YOU PSYCHOPATH!"

"I faked it all until now. Every pregnancy test, everything, all a lie," she says, wild freedom in her steadfast voice. "I always told myself that I did it all because you would've gotten rid of me if you knew the truth, you could've killed me. But I think I liked it, the fantasy, the pageantry of it all. And yes, I faked the fuck out of that miscarriage. Because, Leon?"

He reaches out to grab her. "You're insane. You sick bitch—"

She smiles wide, her nearly toothless grin. "This whole time, you've been sticking your dick into a dirty lying tranny with a surgically constructed cunt that they made out of my big fat fucking cock."

Disturbed by the depth of her depravity, he gags. For a moment, it seems like he's unsure, wondering if in some crazy fucked-up way she might somehow be telling the truth.

But there's no time to care what Leon thinks—Martha must save her baby.

With all her might, she charges at him, knocking him over.

He yelps as her massive body falls onto him. She winces as she hears the distinct crack of his skull slamming against the concrete. She rolls over, panting heavily. He looks at her with bloodshot vacant eyes, dark red pooling out of his skull and onto the concrete. He barely manages to mutter, "Baby."

With the truth in the air, Martha feels free. For years, this was what she feared most in the world, him knowing the truth, losing him. The knot of intestinal tension that she thought was unbreakable has finally come loose.

She looks at his dying face, that handsome face with the distinguished wrinkles and green eyes that told her he loved her a thousand times before. This was not how she wanted it to end, without him. She loves him; even after everything, he's still the man she's loved most in this world.

She reaches out to touch him, to help him, but she pulls her hand back as Leon's half-dead body multiplies in her vision, three of him swirling around on the sidewalk.

A migraine, the worst she's had, no longer a gunshot but a cannonball shattering her cranium. The pain is so intense, she feels as if her head might explode.

Another sharp pain stabs at her abdomen. She howls in agony as she feels more wetness at her crotch. She reaches down, an oily slickness between her legs.

She opens her eyes to see four bloody hands.

Her breathing grows raspy, difficult, barely able to fill her lungs. The dry wind chokes her. The intense pain in her skull somehow grows even stronger, blackness creeping in from the sides of her vision.

"No, no," she mutters, focusing her strained breath to stay conscious, but it's no use. Every gulp of air is like sucking in shards of glass, her field of vision growing smaller and smaller, only seeing blood in the center of her vision, not even sure if it's hers or Leon's.

She closes her eyes, her forehead pressed against the cold concrete. Her vitality drains. She, Leon, and the baby will all die on this sidewalk, bleeding out as a family. Everything she did for this child, the past nine months of hope and horror, was all for nothing. Roger was right. She was so pompous, so arrogant to think that she could do this, that she could have a baby, that she could be a real mother, that she wasn't just some freak hell-bent on her own destruction.

Martha hears Bruce rush toward her and say, "He's bleeding, his skull. We need to call an ambulance or—"

Angie follows after. "No, no. You stay with me, girl." Angie grabs Martha, lifts her head, and turns her face up to look at her.

Martha flutters her eyes open slightly to see six sets of Angie's sweaty overfilled lips right above her face. The air barely leaving her mouth, Martha mutters, "It's over."

She can't even keep her eyes open, the black velvet grip of death dragging her to the underworld. She wants to let go, stop fighting, finally accept the fate that she so desperately tried to escape, the one that her mother predicted: a mangled corpse on the cold concrete like all the other girls.

"I will not have another dead sister." Angie shakes her head, her long black hair flying fiercely around her. "You're too cunt to die."

Martha inhales one last raspy breath so that she can barely eke out: "Finish the treatment."

Chapter 45

"Finish the treatment!" Angie yells at Bruce.

"We can't electrocute her, not, not like this."

"She said finish the damn treatment. Bring it out here. NOW!" Angie barks. Bruce gulps and races back inside.

With little time left, Martha feels herself drifting away, falling through the crust of the earth, leaving her wretched body behind. Angie slaps Martha's cheek. "Don't you leave me now, bitch."

"Let's get her hooked back up." Bruce scrambles back outside with the battery and jumper cables, sneaking a glance at Leon's body.

"We're losing her!" Angie says, letting go of Martha so that Bruce's shaky hands can put the clamps back on her nipples. "Do it, do it already."

Martha stops breathing.

Her lungs, filled with glass, feel too tight. She can't do it, she can't do it . . .

Bruce flicks on the machine and electricity pumps into her body through her breasts. She gasps, air filling her lungs. Her whole body buzzes. Her eyes shoot open, looking up at the dark starless sky.

Angie cheers, “There’s my girl!”

Bruce turns the machine off. “You’re, you’re alive.”

Martha sits up, shocked that she’s not dead. She pants, able to breathe again. She turns to Angie and Bruce, just as shocked as she is.

But she can’t celebrate. A painful contraction hits her, her body splitting open. She cries out, “It’s coming, the baby is coming.”

Angie grabs Martha’s wrist. “I am not gonna let you die.” She handles Martha forcefully, positioning her on her hands and knees, legs spread wide.

Another contraction clenches Martha with the most immense pain she’s ever felt. “FUCK, FUCK, FUCK. I’M GONNA DIE! I’M GONNA DIE IN A FUCKING PARKING LOT!”

Angie pulls down Martha’s panties, leaving her completely naked. She looks into the squelching scarlet abyss of Martha’s groin, now pouring out blood.

“I need more juice,” Martha yells at Bruce. “Now, now. He’s coming, ooh, he’s coming.”

“Okay, okay.” He takes a deep breath, turning the machine on.

Martha’s muscles contracts, buzzing with electricity. She screams, shaking: “HARDER! I SAID HARDER!”

“This is already crazy high.”

Angie commands, “LISTEN TO THE WOMAN!”

He turns it up higher.

Blood shoots out of the gristle of Martha’s vagina, spraying right onto Angie and even farther, onto Leon’s limp body, splattering them in the thick garnet slime, glistening in the glow of the streetlight. The wind whips the blood around in the air, back onto Martha, drenched in her own crimson fluids.

“I’m losing, I’m losing the baby,” she cries, feeling her life force squirting out of her in buckets of dark red plasma, now completely covering Angie.

But the old woman beams, her lumpy lips curling into a bright smile to reveal white teeth, the only part of her not covered in blood: "I see a gorgeous little head!"

Martha yells, "GIVE IT TO ME ALL THE WAY!"

Bruce turns it up to the highest it'll go. She strains to keep pushing as the violent shakes of energy course through her. The lightning rattling her bones surges more blood out of her, sputtering like a Satanic fountain.

"Almost there!" Angie cheers, unafraid as Martha's fluids get in her mouth, coating every inch of her. "THIS CUNT! LOOK AT THIS FUCKING CUNT STRETCH!"

Martha lets out one final earth-shattering scream, pushing with all her might, pushing with the weight of every injection, every pill, every surgery, every hair follicle zapped, every kiss, every lie, every time he came inside her, every migraine, every sleepless night, every bite of rancid steak, every squirt of gasoline, everything.

The most heavenly unexpected sound breaks out in the parking lot: a baby crying.

Bruce turns off the machine. Angie holds the wailing baby, wiping Martha's viscera off of its face. Angie cackles, "A girl, a beautiful little baby girl."

Martha manages to turn herself over, lying on the cold concrete, completely drained, drenched in sweat and blood and who knows what else. Bruce looks at Martha and the baby, utterly amazed. Angie scoots over to hand Martha the child, breathing, crying, bloody, fresh.

"This is your mama," Angie coos, laying the infant softly onto Martha's bosom.

Martha looks at her baby—no scales, fangs, talons, antennae, fins, tusks, whiskers, hooves, wings, or tails. Not the boy she had been imagining, but her precious daughter. She will never forget today, her child's birthday—May 22, the day after her fortieth birthday, although only a sliver of sun has broken past the horizon.

Her heart fills with such warmth, such immense gratitude, to be holding her perfect beautiful baby. Maybe she's not one in a billion, but one *of* a billion. She's just a woman, a mother, like all the other billions of women who've given birth, terrified of what was going to happen to them, only to find, at the end of it all, something magnificent.

The little angel looks up at her, big open eyes. Martha coos, "You're my baby, you're my baby."

A police siren rings out in the distance. Bruce and Angie look to Leon's body in a pool of blood, then to each other, then to Martha and the infant.

"I'm newborn-baby cunt."

Epilogue

"English, sorry," Martha says in a stunning posh British accent. The butcher nods. "Can I get four of those pork chops? Cuatro."

The butcher wipes his hands on a bloodstained apron, a disarming smile peeking out behind his goatee. "Sí, bonita."

Martha's a vision in a lightly stained white dress with colorful embroidery. She looks tan, healthy, normal. Her hair is jet black, cropped short into a bob—drastic times call for drastic hair changes. Her face wrinkles when she smiles, getting a lot more sun and not a drop of Botox.

He hands her the pork chops in butcher paper.

"Gracias." The British accent is a bit much, but she has so much fun doing it. She likes Mexico more than she thought she would. She knows it's a bit of a cliché, American escaping the authorities south of the border, but she didn't have many options. They took Angie's old beat-up car and raced out of there only moments before the police arrived. She thinks her new locale is beautiful, even if she's constantly sweat-soaked, chubby from too many tacos, hair frizzy from the humidity. She's too preoccupied with bath time and grocery shopping and bilingual language development to worry about that stuff. "And can I get five kilos of the chicken breast, that one with the skin and bone," she points. "Cinco kilos."

"¿Fiesta?"

"No, no. Just for family."

She realized her greatest skill is not her smarts or creativity, not even her uncanny talent for deception, although she did end up winning the Oscar, after all—suck it, Meryl. No, her strongest asset is her ability to completely change her life, jumping off the cliff of her existence without a parachute and landing in unknown terrain, where all the rules have changed. She rolls as she hits the ground, dusts herself off, and walks away cheerfully as if she didn't just fall out of the sky. She keeps her past selves inside her; nesting dolls, so many of them now, clinking against each other as she walks, but never breaking through her painted hardwood exterior.

Sure, in moments like these, watching the butcher prepare her chicken, her mind does sometimes drift back to Los Angeles. She knows that Christine and the other mothers at school must have lost it when they saw the news, providing at least a whole semester of gossip as they interrogate every single detail in order to conclude that they all actually saw it coming. Martha wishes she could speak to Roger; she misses his lilting gay drawl. And she wants to brag—his warnings were wrong. She hopes that Bruce was able to start up the treatment group again since the warehouse had to be abandoned, a crime scene. Her hole still puckers longingly at the scent of gasoline, thinking of him.

She still can't quite believe that Leon is really dead. She worried constantly about what he would do to her when he learned the truth, but it was he who had to be worried, dying alone under a streetlight, killed and abandoned by the woman he had loved, smuggling his baby away in a getaway car. She doesn't miss him as much as she thought she would, but she does miss their house, the air-conditioning, and her beautiful throne of a toilet.

But Enid, sweet Enid who did nothing wrong, who lost not just her father but also yet another mother, that haunts her. Late one night, she actually saw Enid, speechless at the ghost glowing in the dark before her. No, not walking down some Mexico City back alley, but in the pixels of her phone.

Martha never googled anything, worried that they somehow might trace the murder back to her. But she couldn't give up TikTok. She made a new account on her new phone. She told herself it would help with learning Spanish, but her algorithm quickly adjusted to feed her a sunny stream of LA content in English, a window into her old life. That's where Martha saw her, her face longer, eyes sharper, voice less squeaky. Martha held her breath, like she might somehow scare the phantom away.

It was a Get Ready With Me video: Enid, now thirteen, doing her makeup before school. Here she was, sitting in her redecorated room, adeptly smacking on foundation, concealer, contour, and blush with a beauty blender, sipping from the straw of a big pink water bottle. To Martha's relief and surprise, the girl seemed okay, just like any other rich eighth grade girl, gabbing about Sephora and homework and Taylor Swift.

"It's time to go!" Amy, unseen, yelled from the other room to an eye roll from the girl.

"Well, before I go," Enid said, whipping out a gray-and-gold tube of mascara. She held it up to the camera before applying it. "This is my secret: L'Oréal Voluminous Original. You're wasting your money on anything else. All a girl needs is a waterproof drugstore mascara."

Martha watched the video on repeat, studying every aspect of the girl's changed face, the new tilts of her voice. Martha wanted more than anything to say something to her, write a comment, send a DM, call, return to her, keep the promise she made the night she left. But she can't, she won't. She deleted the app, never opened it again. Alone in her bed, she wiped carbon-black tears off her cheeks.

The butcher hands back the chicken. "¿Más?"

"That's it. Thank you, love." With the high heat and humidity, food spoils quickly here. She pays and puts the meat in her tote bag.

"Janine! It's time to go." She turns to the toddler, plucking a pink flower from the bush outside the carnicería. "Very pretty, but your gran's telenovela ends in a minute. She'll be waiting for you." Martha smiles as the toddler patters over. "There's my girl."

Martha scoops up Janine, plump rosy cheeks and a ribbon in her hair. She looks just like her father, kind green eyes and a wide smile. Maybe that's why she doesn't really miss Leon; she still has him, a version of him that is unblemished, that still truly loves her. One day, she should tell her child the truth, the whole truth of her origin, but that day is not for a very long time.

Happy to be held in her mother's arms, Janine coos, "Mama," the first word she ever said and the one she still uses the most. Martha loves the way it bubbles out of her daughter's mouth, her lips clumsily gurgling, knowing that one day, the girl will say it crisply. Living outside Martha's body with a beating heart all her own, this little girl and even motherhood itself are nothing like Martha imagined when she was pregnant—both are much more magical.

"When we get home, I don't want to hear any fussing when Gran watches you for a bit." Martha gives her daughter a big kiss on the cheek. "I need to do my treatments."

Acknowledgments

Thank you to all my readers: Wilhelm Sitz, Jenny Truong, Jess Rosenberg, Jack Dailey Barnes, Alizay Mack, Danielle Martinez, Lauren Kilbride, Sophie Benson, Isabel Berg, Nandeeta Vaswani, Kathryn Winn, Matthew Kerr, Manu, and Jordan White. This book was shaped by your intelligence, insight, care, and belief in my work. And thank you, Jack, for taking my fabulous photo and respecting my good side.

Thank you, Dan Milaschewski and Ethan Schlatter, for picking me out of the slush pile and lending your incredible wit and talent to help me bring my weird monstrous fetus into the world. And thank you, Rosie Pierce, for your incredible wit and talent as well and for taking this on overseas. You all impressed me at every turn, able to see what this book could become when it was still rough around the edges. And for answering all of my endless questions. I could not believe the levels of wheeling and dealing. You all changed my life completely, made my wildest dream come true—I'm forever grateful. To many more books and steakhouse dinners.

Thank you, Ruoxi Chen, Katie Bowden, and everyone on the Putnam and 4th Estate teams for nailing the delivery. Your expertise and genius made this book far sharper and brighter. You both immediately understood my perverted vision and only made it bigger, shinier, nastier. I feel lucky to have had my words pruned and plucked and cared for by you both. I knew my baby was always in the best hands. Lindsay Sagnette, thank you for your support in getting this book out there and really advocating for it. Molly Donovan and Lola Downes, thank you for keeping everything running smoothly. Ryan Richardson and Mary Beth Constant, thank you for your keen eyes and expert copyediting. Nicole Biton, Maggie Leone, Olivia Checchio, and Brennin Cummings, thank you for your excitement in championing this book and bringing it out into the world. Freya Alsop, Nicola Webb, and Olivia Marsden, thank you for taking my baby out across the pond. Tyriq Moore, thank you for the masterful work on the cover and book design—the chicken is absolutely lovely.

Thank you to all my writing teachers for your guidance in my craft. I want to especially thank Caitlin Donovan and Maureen McHugh. Ms. Donovan, when I was sixteen, you encouraged my disgusting, provocative, but heartfelt visions and made me believe that maybe other people would enjoy the beauty and hilarity I found in bodily fluids. I remember hoping I'd be half as effortlessly cool as you one day. Maureen, you taught me how to turn those teenage perversities into something like real writing and made me believe this really could be my career. Your incredible guidance and sharp eye nurtured not just my work, but the person you knew I could become.

Thank you to my doctors, surgeons, psychologist, speech therapists, and electrologists for your knowledge and bravery, giving me a body I can call home.

Thank you to all the dolls past, present, and future—your glamour and courage, the forever inspiration.

Thank you to the music of Macy Rodman, Natalia Kills, RuPaul, Ethel Cain, Hole, Mitski, Beyoncé, Kim Petras, Lady Gaga, Patsy Cline, Lana Del Rey, Sara Bareilles, Rentboy, Shirley Bassey, Björk, Billie Holiday, Lykke Li, Brenda Lee, the Dare, Judy Garland, Slayyyter, Connie Francis, and Sky Ferreira for keeping me company in the long and lonely hours of writing.

Thank you to the members of my convoluted interlocking group chats and all my friends in Los Angeles and across the world—there are far too many of you to list. Thank you for filling my days with panties-pissing laughter. I know that the best parts of myself I have stolen from all of you. This is a book about found family—the cost of losing it, the thrill of finding it again. I'm so lucky to be able to say after five, ten, twenty-five years of these life-giving friendships that you guys truly are my family. To so many more years with you guys by my side, or at most a phone call away.

Thank you, Grandma and Grandpa. I'm grateful to have had grandparents as immensely supportive and hilarious as you both. When you told me this was the grossest thing you ever tried to read, I knew I was on the right track. Here's my "great American novel" you always asked for.

Thank you, Mom and Dad, for your endless love and support. While I imagine you expect me to thank you for raising me and all that stuff, I want to thank you for going through the tunnel of my twenties with me. Even when it wasn't always clear if there was a light at the end, you went with me; I woke up from anesthesia to see your faces as mine forever changed. Now we both can see that the other side is sunnier, brighter than we could have ever imagined. And thank you, Mom, for answering the nitty-gritty medical questions and proofreading. Most of all, this is a book about motherhood. So thank you for being my mother in all your glory. I don't know if I will ever be a mother in any traditional sense, but I know that I will Mother ferociously because you were mine.

Thank you to everyone who has ever driven me around—I wouldn't be here without you.

And finally, thank you, Chatham Moser. Somehow the stars aligned, gay boys yelling at you on the balcony, for our paths to cross and crack each other's eggs. Thank you for your beauty, grace, and humor guiding me all the way. As we both changed, blossomed, metamorphosed, I'm so grateful we got to spend this tender sacred time together. I miss every second of our sister/motherhood from the Hollywood Ardmore to the Rattanachol Hotel, but I know our lives will be intertwined forever; I'll still be comparing you to a skyscraper when I'm in a retirement home. Even as I wrote this in my notes app on a walk, a beat-up Honda Element passed by. If every book is really a love letter, I wrote this one to you.